Praise for *Journey to the*

MW00946764

"John Lundin has written a book, Journey to the Heart of the World, that carries ancient wisdom, wrapped in a vision quest, inside an adventure story."

- Michael Brune, Executive Director, Sierra Club

"The world is so weary and filled with fear; our souls are longing now for enchantment and hope. John Lundin has traveled to the heart of things, emerging with the light that guides our fearful hearts back home."

- Marianne Williamson, #1 New York Times best-selling author of *A Return to Love*

"Every voice that comes out of Colombia's Sierra Nevada de Santa Marta is a vision of hope. John Lundin writes from the heart, and the heart that he invokes is the very heart of the world, the mountains of the Elder Brothers, the homeland of the Kogi, Arhuacos and Wiwa. His book, like their message, is a road map to a new dream of the Earth."

- Wade Davis, National Geographic Explorer-in- Residence, best-selling author of *The Serpent and the Rainbow* and *The Wayfinders: Why Ancient Wisdom Matters in the Modern World*

"One can only admire John Lundin's commitment to seeking personal enlightenment by integrating his search for spiritual meaning, his love and concern for the natural world and the expression of these passions in an artistic statement. This novel is the story of a personal journey seeking universal truths that only the natural world can offer. It's a tale for both young and old to learn and be inspired by."

- Ed Kashi, photojournalist, filmmaker, VII Photo, NatGeo contributor, founder of Talking Eyes Media

"Journey to the Heart of the World is an imaginative adventure story which urges us to pay attention to our relationship to the Earth. A real reflection of the environmental destruction the planet faces today, the story inspires and reminds young readers to listen to the natural world to recover love for the Earth. It is a journey to help us remember the real magic of life that we have forgotten, to reconnect with the great conversation of life."

Llewellyn Vaughan-Lee Ph.D., Sufi teacher and author of *Spiritual Ecology: The Cry of the Earth*

"*Journey to the Heart of the World* is a journey home. Though life circumstances are different for each of us, we are all being called home again. We are being called to remember that we are all indigenous to this sacred Earth that gives us life. We are being called to understand that every action we take determines the kind of world we will leave for future generations. This story reflects this journey in such a beautiful breathtaking way that it will inspire readers to connect the dots in their own lives toward real change. Future generations are counting on it."

- Xiuhtezcatl Tonatiuh Martinez, 15-year-old environmental activist and Youth Director of EarthGuardians.org

"There are other worlds on this beautiful planet of ours. What a tragedy that so many never experience them — their flowers, birds, butterflies, trees, and the peoples who live among them. So, it takes a dream to get this story's hero to make his journey, but it is a profound one. Loving the natural world is not merely a spiritual prescription, but practical advice essential for our survival conveyed by those who live in closest contact to it."

- Dr. Stuart Pimm, professor of conservation ecology at Duke University and president of SavingSpecies.org

"When we begin a journey it leads us through some of the most amazing trails! One of these trails can be an inspiring step into a world filled with experiences that perhaps would seem to be a dream. Yet, it is real, then it's surreal - because the sights and sounds around you are so illuminated by the elements in their most natural state, and the people are also illuminated in their relationship and understanding of the world. *Journey to the Heart of the World*, a novel by John Lundin, is a subtle reminder that there are experiences and trails that lead us to the top of the mountain where one will see the world from a whole new perspective. Reading the book gave me moments of wonder and a knowing smile - I could relate.

- Mona Polacca, Havasupai, Hopi, Tewa, International Council of Thirteen Indigenous Grandmothers

"Every now and then, a book comes along that uniquely and powerfully points the way toward a new and important wisdom that humanity must embrace: John Lundin's *Journey to the Heart of the World* is just this kind of book. Taking you from the mountains of New York to the mountains of Colombia and back again, this journey has so much of value to start the next generation on the right path, and to help those of older generations find the path that can bring harmony to our relations with one another and with the Earth."

- Todd E. MacLean, Editor-in-Chief, *Global Chorus: 365*

"Journey to the Heart of the World is a story as epic as the mountain where it is set, as timeless as the traditions of the world's indigenous peoples, and as poignant as the future of our planet. It's a story that had to be told."

- Richard Emblin, editor, *The City Paper Bogotá*

"The indigenous peoples of la Sierra Nevada de Santa Marta certainly rank among the most intriguing cultures on the planet. John Lundin's new book, Journey to the Heart of the World, provides real insight into the world and wisdom of these most extraordinary people. A great read!"

- Mark Plotkin, author of Tales of a Shaman's Apprentice, president of the Amazon Conservation Team

"John Lundin's *Journey to the Heart of the World* is the kind of book that prompts you to thank all of nature - the skies, sun, clouds, rivers, lakes, mountains, trees, shrubs, flowers, birds, animals and fish - for being part of your life each and every day, and letting you be part of theirs. We need such prompters in today's hustle and bustle world."

- Dr. Antonia Neubauer, president, Myths and Mountains, Inc.

"Journey to the Heart of the World' is a good example of the new genre of cli-fi that explores the interface between the natural world and humankind, pro and con, the harm we have done and the good we have done, the trouble we have caused and the joys we have uncovered, the green fields we have paved over and the deserts we have helped to bloom. But in all this there is a major problem we need to face: what will the future bring and how will our descendants live and will they live? Lundin's book explores these cli-fi questions with cli-fi aplomb and bravo. It deserves a global readership as these are global issues."

- Dan Bloom, curator, The Cli-Fi Report

'Asimov wrote about it, from a pragmatic scientific perspective; accepting obliteration as a foregone conclusion. Bill Moyers produced brilliant, insightful, programs about it. Jacques Cousteau explored it, and made incredible inroads towards raising awareness for preservation. Meanwhile? John Lundin lived it: spirit and myth, as an integral part of our biosphere. And now he successfully transfers all of this to a new generation; neatly contained in a charming allegorical adventure story. A young man's transformative *Journey to the Heart of the World*. Simply magical, an enjoyable read; and thereby, incredibly powerful!"

-- Patrick Mahoney, author of *To Be Fit For Life*, and founder of the Annual Convocation for Peaceful Coexistence, Ornans France.

"Once a Christian minister, then a Buddhist acolyte, John Lundin takes the reader backwards in time to the mountains of Columbia where his hero receives ancient teachings from the first Americans on the true nature of reality. Blending science, religion and imagination into an intriguing and compelling fantasy, Lundin takes us on a sincere and engaging fictional journey which the reader will be grateful to have experienced."

- Ace Remas, Buddhist teacher and author of
Just Passin' Through: My Rough Ride to Buddha Land

"*Journey to the Heart of the World* is a profound mythical story with deep ancient roots that will beckon you on a journey of enchantment, discovery and transformation. It will leave you with a powerful and unforgettable connection to Mother Earth."

- Dawn Parker-Waites, co-founder of Echo Eden
and Planet One Solutions.org

"John Lundin's *Journey to the Heart of the World* is not just his journey, but ours: a journey to the heart of the earth, but also a journey into ourselves. At the end of any journey, we can look back and find something that we have learned. What we learn here is a way to live and a way to think, and a way to a better world--and to our own hearts."

- Michael Green, Ph.D., professor of history UNLV, writer, author
of *Nevada: A History of the Silver State*

JOURNEY TO THE HEART OF THE WORLD

a novel by John Lundin

Please direct all inquiries
regarding this work to:

Humanitas Media Publishing
info@humanitasmedia.com

Website:
http://www.humanitasmedia.com

Additional Work by John W. Lundin:

The New Mandala:

Eastern Wisdom for Western Living

Written with His Holiness the Dalai Lama

for

Jwikamey, Bunkey, Dugunawi and Dwiaringumu

Chapter 1

It Began with a Dream

I am writing this book for you. It's a true story, drawn from my life and lives. This story was not written as a book, it was lived for real, only later to be remembered and shared in a book. Some of the details have clearly come from my imagination, but that does not make them at all untrue. In fact, the imagined parts probably contain the greatest truths of all. This is my story, but in many ways that will become apparent in due time, it is also a universal story - your story and your children's story and your grandchildren's story. It is for this reason that I'm sharing my story with you. It is far too important to keep to myself.

I was born on a Wednesday, March 9th, 1988, at 10:55 a.m., in Torrington, Connecticut, a small part of that plot of land arbitrarily called the United States of America, and just as arbitrarily referred to as North America, presumably to differentiate it from the "other" Americas located much further south. I don't actually have any distinct memories of that day, of course, but this is what my mother has told me, and I have pretty much always found value and truth in most anything my mother has ever seen fit to tell me.

I was immediately named Adam. Adam Joseph Rivera. I don't know why Adam. Maybe because I was my mother's first born son, the first male. Maybe because my mother's name was Eve. I don't know, but I think it's because *adám* actually means soil, earth. My mother always knew I was going to be a child of the earth. Rivera was my dad's name, and it means little river. Joseph was oddly enough a very common Mohawk name, from my mother's side of the family.

The story I'm about to share with you here, however, does not so much begin with my rather unremarkable birth in the year nineteen-hundred and eighty-eight, but instead begins with a series of events that unfolded in the spring of my eighteenth year.

It all began with a dream, a most unusual dream. At least I thought it was a dream. Today I'm not so sure.

I was in the woods, a very dense and dark forest that looked more like a jungle than any forest I had ever seen before, when I heard a voice calling to me.

"Adam."

I looked all around but saw no one, nothing but the greenest trees and plants and the most colorful flowers I had ever seen. I could hear birds, lots of birds, singing and chirping, but I couldn't see anyone who was speaking.

"Adam."

The voice called me by name, very clearly, but still I could not see anyone.

"I'm here. I'm in the trees, on the leaves."

"I can't see you," said I.

"You can't see me because you don't know what you're looking for. Open your eyes. Widen your vision. Don't look for me, just be open to seeing me. Let go of everything that is blocking your vision. Let me appear to you."

I did. And then she did. She appeared to me. From out of the tree, from the very leaf where I had been looking but not seeing, came the biggest butterfly I have ever seen. And on her wings was a vivid image of an eye, what appeared to be a bright yellow eye of an owl. And she began to flit about, flying all around me in circles while flapping her big wings much slower than smaller butterflies do. She was bronze and gold and silver in color – except for that big yellow owl's eye.

"Reach out to me."

I held out my hand and the Owl Butterfly came to rest on my finger. Her touch was so gentle I could barely feel her on my finger, and her antennae were moving continuously like she was feeling the air between us. She appeared to be looking directly at me, deep into my eyes. Somehow it felt like she knew me, like she was confirming I was the one she was calling out to.

"Follow me," I heard her say, and she flew off my finger and began flitting back and forth through the air in front of me, teasing me, seemingly beckoning me to follow.

"Follow me," she said again. And so I did.

But at the same time I was thinking to myself, "This can't be real. Butterflies don't talk. This must be a dream."

Apparently the Owl Butterfly heard my thoughts. "I know you think butterflies can't talk. All animals can speak to you. All the birds and the plants and the trees can speak to you, even the waters and the clouds. If you will listen."

The Owl Butterfly continued to lead me forward, and I continued to follow. And she showed me the way out, out of the dark jungle forest into a bright clearing. Ahead, I saw what appeared to be a little river or stream, some ribbon of water anyway, and beyond that mountains rose through a distant mist, up to the clouds, with snow-covered peaks. I remembered thinking, "How could I be in what feels like a jungle and be looking at snowy mountains."

Here, at the edge of the clearing, the Owl Butterfly circled me three times, flew directly over my head where she fluttered her wings like she was hovering above me, and then landed gently on my shoulder, not far from my ear.

She seemed to whisper to me now: "Adam, your mother is gravely ill. She wants to speak to you. She has a message for you. And your elder brother has an important message to give to you as well."

I knew my mother was ill, that was no surprise. "But I don't have an elder brother," I protested, not really believing I was having such an unlikely conversation.

The Owl Butterfly did not answer me, but continued, "I will find you and I will call for you, and you will come. You won't know how or why, but you will build a cocoon in your own way and at the right time, and you will emerge as a new you in one of your new lives. This life you are experiencing may actually be a past life of one of your future lives - you will come to learn that time is not a straight line from here to there, it goes round and round."

With that, the Owl Butterfly began circling me again, round and round above my head it circled, as if she were looking me over.

"Watch for me. Watch the water. Watch the birds. Watch the sky. You'll see me again in the trees, on the branches and on the leaves, in the skies, and beside the sparkling waters. And when you see me, listen to me and follow me. I will lead you to your mother and to your elder brother. I will lead you to where you need to go, to where you need to be. Follow me."

She flew off my shoulder and again I began to follow. But soon she was flying too fast, and even though I was running through the field now I was falling behind. Then I tripped and fell. I must have hit my head because everything appeared to swirl around me, and then all went dark. Either I fell back to sleep, or I began to awaken. I'm not sure which.

I was only once again aware of my surroundings when I heard my sister's familiar voice.

"Are you O.K?"

I was a bit startled and disoriented, but as I quickly realized, I was laying on the grass in my own back yard.

"Were you sleeping? Sleeping on the grass?" asked Sarah with a puzzled look on her face.

"I guess so. I'm not sure. I guess I was."

As I looked around the familiar grassy field, I became aware of how similar yet clearly different it was to the grassy clearing in my dream. The difference was this was the Catskills of upstate New York, not some lush tropical jungle. Then I caught myself looking around for a butterfly. No butterflies here, not this time anyway.

"Mom seems to have taken a turn for the worse. She wants us to come to the hospital, Sarah said with a concerned sadness in her voice. "She said she needs to talk to you." Again I looked for the butterfly.

"She needs to talk to me – not just to us?"

"That's what she said. She wants us both to come to the hospital, of course, but she specifically said she needed to talk to you."

Still no butterfly. And nothing was said about any elder brother. But it all seemed very strange, nonetheless. And the dream – or whatever it was – continued to seem very real. In fact, it almost seemed to be continuing.

I got up from the grass and dusted myself off and followed my sister back to the house. We lived on a small farm near Woodstock, New York, having moved here from Connecticut when I was five, when my dad left us. We grew lots of things on the little five-acre farm, all kinds of fruits and vegetables and lots of herbs and spices - parsley, sage, rosemary and thyme - and much, much more. Woodstock Farms was known throughout the Catskills, and across the country, too, as the best farm stand for every kind of natural organic fruits, vegetables, herbs and spices imaginable. Sometimes in the summer I'd help out by selling the vegetables and plants and spices, even seeds.

Mom was sort of one of those hippies who never really grew up, very much in touch with nature and also very artistic. In addition to the farm in the country, we had an apartment in New York City, in Brooklyn, actually, because Mom was also an artist and a musician, and a teacher. She was sort of a traveling art and music teacher in the New York public schools. The schools had cut way back on their art and music programs, like so many other schools around the country, and my mom went from school to school teaching art and music classes to fill the void. So I grew up with one foot always in the country, and the other firmly planted in the big City. And I liked that.

It was very surprising that my mom, of all people, would wind up with cancer. She had always lived a very healthy lifestyle, pretty much a vegetarian, and always growing and cooking and eating the very best fresh fruits and vegetables. She was into "organic" before most of the rest of the world knew what that meant. She exercised, did yoga, even meditation. So of all the people I knew in my life, she was the last one I would have ever expected to develop cancer. It was metastatic cancer, they called it, the worst kind, that started with a small tumor in her head. Because it was embedded in her brain it could not be removed, and it was spreading, broadcasting the cancer to other parts of her body.

Mom believed the cancer was simply the inevitable result of the environment we all live in, things she had no control over. There were chemicals in the water, pesticides in the plants and the ground, pollution in the air. Even eating healthy and exercising can't fix things if the water and the air, the most basic elements of life, are poisoned, she would say.

My mother was dying. My sister and I, everyone, knew that, but we didn't want to believe it. It was as though we were in some form of denial. We acted as though we thought that if we talked about it she would die, but if we didn't talk about it, didn't acknowledge the fact, then she wouldn't die. It would just go

7

away. It didn't make any sense, I know, but that's the way we were dealing with it anyway. I think it was in part a reaction to the feeling of helplessness – there was nothing I could do to help my mother, so I tried to pretend she was not in trouble. What could I do? I was just a teenager in New York. What could I do to stop the spread of a cancer that had been caused by air pollution and water pollution that I had nothing to do with, a cancer that was spreading out of control, a cancer that was killing my mother?

Sarah and I started the drive to the hospital. The afternoon clouds were building as they often do in the Catskills in springtime, and it was starting to drizzle. That was a good thing since it had been a very dry spring so far, and that was on top of a winter with very little snow. We were both very quiet, and I couldn't stop replaying that dream in my head. It seemed so real, and yet so much of it made no sense at all. Talking butterfly. An elder brother - an elder brother that I don't have - having a message for me. Then my mother wants to talk to me, and right away it turns out she really does want to talk to me! And that jungle, like something out of a movie.

And then I fall down, black out, and wake up on the grass in my own back yard. And it still doesn't feel like a dream. To this day, I'm still not certain it was a dream.

Sarah was especially quiet as we drove. She and I had never been real close, not like some brothers and sisters are. She was the introverted quiet type and I was always the outgoing one, always doing guy stuff. She and my mom and my Aunt Susan ran the farm, and while I helped out some, most of the time I was playing sports or playing music. And I always had girlfriends, too, though never a really steady one. Except Mary. She lived practically next door most of the time I was growing up, so I never really thought of her as a girlfriend. But she was.

I think both Sarah and I missed having a father figure in our life. We never really talked about it. Being without a father around was all we really knew, and a lot of our friends were in the same situation. Still, it often felt like something was missing in my life. My dad's ancestors were from South America, Colombia and maybe Peru, and the family story was that he was also part American Indian, so I sometimes wanted to know more about that part of my heritage. And just as my mom was very artistic, Dad had been very musical. We still had an attic full of bongo drums and guitars and rhythm instruments that had been my dad's. I think his Latin rhythms still flow through my veins as I've always had a love for that kind of music. But I don't have any real memories of my father. I don't even know where he is now.

Sarah was the first to break the silence. "I think Mom wants to tell us she's going to die soon."

It was raining steadily now, giving the lush green foliage a look that was both melancholy and tranquil, the sort of afternoon rain that causes one to daydream and reflect. As we drove, I was sure Sarah was wondering what the future held if Mom passed away. We would probably stay with Aunt Susan, but I didn't know what would happen to the farm or the apartment. I was going to be eighteen soon, so I'd be able to do what I wanted, but I didn't really know what that was – I didn't know what I wanted to do if I was really on my own. Sarah would probably just continue to help Aunt Susan run the farm. She'd be OK. I don't think either of us could imagine living without our mom. We never talked about it. I still couldn't believe we might actually lose our mother.

When we got to the hospital, the clouds had become dark and it was now raining steadily. Aunt Susan was already there. "Your mother is gravely ill, kids. She wants to talk with you. I'm afraid we're going to lose her soon."

When we got to her room she did look very ill, but she also had an almost angelic calm about her. She looked at peace. She had been undergoing radiation therapy for several weeks, and that had taken a toll on her. She was very pale and had lost her hair and she was very thin, but today she seemed to have come to terms with her situation in her own way. She smiled at us as we all came into the room and sat down beside her.

"You know I haven't got much longer to live," she said almost matter-of-factly. Mom was never one to beat around the bush – when she had something to say, she said it. "This cancer is spreading faster every day, and of course there's nothing they can do. I don't know how much time I have left. I'm not really in pain now, but the doctors say I will be soon. They can ease the pain with drugs, but I've told them no. What's the use? There's no reason to drag out the inevitable. When it's time for me to go, let's get on with it, I said." Even now her voice was sounding weaker. "I may soon be too out of it to be able to talk straight, so I wanted to talk to you both now."

It was hard to see my mother dying and to hear her speak to me, maybe for the last time, without the tears welling up in my eyes and starting to roll down my cheek.

"Aunt Susan will be your guardian. But you're both nearly adults, and you've long been able to take care of yourselves. I don't worry about either of you. You're both great kids, and you're going to be fine young adults, too. I've already transferred the farm and the apartment into a trust, with Aunt Susan overseeing it. They will be yours for as long as you want them. And you know the business is doing well, and I've been lucky with my investments, so there's a reasonable estate that will keep you going after I'm gone."

It was becoming harder for her to summon the strength to speak. This was so difficult, but in Mom's typical fashion, she had thought of everything. That didn't stop my tears, though.

"Sarah, I'm leaving the business to you, and I know you'll continue to run it with love. But I want you to know that you're always free to follow your heart wherever it may lead you. Don't ever feel you have to stay on that old farm just because it was mine. It's yours now. Do with it as you see fit. I'm proud that the world will always know you as my daughter."

Mom seemed to be saying good-bye to each of us now.

"And Adam, my son. You're still half owner of the farm, too. But I know your heart will lead you in a different direction. I've always known that. From the moment you were born, I have always known you were going to live your life as an adventure and make your mark on the world, to make a difference. The Earth is calling you, Adam. Listen to her. Follow her call."

Her voice was weaker now, and her breathing more strained. From under the blanket, she produced what looked like a necklace she seemed to have been clutching close to her. It was a golden figurine on a simple green cord. She placed the figurine in my hand and clasped her hands around mine. She looked deeply into my eyes with her weak but still clear eyes, and said to me, "This is yours. It has always been yours. Like you, it was born from the earth, then shaped by the original peoples of the land. It has always helped me find my way. But it has always been meant for you."

She lifted herself up a bit and pulled me down, closer to her. She placed the green cord around my neck, looked into my eyes, and whispered, "*You are the sun and the rain. Watch the water, watch the birds, watch the sky.*"

Those would be her last words.

The monitors on the wall sounded a warning as the nurses and doctors filled the room. I clutched the golden figurine, and wept.

Chapter 2

Colombia Calling

"Watch the water. Watch the birds. Watch the sky."

Those had been my mother's last words. They were also the words of the Owl Butterfly. What did it mean?

My mother had died too soon. The cancer consumed her and ended her life before her full potential could be realized. Her story did not end the way it should have. She had much more to offer, much more to give. Then again, maybe her story hasn't ended. Perhaps death is, in fact, just the start of another new chapter. I found myself hoping that somewhere, somehow she was already remembering this past life in some new and better future.

One of Mom's nurses had shared something with me immediately after Mom died. She said all the staff in the hospital had been surprised at how quickly and suddenly she had died. "Everyone on the staff - the doctors, the nurses, everyone - they all loved Eve. And it was a shock that the end came so quickly." And then she said, "But people seem to choose when it's their time to pass away. It's like they take care of their 'unfinished business' and then they can die peacefully, knowing it's time for their life's chapter to end, and to pass the story on to those they leave behind.

"Your mother's 'unfinished business' was that golden figurine. None of us knew exactly what it was, but we all knew it was very important to her. She held it close to her always. And it was clear she needed to pass it to you before she could pass away.

I'm sure she knew that she'd continue to live on, because of you, through you, through your life. In her own way, it seems, she needed to pass the torch, to let you know that she knew you were ready to continue her story in your life, in your story."

And what about my story? What would my story be, what would it look like? I think when anyone's parents die it's normal to think about life and death. I wasn't even twenty years old. If I were to die at the same age my mother did, I wouldn't have much more than twenty years left. If I was to live to be seventy or eighty I had all those many years ahead of me. Either way, would mine be a life that anyone would remember? Would it be a life I would want to remember?

These were the kinds of thoughts going through my head as we prepared for the two funerals we would have for my mother, her burial in the Catskills and a memorial service in the City. A lot of relatives and friends had been coming to visit and pay their respects. Mary had come over right away and I was very happy to see her. She wasn't a relative or a friend, she was just Mary, and I had always been able to talk with her about anything. I could share whatever was going on in my head and she would listen, take it all in, and never be judgmental. It always seemed like my thoughts mattered to Mary.

She didn't try to say things just to cheer me up, and she didn't talk about how sorry she was or what a great person my mom had been. She just listened to me, and she made me feel like it was OK to share whatever I was thinking at the moment. With the other people, I was always trying to make sure I said the right thing, or that I was actually cheering them up. With Mary I could always just be myself, never worrying about what she might think

14

of whatever I was thinking or saying. I didn't fully realize it at the time, but she was truly my one best friend.

I shared my mother's figurine with her. She had never seen a figurine quite like it. "Your mom expected you to be someone truly special, Adam. It sounds like she knew one day she would be saying good bye, and that you'd be remaining behind as the presence of her heart in the world."

I hadn't thought of it that profoundly, but that was Mary – always understanding things the way they should be understood.

"What are you going to do now?" she asked, knowing, I'm sure, that I didn't yet know. She knew that was the question I was just beginning to ask myself.

"I don't know. I don't know."

We were starting to look through boxes of old photographs and other memories, finding things to display at the memorial service. It was sometimes sad, sometimes funny as we looked at old family pictures and cards and letters that brought back so many memories.

"It's as though I've been given a blank page and told I can write my own story. I'd known this day was coming, but I hadn't really given it much thought. I don't know what I want to do."

I held up a photo of my mom reading to me. Mom was always teaching, teaching me and everyone else. Mary had often come over to my house just to learn from my mom. Mom made learning fun. I pretty much learned everything I really needed to know from my mother. My mom taught me to think; school taught me to memorize and take tests. Mom's art and music classes weren't like that, though. She taught her school students

15

how to express themselves, how to share what was deep inside their heart and soul. She did that with me, too, of course. High school hadn't been nearly as much fun. I had recently been thinking about leaving school, actually. The truth is, I was bored.

"I may drop out of school," I told Mary, wondering what she would think of the idea.

"You only have a couple months to go before you graduate," she said, not revealing what she actually thought. That was Mary – she'd support whatever I decided to do, but she'd also help me look at all my options seriously.

"I know. But I don't think I'm going to go to college like I had planned. At least not right away."

I knew it was the right thing to do, to get my high school diploma, but I was starting to think I needed some time to sort out my life before going on to college. Maybe I would travel the world, see what life was like outside of New York and the States before going to college. That way I'd have a better idea of what it was I actually wanted to study, to learn, when I did get to college. Right? Well, at least that was the thinking going on in my head at that moment.

"Maybe you should take some time to travel a little. See America, see the world maybe! You've hardly even been outside of New York!" said Mary, again knowing exactly what I was already thinking.

As we continued to pick through the memories, there were photos of Mom when she got married, and pictures of my dad, and more pictures of me and Sarah, too. Pictures of the farm and pictures of New York City and vacations and holidays. But it was true, nothing outside of New York, Connecticut and New England.

"What do you think I should do?"

"It's not for me to decide. And I'd be a little sad not having you around if you left, if you want to know the truth. But maybe it could be a good opportunity for you – maybe even life-changing. You've got to give it a lot of thought, though." She smiled and added, "And don't worry about me, about leaving me behind. It would be the same as if you went away to college, right?" Again, she was right, of course.

We were looking at all the photos of Mom, but there were many of my dad in there as well. The photos of Mom were all pretty much familiar. I knew my mom better than anyone else in the world. I knew everything about her, and I knew how much of her had rubbed off on me. We had shared my whole life together. We had shared the same experiences and had come to share many of the same interests and passions, even some of the same habits and quirks! But my dad was a whole other story. I had never had a chance to really know him. We had not shared a lifetime of experiences. I had no way of knowing if we shared the same interests or habits or quirks. Even the photos taken when he was a part of my younger life were vaguely unfamiliar. I sometimes found myself wondering about my unknown father – who he was, and how much of him was a part of who I had become.

Mom was a true all-American mix - one half was Dutch, the other half mostly Mohawk. Dad, on the other hand was another kind of American – a South American, a Colombian. There were family stories that he had some Italian in him, some Sicilian was the rumor, and maybe even some Native American, but mostly he was a true Colombiano and a true Latino. The

17

Latin rhythm in his genes gave him his love of music, and the Latin lover in his jeans got him in a lot of trouble! It was his eye for women that ultimately led to him leaving us. Maybe he left, maybe Mom kicked him out. I was never sure.

There were photos of my dad I had never seen before. As we looked through some of them together, Mary held one up and remarked, "You look just like him, Adam - or he looks just like you!"

I spotted one of Dad and me playing the bongos together. "I was probably only three years old or so at the time, but look at that big smile on my dad's face as I'm banging away on the drums. A future Latino rock star!"

And then I saw the actual bongos, and more drums, a lot of drums, all lined up along the wall at the very back of the attic. A couple pairs of bongos, a tambour, a big conga drum, and other rhythm instruments as well – cowbells, maracas and more. I cleared a path through the stuff on the floor and couldn't resist beating out a rhythm – tap, tap, tap, tap-tap – tap, tap, tap, tap-tap. I played keyboard and the sax, but it was always the beat of the drum that touched my heart. The Latin rhythm was as natural as walking for me, as natural as the primal urge to dance. As I got into the rhythm Mary stood up and started to move, rocking her hips and moving her feet to the beat. Even in a time of mourning, maybe especially in a time of mourning, the soul naturally responds to rhythm.

About that time, Sarah came into the room. She had been going through Mom's things, too. She reached her hand toward my neck and gently took hold of the golden figurine, looking at it closely.

"That figurine was very important to Mom. Dad gave it to her. I don't ever remember her wearing it after Dad left, but I know she carried it, carried it close to her always. I remember her saying she wanted you to have it one day, Adam."

I looked at it. It was a small golden figurine on a simple cord, a green cotton cord. The figurine appeared to be Mayan or Aztec or something like that, the figure of an ancient man with hands open and raised in what appeared to me to be a gesture of peace. He was topped with what looked like a feather headdress, the feathers fanning out from his head like the rays of the sun, and it looked like real gold. It appeared to be very old. The necklace and the figure looked like something a Native American warrior from Mexico or South America might wear, I thought. It might even have been from one of Mom's Mohawk ancestors.

"And you remember Joseph Eagle Feather? He was Mom's friend from way back, and Dad's friend, too. He's agreed to give a Native American prayer at Mom's burial, and since he's a Mohawk he might know more about exactly where that necklace and figure came from, something about its history."

Then Sarah continued with more about how Mom had taken very good care of the business and in turn taken very good care of the two of us: "Mom was never one to pursue money. But she did take care of the money she earned. She ran the business of the farm well, always saying that was her job – taking care of what she had been given. Caring for the earth was her number one job, but taking care of what it provided her with was job number two in her mind. So the bottom line is this: she has left you and me enough to care for us for the foreseeable future, if we take care of what has been given to us now. We're not rich, but we will each have enough that we can live comfortably and choose what we want to do with our lives. That is an amazing gift our mother has given us."

I was a bit overwhelmed with a whirlwind of emotions. I was grieving, sad, in pain over Mom's sudden and premature death. And at the same time I was thankful for all she had done for me, her being the best mother a boy could ask for. And now even caring for me in death. And I was also confused, and perplexed. What was I going to do with my life? What was I going to do now, right now, and what was I going to do in the future? And the bigger question, the one it seemed my mother's last words were pointing to, was this: What is my purpose in life? I was suddenly beginning to feel the weight of this question at only seventeen-going-on-eighteen, and I didn't have anything close to a clear answer.

The service was at the local funeral home on Friday. It wasn't at a church, since Mom had never been religious in the traditional sense. She believed in God, but not in the religious definition of God. She didn't believe in defining God too narrowly, in fact believing that a 'definition' of God was not needed at all. God was an infinite mystery to her, and she was happy leaving it at that.

During the service, I spoke about my mother: "Mom was my teacher, in more ways than one. She gave me my education, and she taught me about life. She could grow anything. She loved nature and the earth. And she taught me everything from that love. She used to tell me, 'We aren't born with knowledge. We have to learn things. And our best teacher is the Earth itself.' My mother gave me life, nurtured me. I know, that's true for everyone. Everyone knows it, but not everyone feels it. I felt it. I remember Mom teaching me about Thomas Edison one day, and a quote from him has always stuck with me. He said, 'My mother was the making of me. She was so true, so sure of me; and I felt I had something to live for, someone I must not disappoint.' Well my mother's heart has been given to me. For me, she is the one I must not disappoint."

After the brief service at the funeral home, Mom was laid to rest in the simple country cemetery near Woodstock. Joseph Eagle Feather offered a heartfelt Native American prayer: "Where does all life come from? The Earth. Where does everything return to? The Earth. Where do values come from? The Earth. Many people are lost because they don't know the importance of connection to the Earth. They connect to things, to relationships, to success, to goals. When we are disconnected from the Earth, we have feelings of being sad or lost. When we are connected to the Earth, we feel warm and secure. Great Spirit, help us to stay connected in all ways and through all our days to our Earth Mother, and to Eve, the best friend our Earth Mother could ever have." And with that, Mom was lowered into the Earth. Silently we all passed by and each tossed a handful of Catskill soil onto the casket.

Afterward, everyone came back to the house for a little reception. I thanked Joseph for his beautiful prayer, and I introduced him to Mary, who also told him how much she liked his prayer and how appropriate it had been. Joseph is a wise elder, a Mohawk Indian whose grandfather was a famous Mohawk Chief, and I had always appreciated his calm wisdom.

"Mom was part Mohawk, herself. Your prayer meant a lot to all of us," I told him. "Your prayer about our Earth Mother reminded me of what I repeated at the funeral service, something

Mom often said: 'We aren't born with knowledge. We have to learn things. And our best teacher is the Earth itself.'"

I was wearing my mother's golden figurine now, so I showed it to Joseph and asked him if he knew anything about it, about its history.

"Mom said it was 'born from the earth, then shaped by the original peoples of the land.' She said it has always helped her find her way."

He looked at it carefully for some time, turning it around and around and looking at it from all sides.

"I'm sorry son, I don't really know too much about it. It seems genuine, real gold and not a replica, and my best guess is that it comes from my brothers and sisters, the original peoples of Central or South America. It would have been a very sacred object for them, like an ancestor. Wear it with great respect. It has energy. It can guide you, protect you, if you let it."

And then he caught me a little off guard with what seemed to be a change of subject and a simple question:

"So Mary is your neighbor, young man?"

"Yes, sir"

"Then she's your sister."

"No, sir, she's not my sister," I said with a smile.

"Hmmm…I think she is, boy…and that mountain over there, that's one of your ancestors, and that bird and that tree…those are your cousins. And that gold talisman you're now wearing about your neck, that is your Mother, the precious golden energy of your Earth Mother."

I have pondered that profound thought often since that day.

The memorial service was the next day, Saturday. We had gathered up a bunch of Mom's things, pictures and other mementoes, to display at the service, and then drove down to the apartment, and to a public school auditorium where the memorial service for my mother the teacher would take place. We unloaded the pictures and mementoes and several pieces of Mom's art. She had been an artist all her life – a painter, but really an artist in everything she did. She recognized beauty wherever she found it, and that was pretty much everywhere. She painted, she played piano, even her garden was a work of art. For her, all of life was beauty, and living life was an art.

As we carried the boxes of things into the small auditorium where the service would be held, we passed a poster in the entry, one that almost made me drop the boxes I was carrying. "That's the butterfly! The Owl Butterfly in my dream!" It was a poster for the New York Public Library, with an image of the Owl Butterfly resting on the finger of a young boy, and the headline, "Spread your wings and fly."

"That's my butterfly, the one with the eye of an owl!" I called out to the surprise of everyone. I remembered she had said, "Watch for me…you'll see me again." I thought to myself that if we had time I needed to go to the library and discover more about the Owl Butterfly.

Inside we arranged the memories on a table in the entry – the photos and some of Mom's art, even colorful seed packets she had designed. I had wondered if I should display the golden figurine, but I decided that was for me and not for everyone, so I continued to simply wear it. We talked with Mom's friends as they arrived. Mostly they were artist friends and teachers that I didn't know very well, but there was also Joseph Eagle Feather, this time with another group of Native American artists and musicians. They had brought a drum, the biggest I had ever seen. It was a flat drum, maybe five feet in diameter, with an animal hide stretched across the top of the frame and pulled taught with an intricate pattern of cords crisscrossed on the side. There was a colorful pattern of flowers and Native American symbols painted on the side, and the skin of the drum had been painted with a striking image of four arms - red, white, black, yellow, one from each of the cardinal compass points - all joined in a handclasp at the center. It was an amazing image. Several men carried the drum into the room and placed it on a low stand in front of the podium.

Joe and his musician friends shared with me the flutes they would also be playing. There were hand-carved wooden flutes, and ones made from animal bones. But the most intriguing were ones made from bird feathers, simple flutes with holes carved in the hollow feathers of eagles and hawks and Macaw parrots, Joe explained. One of the men played a simple tune. As his breath filled the hollow of the feather, music filled the room. It seemed somehow fitting that such a soulful sound, like the human voice crying aloud, would come from the wings of a once majestic bird.

Soon everyone took their seat in the auditorium, and friends of Eve spoke in turn. The dominant theme was beauty – music, art and beauty. One friend explained that Eve always thought of art for art's sake alone – for the value of creativity and imagination, not for the money. "People pay big prices for art because they think they can find happiness in owning things," she said, "Eve knew that happiness came through an appreciation of the beauty itself. For her, beauty was a way of living, a verb not a noun, an action not an object. She knew in her heart that no one can ever purchase beauty – or purchase happiness. The true beauty in the world is all around us, and it's not for sale. The colors, the paint and the brushes, are the trees and the birds, the waters and the clouds, the plants and the animals. And they speak to us in their beauty. The artist hears the colors in her heart. That was Eve. An artist who knew how to listen, to listen with her eyes as well as with her ears, and most of all with her heart."

Another friend compared her to an impressionist painter. "The artist doesn't try to create a photographic record of every line and detail of what is before her eyes. Instead she uses her brush to awaken our eyes to an impression of what she's discovered in her heart. If we focus on only the dots and lines, we miss the big picture. If we step back and absorb the meaning of all the dots and lines and splashes of color taken together, allow ourselves to enjoy the big picture as a whole, we come to know the beauty the artist had known. Eve's life was all about sharing her vision, her impression of life, its rhythm and beauty, with us."

Several of mom's public school students had come to pay their respects. One of them also rose to speak. "Miss Rivera changed my life. Without her I would never have learned to play the flute. On a simple wooden flute she taught me about music - about rhythm and harmony. She taught me to appreciate all types of music I had never heard before and that I would never have heard or appreciated if it wasn't for her. She gave me an opportunity to express myself. She showed me the way. And next year I'm going to college. I'm going to study music and the arts. I want to be a teacher just like Miss Rivera."

And then the butterfly appeared again! It's true! My mind had drifted away momentarily, but was brought back instantly with the mention of a butterfly.

"Eve's beauty was like that of the butterfly," said another friend. "It's appropriate to grieve at her passing, but our grief should be colored with joy – joy that we were blessed to have had our lives brightened by the beauty of Eve's life, and joy in the knowledge that, like the colorful butterfly, she showed us how to spread our wings and fly. And we find hope knowing that what appears to be the end of the world for the caterpillar is for the butterfly a beautiful new beginning."

There were prayers – Christian prayers, Jewish prayers, Baha'i prayers, Sufi poetry, Buddhist chanting. I liked that. It was 'artistic' in its own way.

And there was music. Bagpipes. Piano. A string quartet playing chamber music. A Celtic flute. And then the Native American flutes – and the drum. Everyone was invited to gather around the drum and participate, and many did. I did. A Mohawk leader began striking a simple heartbeat-like cadence – a throbbing boom, boom, boom, boom – and everyone around the drum joined in. Boom. Boom. Boom. Boom. Like a heartbeat. Soon we were all one, all a part of the same sound, all a part of the one heartbeat, all a part of making the one heart beat in a gentle rhythm. We became that heartbeat, became that simple rhythm. And then the flutes joined in – the wood flutes, the bone flutes, the feather flutes. It was magical. Everyone around the drum, everyone in the room let go of their self and for a moment became joined with the One through the beauty of the sounds, the rhythm of the heartbeat, and a gentle wind dancing through flutes and feathers.

The memorial service had ended, but the music continued for some time. The circle of friends was caught up in the spirit of the moment, sharing the rhythms of life they were feeling, and sharing the connectedness of which they had become a part. The drumming, the spontaneous chanting that arose, the impromptu dancing, the flutes and the gentle joy didn't seem to want to end.

But end it eventually did, and soon Sarah and I were greeting friends in the reception that followed, with Mary at my side. Everyone had a story to share, a story of Eve, my mother. I was struck with the fact that it's through our stories that we discover who we are, who the others in our lives are. We tell stories. If I want to tell you who I am, I tell you a story, perhaps one as brief as, "I was born in Torrington, Connecticut and moved to the Catskills when I was five. I live on a farm where my mother grows the best vegetables in the world." It was those kinds of stories that people were sharing about my mother – who she was and how they had been blessed to come to know her. And the stories people were telling about Mom, stories they were eager to share with me and Sarah, all seemed to have a common thread running through them. Most everyone would say something like, "Your mother was a great teacher." They all seemed to have a story of how my mother had taught them something. Every story confirmed what I already knew – my mother had always been my best teacher.

Some of my New York City friends were there, too. I had been fortunate growing up, living in the city and in the country, and I had a bunch of city friends. There was Tony who worked at a music store and Miguel, who played guitar and sometimes played in a band. And Oscar, who was the best soccer player I ever knew. I didn't have many close girl friends in the city, but there were many good guy friends. And whenever the guys would get together there were always plenty of girls around, but I never become close friends with any of them, maybe because I was always returning to the farm. Or maybe because I had Mary.

Tony started talking about Mom, and then the others joined in. Again it seemed everyone had a favorite story, and again they all seemed to think of Mom as a teacher in some way or another. They knew Mom was a school teacher, and she often schooled them, too. "You were lucky, dude," Tony said. "Your mom was your best friend and best teacher. She was a friend and a teacher for me, too. Living here in the city, she opened my eyes to what there was outside the city, to nature. And she helped me see how much natural beauty we actually have right here in the City. Most people walk right past the parks and the flowers and the trees, they miss the birds singing. Not your mom. She didn't miss a thing, and I learned some of that from her." There were other stories like that from the other guys.

"Why don't you bring Mary by the music store later? Show her around. And then there's a party tonight, at Miguel's. Some guys from his band are gonna be there – it's gonna be a big jam. You can come over to my place first, then we go to Miguel's and party - make some music, dance, drink, smoke - then you can spend the night at my place. " It sounded like a plan. I told him we'd be there.

Sarah took care of gathering up our things and helping the people with the cleanup as the reception wound down, and Mary and I slipped out the door and back into the sounds of the city.

"Let's go see the music store, and then you know what else I want to do? I want to stop at the library. I want to see if I can find that Owl Butterfly. Is that O.K? And then tonight we go to Miguel's party. But first I want to go to the park. I want some

28

quiet time, time to think, to think about Mom, to think about what's happened, about life. I need to get my head together. I'd just like to walk around the park for a while, with you. OK? " So that became the plan, and we were off.

Central Park was just across the street, across Fifth Avenue. I loved Central Park. I liked the city, of course - the excitement, the sounds, the lights, everything the city had to offer - but I also liked getting away from all that, returning to my country roots, sort of, and entering into the solitude that nature seems to nurture. And at this moment, I needed that.

So we just walked. Silently at first. As we walked alongside the lake I looked at the trees, at the flowers, at the birds and the squirrels. It was spring, and everything seemed very much alive. And I looked at Mary, into her eyes, her soft smile, and I held her hand. It was a little thing, but we didn't usually hold hands. In fact this may have been the first time I ever took her hand in mine. She squeezed my hand gently, and seemed to be silently saying everything's going to be alright.

At first neither of us said much of anything. Mary knew I needed a little time to think, to work through what had happened, what was happening. But soon I was thinking out loud.

"I'm gonna have to make some choices, Mary. A lot of choices. A few days ago I wasn't paying much attention to the future, to what I was going to do with my life. But now it's important. It's like my future is suddenly now. It's like I had been ignoring it, but now I have to face it. What I had always thought was going to be 'someday' is suddenly now, today. And now it's about choices. I suddenly have so many choices to make. And I know the choices I make now are going to affect my entire life, my whole future. And there's no one to tell me what choices to make. I'm the only one."

Mary didn't say much. She gave me the space and the time to work things through in my head in my own way. But when she did say something, it was always just what I needed to hear. "The fact that you know the choices you make now are important means that you're paying attention to your choices, seriously looking at your options, and that you'll probably make the right choices."

The sparkling water of the lake again reminded me of Mom's final words, and of my dream. They both said watch the water, watch the birds, watch the sky. I held the golden figurine in my fingers. As I did, I was aware of several colorful butterflies flitting around – not an Owl Butterfly, of course, but butterflies nonetheless. I thought of what had been said at the memorial, that Mom had spread her wings and flown. Perhaps she was flying before me now. And I thought of the Owl Butterfly saying I would build a cocoon of my own, that I would be changed, then spread my wings and fly. What did it all mean? So many choices. I found myself asking again would I make the right choices? Would my life be a life anyone - my mom, myself, anyone - would want to remember?

I was actually starting to worry about all the choices I might make, all the choices I needed to make, and make soon. My mom had always helped me find my way, guiding me through the choices in my life before. But I was on my own now. It would only be what my mother had taught me, what she had shown me, that would guide me now. And where would my choices take me? My fingers touched the golden figurine and I heard her words, "The Earth is calling you, Adam. Listen to her. Follow her call."

And I thought of the Owl Butterfly, what my dream may have said about where to look for answers, whose advice to follow. "All the birds and the plants and the trees can speak to you, even the waters and the clouds. If you will listen." I felt like I needed to listen, but listen to who? To what? Maybe that's what the butterfly meant when she said, "you don't know what you're looking for. Open your eyes. Widen your vision. Don't look for me, just be open to seeing me. Let go of everything that is blocking your vision. Let me appear to you." Maybe the butterfly didn't mean she would appear to me, exactly, but the answers I needed would appear to me. If I let go of the things that were blocking my vision, if I was open to seeing the answers. I hoped so.

While I didn't really sort out all my thoughts or come up with all the answers for what I should do with the rest of my life, I did manage to bring some calm and peace back to my mind. Returning to nature – even in the midst of the city – can help a person find that calm and peace, for sure. It was like Joseph Eagle Feather had said: when we are disconnected from the Earth we have feelings of being sad or lost. When we are connected to the Earth we feel warm and secure. While I didn't yet have all the answers, I was feeling more secure about my ability to discern them and to make the right choices eventually.

"Let's go."

Mary squeezed my hand gently as if to say, "OK."

We took the subway to the Times Square station, and once again there was that poster of the Owl Butterfly, looking right at me as we got off the train. Weird.

31

First stop, the library. I loved the New York Library. Mom had taken me the first time as a very young kid, and I never outgrew the curiosity that place awakened in me. As I saluted the famous lions out front, there it was still again – the poster with the Owl Butterfly. "Spread your wings and fly!" This was starting to be more than coincidence, I thought.

Up the huge stairs we went, and then it was off to 'the stacks.' I found the animals section, then the insects aisle, and then the butterfly books – lots of butterfly books. Field guides, butterflies of North America, butterflies and moths of the world, even butterflies of New York.

"Is this it?" Mary held up a big picture book of butterflies, with my Owl Butterfly right there on the cover!

We took that book and a couple more, and sat down and read. It turns out my Owl Butterfly was actually called just that, the Owl Butterfly. The scientific name is *Caligo,* and they're found in parts of Mexico, Central and South America - not in New York! They're among the largest of all the butterflies, and the biggest are found in Colombia, in the jungle forests of the Atlantic coast, where they're called "mariposa búho" – Owl Butterfly.

"Look at this." Mary had found a book that told of a legend surrounding the Owl Butterfly:

The indigenous peoples of the South American mountains believe that when an Owl Butterfly flies directly over you, and then circles you three times, she will drop a fine dust from the underside of her wings, a dust that imparts wisdom to the person upon whom it falls.

Butterflies, the books all said, are very adaptable to change, because their life-cycles are so short – going from caterpillar to butterfly to laying eggs and then starting the whole cycle all over again, over and over in a very brief span of time. The Owl Butterfly has evolved over thousands of years, maybe millions, developing the eye pattern on its wings to fend off predators. The Owl Butterfly is so big that it flies slowly and only for short distances at a time. This makes it vulnerable to predators, especially rats. The 'owl eye' fools the predator into thinking it's an actual owl, one of the rat's most feared predators. I couldn't help thinking how amazing nature is.

And I couldn't help wondering how it was that a butterfly from South America, one that doesn't exist in New York and that I had never seen or known anything about before, somehow appeared in my dream. If it was a dream.

"That was my Owl Butterfly, Mary. It told me to look for it, to watch for it. And I keep seeing it, in the poster, in the auditorium, in the subway. And she told me, 'when you see me, listen to me and follow me.' Mom's friend talked about the butterfly at the service this morning – about the end of the world being a new beginning. I think my butterfly is still talking to me, Mary. But how do I follow? How do I follow a butterfly that's in South America? And only in my dreams? I don't know what it means. Maybe nothing."

Next, it was off to the music store. It was the one my mother was always taking me to, and where she sent her students. Mary had never seen anything like it. It's more than a music store, it's history. There are photos on the walls of famous musicians and their instruments. And there's every instrument you could imagine, and all the amplifiers and mixers and speakers to go with them. The instruments tell a history, too. There are old instruments and the most modern, a history of music and the

33

way that people have made music through the ages. Polished Spanish guitars, and gleaming rock star electric ones. Classic pianos and the latest and most sophisticated electronic keyboards. Flutes and horns, from the ancient and simple to the new and brassy.

But for me the most fun were the percussion instruments - modern electronic drum pads alongside the most primitive African drums, tambourines and cowbells, Native American tom-toms, all the way to entire digital rhythm synthesizers. And I showed them all to Mary. There were the drums sets, like the rock bands use, with their snare drums and bass drums and toms. Even the timpani from the orchestra. And there were the Latin and African ones – bongos and congas and more. Even drums from India, a pair of *tabla*. In addition to all the drums, there were the other rhythm instruments like the cymbals – high-hats and rides, crash symbols and splash cymbals – and tambourines and maracas, shakers and guiros and claves. I think it was a bit overwhelming for Mary, but for me it was being like a kid in a candy store. Drums had always been a part of my life. Dad's drums were always around and I was always drumming. Somehow I always knew I had my dad's Colombian rhythms in my genes and running through my veins. I could feel the rhythm in the instruments just by looking at them or touching them. But that didn't hold me back from pounding out a few rhythms on them as well!

As we were looking around, Tony and Miguel returned to the store. Miguel was a guitar player, but he knew his Latin percussion as well. He started beating out some salsa rhythms on the conga and Tony took sticks to the timbales, both of them really getting into it. Customers in the store stopped and listened, and some even started dancing. The party had already begun!

What had been mourning only a short time before was now dancing and laughter. Music and its rhythms can do that.

"That service for your mom was really something, Adam. Your mom was something else, and all those people there today, they knew it." Tony had always liked my mom. He spent a lot of time with me whenever I was in the city, but I think it was really so he could spend time with my mom. Just as I was always learning from my mother, Tony and Miguel and my other friends also knew they would always learn something by being around my mother. She was everyone's teacher.

"And that drum," said Miguel. "That big drum was awesome! I've never seen such a beautiful drum. And when everyone beat out the rhythm together, the beat, the heartbeat, it was like we were all one. And like your mother's heart was still beating and we were connected to her. Everyone in the circle was connected to each other, and connected to your mother. And you could feel the love. It was awesome. I don't know any other word for it."

I told Tony and Miguel it was Mary's first time in the store. Tony told her, "This place is amazing. So much musical history in this place. A lot of music you hear every day was actually born here. The great musicians have bought their instruments here, and musicians have met musicians here, exchanged musical ideas. Adam loves to hang out here. I think music is in his veins, but maybe his love of music was born here. Salsa – my kind of music – was sort of born here. This place is a salsa, a sauce, a stew, a mixture of everything, just like the music. Salsa flourished in places like Colombia, but the sauce, the stew – the original salsa – was put together right here. Puerto Ricans, Cubans, Africans – all the immigrants from all the neighborhoods and from all parts of the world – brought their instruments and their rhythms with them and tossed them all together into the pot right here. A lot of people don't know it, but salsa is a New York invention, and a lot of the drums and cowbells came right from here. And who knows how many future musicians your mom inspired, Adam."

Tony and Miguel again told us to come to their place in the evening. There would be lots of friends and lots of music. Members of Miguel's band were coming and they planned to really jam some salsa and more, and get everyone dancing. It sounded like fun, and just the right diversion on this melancholy Saturday night. We said we'd be there, and then we headed back to the apartment, and to look for something to eat. We realized we had hardly eaten all day. Katz's Deli took care of that. We met up with Sarah there and together we shared pastrami sandwiches and matzo-ball soup!

Then it was back to the apartment for a little nap. Actually the girls took a nap. I kept pondering my future. Choices – lots of choices to make. And of course my mind was full of thoughts and memories of my mother. Again her last words spoke to me in my head: "I have always known you were destined to live an adventure and make your mark on the world, to make a difference. The Earth is calling you, Adam. Listen to her. Follow her call. Watch the water, watch the birds, watch the sky."

The day had been special, a mix of grieving and celebration, celebration of my mother's life and also a reminder of how important it is for each of us to fully live our own lives, to celebrate the miracle of our lives every day. The evening would be special, too, and also a celebration of life, the mysterious rhythms of life.

Tony's place was just across the river. The neighborhood was a bohemian hotbed of music and the arts. It was always alive, no matter the time of day or night, with music, with dancing, with street artists, with colorful sights, sounds and people. And tonight Tony's house was all of that. There were Colombians, Italians, Puerto Ricans, Hispanics, Africans and Caribbeans, young and old, rich and not so rich. It was New York, all in one funky house.

It was a big house, typical of the City, a lot of guys lived there. It had a big back yard and a big porch. The party spread out and filled it all. There was food – all kinds of food – and plenty to drink. And plenty to smoke, too, if that was your thing. And of course, music. It seemed like everyone had an instrument, and there were drums of every kind, and guitars and amplifiers and speakers – big, loud speakers. The party was already well underway when we got there.

I had a couple of beers, and so did Mary, and soon we were dancing. I was a pretty good dancer, for a 'white guy.' I'm sure it was due to the Colombian genes from my dad, and maybe a bit of that Mohawk, too. And Mary could dance. So together we started really getting into it. There was plenty of salsa but other rhythms as well. Everyone was just jammin'. For those making music, it didn't feel like anyone was 'performing,' but more like the music just flowed together naturally, like everyone was just having fun making music together. And no matter what type of music it was – from the salsa to techno – there was rhythm, lots of beat. It was the kind of rhythm that brought everyone together, like the drum beat of this morning, but it was also rhythm that called you to move. Everyone was dancing, even if it was just tapping their toes and swinging their hips.

37

I made a little music myself. When I was much younger, from around the age of eight I guess, I had played the saxophone. We had always had a piano in the house – that was Mom's music – and later Mom had bought me an electronic keyboard, a synthesizer, one that had all the sounds and rhythms I could play with. So I became a bit of a keyboard artist, painting musical pictures with my hands. I liked the keyboard because I could be a one-man band, making pretty much all the sounds of an orchestra at one time, by myself. But to really make and feel the music, it's still the very best when you can make it with someone else, with others. I remember my mother teaching me, "You can't make harmony by yourself. You have to create harmony with 'others.'"

So this evening I played a little sax with all the great 'others' in the room, and I took over the keyboard a few times, too. And everyone, whether they could play an instrument or not, could help create the rhythm with any of the many drums and tambourines and rhythm sticks – and they all did. Me, too. I got in my share of rockin' the rhythm on the drums, and so did Mary. She liked music, though she didn't really play any instruments herself. And she especially liked it when I played. She had always liked my music.

Even with all the loud music, there was also plenty of conversation. It was a party, after all, not a concert. And if it was too loud to talk in the house, we'd step outside. We talked about my mom, we talked about music and rhythm, and we talked about life – mostly my life, my future. I guess I sort of monopolized the conversation at times. I talked with Mary, with Tony and Miguel – pretty much everyone at one time or another. There was a guy from Peru; he played the flute, naturally, and a young couple from Brazil. She was a singer and played the tambourines and the maracas and other rhythm things. The guy had a great-grandfather who was an Indian from the Amazon, from the rainforest. Lots of fun and interesting people, people from all over the world, and I think we talked with all of them at least a little. I was grieving the loss of my mother, of course, and for me sometimes talking with others was the best way to work things through.

Miguel introduced me to José, who was often called simply Joe, and who was the leader of the band Miguel played with. José was walking around the house with a parrot on his shoulder all the time, a big red and yellow and blue parrot! José was from Colombia, maybe the parrot was, too.

"This is Guaca – short for Guacamaya. That's what they call macaws in Colombia, she's a guacamaya. And that's the name of our band – Guacamaya. We make a big sound, we sing, we dance - just like Guaca here. Did you know that parrots are just about the only animals in the wild that respond to rhythm? It's true! Some animals, like dogs and stuff, even monkeys, they can be taught tricks that make it look like they're dancing or responding to the rhythm, but in fact they don't have any sense of rhythm at all. Only parrots. And people. They'll rock their head and move their feet, their claws, just like we do, when they hear the beat, feel the rhythm. Guaca goes crazy when the band really gets going. She really gets into it!"

And she did. When the band was playing she was bobbing her head like crazy. And she could sing, too – sort of. She would screech loudly, and she could also talk, a few words anyway. She would call out her name whenever she wanted attention – "Guaca! Guaca!" – and some Spanish words, too, like "Hola" and "Chao." Before long no one really noticed her. She was just like everyone else at the party - except that she was always on José's shoulder.

Mary was sort of on my shoulder all night, too. After a few beers - and a few rum drinks as well, I think - I was holding her and hugging her, even stealing a kiss or two when a dance number ended. We sat together on the couch, and we talked together on the porch. By the end of the night the hugs and kisses had become seriously passionate.

But mostly we talked. Mary and I talked about my future, even *our* future. And about Mom. And we talked with Tony and Miguel and José, mostly about music, but about Mom, too. And about me and my future.

One conversation in particular pretty much included everything we talked about all night. About rhythm. And the rhythms of life. José knew a lot about music, especially Latin rhythms. It was in his blood, in his Colombian genes, to be sure.

"Rhythm is natural and also learned," he said. "In salsa, in the Latin beat, the rhythm is called clave. It's a rhythm pattern - one, two, three, one-two; one, two, three, one-two - a pattern that's both natural, almost primal in folk with a little Latin blood in them, and that also needs to be learned. Adam, here, he picks up the Latin beat easily 'cuz he's got it in him. He responds to the Latin rhythms that are sort of imprinted in his DNA. But he still has to learn to really make it a part of him, to really make music with the others in the whole band. The point is, we're all born with a natural rhythm, one that beats in tune with our natural heart rhythm, but to really be in harmony with the music that's all around us, we need to learn – we need to learn how to be in harmony with others, not just going off on our own rhythm. And that's one of the things that makes music so powerful for me. It's taught me that we are all born with a genetic rhythm, a natural connection between the heart rhythm and the natural rhythms of nature, but we still need to learn to follow them, to respond to them, to live in harmony, to transcend our individual contribution and to begin to understand and respond to the rhythm of the whole. And to learn how to make our little contribution, our rhythm, fit in and make the whole greater. A bunch of people making beautiful music together, in harmony, all in touch with the same rhythm – that's a beautiful thing."

I was struck by that. It made sense to me. The idea was like the rhythm itself. I already knew what José was trying to say, it was intuitive, I understood it at a gut level. But I needed to learn it from him, too. It was something I needed to look at, to examine, in order to really understand.

"The natural rhythms are a part of us, of who we are. Some of us are born with more natural rhythm in our DNA than others," he said with a smile. "You white guys," he said, looking at me, "maybe have to work harder at it than I do. But anyone can learn. What we all really need to do is learn, to learn how to be fully aware of the rhythms, to pay attention, to listen and to hear them – in the music and in the world around us. People – all people, Latino or not – need to learn harmony. The rhythms already exist. The harmony takes practice. Weaving the rhythms into a harmonious whole takes practice. It takes effort. But when the rhythm and harmony are all together, when everyone is paying attention and making the same music together, when we're all interwoven, it's perfect! But you have to learn to listen for the rhythm pattern, you have to listen carefully to find it. Listen for the other parts. You have to listen carefully to find the individual parts, the individual players. You have to listen to the other parts to find your part, to find where you fit in, how you contribute to the whole."

41

I thought about that, and I've thought about it often since. That night it spoke to my future. Where did I fit in? What part of the music, the rhythm, was I already in touch with, and what did I need to learn? And what part of the harmony should I be playing? What was the music saying to me and where was my place in the whole sound?

Mary and I talked about that well into the night, into the early morning, in fact. Mary helped me continue to sort through my thoughts, not by saying much, really, but by listening to my random rambling. I guess it was a little like playing music – it always comes out better if someone is listening to it, paying attention.

I had so many options, and so many choices to make. Maybe I should pursue my music. With a lot of that practice José talked about I could probably make a living making music. I didn't need college for that. Well, maybe I did. There was still more to learn, even about making music. And should I live in the city or in the country? Or maybe travel, even leave the country. I wanted to know more about the world. I wanted to know more about my roots, my dad's Colombia, my mom's Mohawk and Dutch roots. And I wanted to explore my own backyard – the City and the other states. I wanted to explore nature, to really get in touch with the land, but I also loved the excitement and the energy of the City. Maybe I should just enjoy sex, drugs and rock and roll for a while! No, that's not really me. Should I buy a car? If so, what car? Or should I just travel for a while. Or go straight to college. And if college, where? I didn't even know what I would study. I didn't know what I wanted to be when I 'grew up.' I didn't know if I wanted to grow up! Or maybe I was already grown up.

All these random thoughts and questions flitting around in my pleasantly inebriated brain were starting to point me toward the three real questions I knew I had to answer: number one, what did I want to do, what did I like doing; number two what didn't I like, what did I not want to do; and finally, what *should* I do? That was the big one, for sure, but finding the answer for myself required answering the other two first.

"What am I going to do, Mary? What *should* I do?"

"I can't tell you, Adam. I can't really even give you any advice. But I can tell you this: you're gonna choose what's right. I know you are."

Somehow, deep inside, I knew she was right. But the choices still weren't going to be easy, and finally resolving that question of what was right for me was going to take time, a lot of time, maybe even the rest of my life.

We talked and talked and talked, all night, but we also danced. When José talked about rhythm earlier he talked about how everyone has this need to make music together, and he added we also have an inner need to respond to that music.

"When the rhythm touches you, caresses you, when it resonates with your own rhythm, beats in time with your own heartbeat, you no longer have a choice – you must get up and dance. The rhythm is your lover; she seduces you and calls you to consummate your passion, to be joined as one. The beat is a lover that never disappoints and, like all lovers, it demands one hundred percent surrender. It has the power to seduce moves we couldn't dream. It grabs us by the belly, turns us inside out and leaves us begging for more. The beat is bad, wicked, sick –whatever the word is. The Native Americans say we dance to fall in love with the spirit in all things."

So Mary and I danced and danced and danced, and I think she seduced me. Or maybe I seduced her. Or maybe both. Anyway, the rum and the beer had certainly filled us with plenty of 'spirits,' so it was not at all surprising that we were falling in love, in love with the spirit in each of us. Well into the wee hours of the morning, with the rest of the party having departed, we collapsed on the sofa, wrapped in each other's arms. And we made love. We didn't just have sex, we made love. It was the first time, but it felt so perfectly natural it was as if we had been lovers forever. And perhaps, in a very real sense, that was the truth. She laid her head on my chest, I held her close, and we smiled ourselves to sleep.

"Squawk! Squawk! Squawk! " I was awakened by the sound of the parrot, the macaw, Guaca. I opened my eyes to see where she was, and in the early morning sunlight I immediately saw that something was out of place. In fact everything was out of place. I was no longer on the sofa. I was outdoors. I was in the woods, the forest, maybe the jungle.

"Squawk! Hola Adam!"

The parrot was perched on a branch of a tall tree directly in front of me. I looked around and noticed the forest was vaguely familiar, not unlike in my butterfly dream. Huge trees, colorful flowers, everything so green. Birds were singing and chirping, and the sun shining through the trees felt very warm. And then there she was, the Owl Butterfly! She fluttered her big wings, right in front of me, then flew above me, flitting back and forth and then in circles above my head. Three times she circled my head. And then she flew to the tree and landed on the branch next to the parrot.

"Follow me. Follow us."

The Owl Butterfly was speaking to me again. "Follow us as you would follow your heart. Follow us to the Mountain across the sea. Follow us to your Brother. Follow us to your Mother. Follow us to the Heart of the World."

Then both of them, Guaca and the Owl Butterfly, flew off the branch and began flying back and forth from tree to tree in front of me, leading me toward a path through the jungle. I didn't hesitate. I followed. I followed as though I had been expecting them to come to me, expecting them to show me where I was supposed to go.

Through the trees I could see snowy mountains in the far distance, below them nothing but trees and jungle. The parrot and the butterfly called to me to follow. Soon the path narrowed, and the jungle became even more dense and dark. The path was steep, we were clearly climbing the hill, and at times the trees blocked the sun so completely it felt almost like nighttime. I kept following. To the left and right I saw colorful lizards, even a bright green iguana, and in the trees were monkeys. And birds - lots of noisy colorful birds. There were red and yellow and pink flowers all around, and orange and red and yellow fruits of all sizes and description on the plants and trees. Some of the trees were big around and looked to be hundreds of years old, with gnarly trunks and long roots on the ground and long, low branches that looked like arms – the trees seemed to have a personality, a character of their own. The path kept getting narrower and narrower and darker and darker.

45

"This is the path to your future, Adam." It was the Owl Butterfly talking. "The path is here. It has always been here. We have led you to it, but you are the one who has to walk it. We can show you the way, but you have to discover for yourself where it leads you."

"Water! Water!" The parrot could have been saying "Guaca! Guaca!" or "Agua! Agua!" - but I swear she said water. And sure enough, there was light ahead of us, a clearing at the end of the path, and soon I could see water - a beautiful blue ocean and a long sandy beach shining in the bright sun. It was stretched out before us, just below our perch in the hills at the edge of the jungle. The sea was a beautiful aqua blue, and the sand a brilliant white, and there was no one there. The beach was deserted.

The butterfly and the parrot led me down the path, down the hillside to the beach. And then they led me down the shore, past massive boulders that were half on the beach, half in the sea. Past lagoons and groves of palm trees, coconut palms, I think. The parrot and the owl kept leading me on, and I kept following. It was a long hike but I never felt tired. There were several inlets, little bays, each one more beautiful than the next, and each one deserted, but my animal guides kept calling me to keep going. I saw that the beaches were a big arch, and I could now look back toward where I had been, and I could see the snowy mountain peaks again. They were once again in the hazy distance, but this time almost behind me.

We came to a point of rocks that were like a finger into the sea that blocked our way. The parrot and butterfly led me to another path that took me over the rocks and up a little hill. In front of me was the gentle curve of a beach, a beautiful bay, and this time there were people on the beach. Lots of people. As we got closer, I could hear music, and then I could see people were dancing on the beach. There were young people dancing, and old people. Black people, brown people, white people. And children. And what looked like American Indians wearing colorful feather headdresses. And dark-skinned natives wearing not very much at all. Drummers on bongos and other bigger drums were providing the rhythm and flutes made the music.

"They want you to join them, Adam." I don't know if it was the Owl Butterfly or the Guacamaya talking. It didn't matter.

"Where am I?"

"This is your home. This is the Heart of the World. And this is your family. The sea in front of you is your Father and the snowy mountain over there is your Mother. The waters from both is in your blood. And your brothers and sisters are down there, waiting to dance with you. They've been expecting you."

Guaca and the Owl Butterfly led me down the path to the beach. As we drew closer to the dancers I could hear they were calling to me. I don't know what they were saying but it began to sound like a chant. It was "Hola!" or "Welcome," maybe, but soon it just sounded like they were chanting, "Colombia! "Colombia! Colombia!"

"Adam, wake up wake up. It's OK, it's OK."

It was Mary. She was on the couch, but I was standing.

"Where am I?"

"You're right here with me, Adam. You were having a nightmare. And you were yelling, 'Colombia, Colombia, Colombia,' when you jumped up and started dancing – dancing in your sleep!"

47

"It wasn't a nightmare, Mary."

It was then that I saw the path. I looked around the cluttered room, but in my mind I saw only jungle. Through what had been darkness I saw a clear light, the sea, the mountain - and the path. Suddenly the path was clear.

"Colombia! That's it! I have to go. I'm going to Colombia!"

Chapter 3

The Elder Brother

I think it was then that I became a man. My mother was gone, my father was gone. It was then I realized that life is all about choices. All the experiences I would ever have in life, that story I would remember, would be determined by the choices I made. Millions of choices, big and small, the important and the seemingly inconsequential. In truth every choice I would ever make would matter – somehow, somewhere, some day. And no one could make my choices for me. Not my mother, not my friends, not my teachers. I am responsible for every choice I make. We all are. Today I had a blank page in front of me. It was up to me to start making the choices – to choose what I would write on that page, what images I would draw, and what many colors I would fill them with.

I had made up my mind. I was going to Colombia. I was going home, to a place I'd never been before.

The mysterious dreams, both dreams, had been so real I still wasn't sure they were even dreams at all. And I didn't know what the Owl Butterfly meant by leading me to my brother and leading me to my mother but somehow I trusted it all. It was as though the dreams had come from my soul, and my heart was speaking to me. I knew I had to follow. I was certain I was doing the right thing and I would come to understand what it all meant in due time.

Filled with the energy and enthusiasm that came from knowing I was doing exactly what I should be doing at this point in my life, I set about finishing what had to be finished and organizing the launch of what was to begin. I finished school, got my high school diploma. I made the decision to go to college, but only after I had explored the world. I was certain that I would have a much better idea of what I wanted to learn after my world view had expanded and my vision of the future had matured. I organized my finances, got my passport and bought my ticket, and said my good-byes.

Saying good bye to Mary was the hardest part. We had talked about my leaving and our being apart for some time, and she had always said she was good with it, but it was still difficult. I think what made it OK, though, was the confidence I felt knowing that I was doing exactly what I needed to be doing at just the right time. Mary felt that confidence. She, too, knew it was the right thing. We talked about our future, about how our being apart was not the end of our relationship, just one of many separations we would know in our life together. There would be many good-byes, and just as many welcome homes. It was Mary who assured me by saying that, "Relationships never end, they only change. They change constantly. How many times has our relationship changed already? Many times. This is just another change. Your exploring will change you and make you a better person. And when you return, it will make our relationship stronger, richer, fuller. We've know each other for years and we've changed a hundred times, a thousand times, during that time. The relationship always survived, in fact grew. That's what'll happen this time. I'll be here when you return, ready to kiss you again and eager to hear all your stories. I love you. I always will."

That may have been the first time either of us had ever said I love you. We had thought it, we had known it, but not actually acknowledged it, not actually said it aloud, not very often, if ever.

"I love you, too, Mary. I guess I always have. I'll be back. I don't know when, but I'll be back, and I'll be a better person when I come back to you. I'll be a man; I'll know who I am and what I want to make of my life. I'll be ready to start building a better future for both of us."

It had been two months since Mom died when I was packing my bags, but it was as though no time had passed at all. Tony and José had friends and relatives in Colombia, friends I could stay with when I got there. They were in Santa Marta, which I discovered was on the coast of the Caribbean Sea but also at the base of the mountains. I loved the sea and the mountains, it sounded perfect. Mary took me to JFK where we said our good-byes, kissed and hugged like we didn't want to let go, and then I was on my way.

The first flight was from New York to Miami, then a second flight took me directly to Santa Marta. I spent the entire time in the air pondering the last words of my mother and replaying the butterfly dreams in my head. I wondered what South America held in store for me. Would I see the tropical jungles of my dreams, would I find the snowy mountains? I remembered the Owl Butterfly saying I would build a cocoon in my own way and at the right time, and that I would emerge "as a new you in one of your new lives."

Is that what this airplane is? I wondered. Is this my cocoon, my transition from my old life to my new life? Is the old me passing away and the new me preparing to spread my wings and fly? Will I find the sparkling waters, the birds, new skies?

Will I live new adventures? Will I make a mark on the world? Am I really being called? Will I one day make a difference?

     I caught a glimpse of those waters and those worlds out the window as we crossed the ocean, flying over Cuba and Jamaica before touching down in Santa Marta, Colombia.

I guess this young gringo was easy to spot among the crowd of passengers as Carlos and Sophia found me as soon as I emerged from the customs area. "Bienvenido a Colombia!"

I was trying to travel light, but I also knew I might be in Colombia for a long time, so I had a couple of pretty big bags that they put into the car, and we headed to their home in the hills, just a short drive from the city. Santa Marta is the oldest city on the American continent, founded at the time of Columbus, and the architecture is very Spanish. But the old is surrounded by the new. In the short drive from the airport to Carlos' home I saw everything from the old Spanish cathedral to tall modern office buildings, from shopping malls to roadside vegetable stands and primitive open air restaurants. Most Colombians do not own their own car, but the streets are full of vehicles nonetheless - cars and taxis, trucks and buses, as well as donkey carts and pushcarts full to overflowing with fresh fruits and vegetables and more.

Carlos' home was simple but elegant at the same time, not in the city at all but in the hills above the city, in the country, surrounded by palm trees and other plants and trees that clearly announced I wasn't in New York anymore.

I soon discovered that life in Colombia is lived outdoors. There was a big patio with inviting hammocks strung between the trees. It was surrounded by the house which was nearly open on all sides – wide windows with no glass, doors always open, and some rooms with no walls at all, only support for a roof overhead. The kitchen was pretty much outdoors, just two walls, two open sides and a roof. I learned that we were nearly on the equator and the temperature doesn't change much – nearly always perfect for sitting outdoors. There is rain, a little rain most every afternoon, but as long as there's a roof overhead, outdoors is the place to be.

From the patio I could see all the way to the sea. The city of Santa Marta, from the port to the beaches to the city center, was spread along the coast just below the hills, and looking in the other direction the hills became mountains – steep mountains that were covered in green and with peaks that reached the clouds. There were trees and flowers everywhere, a carefully tended garden and yard became a coastal jungle just a little higher up the hill. And birds, lots of birds. Over time I saw toucans and parakeets and eagles and hummingbirds and others whose name I never knew. I soon gave up trying to identify them all and just enjoyed them. There was one that Carlos called a Motmot, a large blue-green bird with a very long paddle-shaped tail. He liked to perch in a nearby tree and watch me. He was as curious about me as I was about him.

Carlos pointed out all the fruits that were growing right there in his back yard. There were bananas and plantains, papaya and mango, even pineapple, and all types of citrus trees – oranges, lemons, limes, mandarinas – but also a bunch of fruits I had never seen or even heard of before – lulo, cherimoya, maracuya, and more. As we were exploring the many fruit trees, I spotted several different colorful butterflies, presumably attracted to the fruit trees as well. There were big ones and little ones, red ones, orange ones, yellow and even big blue butterflies. I asked Carlos, "Do you ever see the Owl Butterfly here?"

53

"Ah, the Búho! Oh yes, very often. You'll see one here I'm sure."

I had found myself thinking often of the Owl Butterfly because while I had arrived in Colombia by airplane, of course, in truth it was the Owl Butterfly who had brought me here.

Carlos and Sophia had prepared a room for me, a guest cottage actually, and they told me to make myself at home. I settled in a bit, then figured out how to get myself into one of the hammocks on the patio, and I took a nap – a siesta. No dreams this time – I was tired from the flight and I was soon out like a rock, sleeping soundly in the hammock until they were calling me to dinner.

Sophia had prepared what she said was a very typical Colombian country meal – a grilled piece of pork and a spicy sausage, a fried egg, some fried plantain, rice and beans, and corn *arepas*. The plantains, or *platano*, were new to me, as were the arepas. The platano look like large bananas, but they are not nearly so sweet and are not eaten raw. In Colombia they're eaten like potatoes, and in fact taste a little like sweet-potatoes. The arepas are like thick pancakes, made from corn meal and fried or toasted. They're served many ways, but mostly as a bread with the dinner. Since pretty much everything grows in Colombia, over time the meals included pretty much everything as well.

After dinner, we sat on the patio and talked into the night. Carlos had lived for a while in the States, in Miami and in New York, so his English was pretty good. I knew a little Spanish, but only a little. Still, we never had any trouble understanding each other. He started telling me about Colombia and the area around Santa Marta. The city is an important port city, sitting right on

the ocean but also at the base of a mountain, the Sierra Nevada de
Santa Marta.

Sierra Nevada means literally snowy mountain, and the
mountain range rises from sea level to over eighteen thousand
feet only twenty-six miles inland. The peaks are covered with
snow year-round, while the lower elevations are warm year-round
and include virtually every climate and topography on the planet
– from beaches and deserts to rain-forest jungle to the peaks of
tundra and glaciers. The mountain and the beaches were home to
indigenous natives until the time of Columbus, Carlos explained.
With the arrival of the Spanish conquerors five hundred years
ago, the indigenous peoples fled to the safety of the high
mountains, and they have lived there ever since, with their ancient
culture having remained nearly unchanged. The city of Santa
Marta, however, is now a modern thriving city. It's a major port
for the export of the bananas that are harvested nearby and the
coal that is extracted from the mountain, and also for the famous
Colombian coffee. Santa Marta and the nearby mountains are also
a source of much of the Colombian drug trade. Marijuana was the
big crop until recently, Carlos said, but now it's cocaine. There's
ongoing violence between the various drug traffickers and the
government military forces and the civilian paramilitary forces.

"It can be dangerous traveling in the jungle and in the
mountains if you're in the wrong place at the wrong time," he
warned me. "The city itself has a long history of being a typically
rough seaport town," he continued. Pickpockets and prostitutes,
pirates and thieves of all sorts, that's been the history of the Santa
Marta coast forever. And now the drug violence. But the truth is,
if you're not caught up in any of that business it's a wonderful
place to live, and to visit. Just use a little common sense and be
careful. For one thing, I wouldn't wear that gold icon you're

wearing, not in the city anyway. Someone's liable to snatch it right off your neck! It's a tempting target for the wrong person."

Carlos was a musician, not surprising since he was friends with Tony and José. I'm guessing he was in his early forties. He had the rugged good looks and darker skin of a *costeño*, someone from the Caribbean coast. His family had been one of the old families rooted in the history of Santa Marta going all the way back to the colonial period when the city was founded. They had a lot of land that had been farm land in years past, coffee and bananas, but most of it was now occupied by large homes and commercial businesses. Carlos helped with the family business, but his real love was music. This was the land of *cumbia*, the country music of the coast and la Sierra, and Carlos played the accordion, the national instrument in this part of Colombia. He also played drums - everyone in Colombia played the drums, at least a little, it seemed. So before long, it was Carlos on the accordion and Sophia setting the rhythm with the clave and I followed along, beating a rhythm on the tambora as best I could, and we were making music together. Carlos said I had a natural Latin rhythm. Maybe so. I had come here to get to know myself, my roots, and I was already starting to feel more in touch with my inner rhythms, the heartbeat that was born inside of me.

Carlos was a walking encyclopedia of Colombian history and of its cultural roots. He picked up on my own interest and started telling stories. The folk music he had been playing, the *cumbia* and *vallenato*, were born here along the coast and the coastal mountains and valleys.

"Around the time of Columbus, Spain used its ports to import African slaves who tried to preserve their musical traditions and also turned the drumming and dances into a courtship ritual. Originally the music was mainly performed with just drums and claves, a very primitive music that was not much more than the primal beat. The slaves were later influenced by the local natives, with their flutes made of wood and bone and even bird feathers. The European guitars were added later by the Spanish settlers.

"According to legend, the accordion was added after a German cargo ship carrying the instruments sank as a cargo of accordions washed ashore on the northwest coast of Colombia. However, it's more likely that German immigrants brought the instrument to the coast in the nineteenth century, and it was later adopted by the local population."

Carlos pointed out that we all have our roots in this music. "The original peoples, the first human beings, the *homo sapien,* evolved in Africa, in the Great Rift Valley, and from there he spread throughout the world. All the peoples of the world descended from these same Africans.

"The rhythms of the coast are primordial, they're the mating dances of our African mothers and fathers. Originally the cumbia was a courtship dance only one step removed from African tribal ritual. For a long time the dance was regarded as too sexual and inappropriate for Spanish society and was only performed by the lower class."

Today, Carlos explained, the cumbia music, along with the related vallenato, are popular throughout Colombia and all of South America. Salsa, too, but the salsa has added many more instruments to the sauce, namely all the brass instruments that are conspicuously absent in the coastal music.

"There is a cumbia festival going on now in Santa Marta. We'll go into the city tomorrow. We'll show you around the town and we can enjoy some music and dance as well."

That became the plan, but for now I was very tired after a day of flying and the introduction to my new home – and my ancient roots. It was well past midnight when I opted to forego the comfortable bed Sophia had prepared for me in my room, and instead climbed back into the hammock and soon fell fast asleep under the stars.

We were all awake at sunrise, and Sophia served breakfast on the patio – fruit juice of fresh lulo, arepas with eggs, and Colombian coffee from freshly ground beans. As the morning sun grew brighter the chatter of birds grew louder. And then we were joined briefly by my friend, the Owl Butterfly. Carlos spotted her first. "There's the Búho! They say if she circles over your head she will spread the dust of her wings all over you and give you the gift of wisdom." This one flew off before circling my head, and she never spoke, but I took her appearance as an auspicious sign anyway. The Owl Butterfly had appeared to me, and it was no longer a dream.

Soon we were off to Santa Marta and more history lessons from Carlos. First stop was the historic center of town, with its government buildings of Spanish colonial architecture, narrow streets and wide parks and plazas. We went into the museum, the gold museum, that holds much of Colombia's treasure of pre-Columbian gold and a lot of other history as well. The history of early Spanish Colombia is a history of gold, and of Spanish greed. The museum exhibits display how the original peoples of the coastal mountains, the ones Columbus called the Indians and who called themselves the Tayrona, would craft beautiful figurines from the gold by melting it down and pouring it into wax molds. Many of the figurines were strikingly similar to the one I had been wearing, the one from my mother, and apparently from my father, and before that from the original peoples of the land. I was not wearing it today, as Carlos had suggested, but I did have it hidden in my pocket. I always had it with me. I couldn't help thinking that perhaps my golden figurine had come full circle, from the coastal mountains of Colombia to New York and back. I saw many figurines in the museum displays that were very similar to mine, but none that was exactly the same. Still, I came to believe in my heart that mine was from the Tayrona.

The museum guide explained that virtually all the gold of the Indians was stolen by the Spanish conquerors. Much of it was carried back to Spain by Columbus and those who followed him and the gold financed still more Spanish wars and conquests. For the indigenous peoples, the gold and the figures crafted from it represented the life-giving energy of the Earth, of their Earth Mother. The gold that didn't get shipped to Spain eventually wound up on the black market, with the Colombian government reclaiming much of it. Today the natives of the mountains, the ones for whom the gold had been so sacred, have none – no gold at all. The search for riches, the greed, that drove Spanish exploration, the search for the mythical city of El Dorado, has stripped the land and its original peoples of their sacred heritage. Figures that were once thought to be alive with the mystical energies of life now sit silent, locked up in glass cases.

It was here at the museum that I learned of the fabled Lost City, *la ciudad perdida*. This was not the mythical El Dorado, the city of gold in legend, but was a very real ancient city of the Tayrona, a city now abandoned in ruin, the remnant of a rich culture that died off following the Spanish invasion. Colombians call it the Lost City because it lay unknown for hundreds of years, hidden in the dense mountain jungle overgrowth, until re-discovered by grave-robbers looking for gold in the 1970s. Because of its isolated location, high in the rugged mountains, it remains largely unchanged from when the Tayrona culture disappeared nearly five hundred years ago. Drug traffickers and paramilitary operating in the secrecy of this dense forest have discouraged tourists from visiting, but with a good guide it is possible to make the two-day trek and visit the site we were told. Since the whole purpose of my coming to Colombia was to reclaim my roots, my heritage, I made up my mind to make a personal pilgrimage to the Lost City if at all possible. Carlos encouraged me and added, "I have a trusted friend who can take you."

Over the next two days I continued to tour the city and explore the Caribbean coast with Carlos and Sophia as my guides. We enjoyed the music and dancing of the cumbia festival, and also visited the quaint fishing villages to the north and the unspoiled beaches of the Tayrona coast. Everywhere we went, every new site I discovered, told its own story of the history of the peoples who had inhabited this place over time – the original peoples who lived here before Columbus and the Spanish and others who settled and built the cites afterward, and the African slaves who were added to the salsa. In a way, this colorful mix of peoples and their colorful history was my story, too, I was realizing. The rhythm and the energy I was feeling were in my heart and in my blood and my veins, and I was responding. I was starting to feel like I was truly home, home in that place where I had never been before.

There was more, much more, that I wanted to discover. I had seen the snowy peaks in the distance, first in my dreams and now for real in Colombia. It was as though the mountain was calling me. I was feeling a need to experience the energy of the mountain for myself, to follow in the footsteps of my ancient past. When we returned home, I pressed Carlos to tell me more of the Lost City. He had not been there himself, but he knew the person who would be the perfect guide for me. It was a two-day trek through the jungle, very steep and rugged, but with his friend I would be safe. A short time later, Carlos found me in my hammock and awakened me from my brief siesta to tell me the arrangements had been made. I would leave tomorrow.

First thing in the morning Carlos drove me to the little fishing village of Taganga where we met up with Ramon who would be my jungle guide. He looked every bit the part, with a thick black beard and dark leathery skin, wearing khaki field clothes and a holstered machete hanging from his waist. Right away I felt this was a guy who knew his way around the jungle and someone I could trust to get me to the Lost City and back safely. Ramon told Carlos that we'd be gone for about a week and that he'd bring me back to Carlos' home when we returned.

"Don't worry about the kid. I'll keep him from the pirates. He'll be safe."

That pirate remark didn't exactly put me at ease, but I trusted Ramon anyway. He said he was in constant conversation with the locals in the area and they had assured him there was no danger at the moment. I climbed into his Land Rover and we were on our way up the mountain.

As we drove Ramon told me a little more about the Lost City, *la ciudad perdida*, and revealed a little bit about himself. His father had been an amateur archeologist, which Ramon explained meant he was actually a treasure hunter, a grave-robber, looking for artifacts that could be sold on the black market. He was especially looking for gold. I suspected Ramon had engaged in more than a little treasure hunting himself. His dad was among those who first stumbled upon the Lost City only about fifteen years earlier. Until that time no one knew it was there, it is so secluded and overgrown and hidden deep in the dense jungle. Real archeologists, not the amateur kind, believe the city was established around the seventh century, making it older than the more famous Machu Picchu, the ancient Incan city in Peru.

"You'll see when we get up there that the city was laid out in a very elaborate and complex pattern, one the archeologists believe was a symbolic representation of the entire world and its place in the universe. It's a maze of paths and carefully constructed stairways leading to and from large open spaces and terraces, the foundations of what once were massive buildings, maybe temples. It was a very advanced society in its day."

Ramon explained that the city was once the heart of a network of villages inhabited by the Tayrona, the ancestors of the indigenous tribes that still live in the high mountains today. No one knows for certain how or when or exactly why the entire Tayrona culture disappeared, but it did, probably soon after the Spanish invasion. The city may have been overrun by Spaniards looking for gold, or more likely the European plagues that killed so many of the indigenous peoples also infected the Tayrona. Whatever the story, the city itself has remained silently abandoned and undisturbed for roughly five hundred years.

"It's believed there are still lost tribes hidden on the mountain, in the jungle, indigenous peoples who have had little or no contact with the outside world ever."

The Sierra Nevada is a triangular-shaped mountain that has its base beneath the ocean, and the part that emerges from the sea, the part we call land, the tip of the iceberg, if you will, rises from the beaches at Taganga and Santa Marta to the towering snowy peaks in a mere twenty-six horizontal miles. So the way up the mountain is steep, very steep.

The road was not very good to begin with, and it got steadily worse as we made our way up the base of the mountain. The cracked blacktop full of potholes soon disappeared altogether and the so-called road was now not much more than a washed-out river bed. The Land Rover earned its reputation as an off-road vehicle, to be sure. The road, or more accurately the path, became increasingly steep and narrow and rough, until it pretty much ended altogether at the base of a much steeper portion of the hill. We would leave the vehicle here and continue on foot.

"This is it, young man. This is the mountain - la Sierra."

Ramon had prepared packs for both of us with sleeping bags and a tent and enough food for several days of hiking. We loaded it all on a burro he hired from the local farmer. He gave me a *mochilla*, one of the woven bags the indigenous women weave and that everyone seems to carry. I hung it over my shoulder and filled it with water bottles and other things we'd need on the trail. We would hike all day today, camp for the night, and then hike another full day tomorrow before arriving at the Lost City the following morning.

It was not an easy hike. The path was narrow and overgrown with tall grasses that required constant clearing by Ramon and his machete. And it was very steep in places. We were headed for a destination that was much higher in the mountains, and getting there helped explain why the city lay undiscovered for so long.

The arduous trek had its rewards, though. It was incredibly beautiful in the lush jungle. Being so close to the equator there was sun every day, and during most of the year abundant rainfall pretty much every afternoon. We were now in the so-called dry season and the previous rainy season had turned the jungle into a lush green paradise. As we climbed the path we were constantly dodging low branches and hanging vines as I tripped over still more vines underfoot. There were palm trees of all kinds and sizes and banana trees and ferns and other plants with the biggest leaves I've ever seen. Orchids and many other flowers were everywhere, some even growing on the trees. And the trees looked alive, too, like they were some multi-armed character, watching our every move. Many appeared to have human faces, some smiling, most looking very stern, even frightening. I fully expected one of them to call out to me.

We occasionally caught a glimpse of a monkey climbing and jumping through the high branches, and I think I saw a sloth, but they look similar to the monkeys so I'm not certain. And of course there were the birds. We spotted several toucans and also what Ramon said was a quetzal, a very colorful bird that is quite rare and this particular one is only found in the Sierra.

There are apparently some small bear and small deer, and small leopards or jaguar in this part of the jungle, but we made it through our first night of camping without hearing any of them. What we did hear, at sunset and again first thing in the morning, was the mating cry of the howler monkeys. We never actually saw one, though. They're always hidden high in the jungle canopy of trees, Ramon told me. And during the night there were several bats making their eerie high-pitched sound as they buzzed around in the moonlight. In spite of them, we slept very well after a full day of rigorous hiking.

It was foggy as the sun rose since we were apparently high enough to actually be in the clouds. After Ramon made coffee and a little breakfast, we were back on the trail. As we walked I kept looking for the howler monkeys. I finally did see a couple, high in the trees. And I saw a big green iguana also high in a tree. Early in the morning the birds were very active and very noisy. The jungle was silent except for the birds and the howler monkeys, but somehow it felt very much alive. As we continued our climb up the mountain I was constantly aware of signs of small animals and lizards and insects and birds and butterflies everywhere. No Owl Butterfly, though. Not this time.

Just beyond a bend in the trail I thought I saw something move, an animal maybe, and then I thought I heard voices. Suddenly several soldiers in camouflage uniforms emerged from jungle and blocked our path. They were all displaying automatic rifles and wearing pistols on their belt. They looked like a serious threat. We stopped in our tracks and I held my breath as one of the men started to speak very abruptly, something in Spanish I didn't understand, but it sounded threatening. Ramon held up his hands in the air, so I did too. One of the soldiers then frisked us both, patted us down all over. And then Ramon removed his wallet from his back pocket. Now I was really scared. We were being robbed! But then Ramon started to take some identification out of his wallet and hand it to the soldier, and he said to me, "It's just a check point. Nothing to worry about," then he spoke to the soldiers and I understood something about "gringo" and "tourista." The serious looks on the men turned to smiles as they returned Ramon's ID and soon he was chatting with them as though they were old friends. He explained that it was a routine checkpoint, just a military presence on the lookout for drug traffickers or bandits. "You don't ever want to cross paths with guys with guns up here, but if you do, these are the ones you want it to be." I'm sure I breathed a noticeable sigh of relief, but I tried to look like I wasn't as scared as I had really been.

We continued on our way, and Ramon told me a little about the history of the drug activity in the area, and the violence. Colombia, and this area in particular, had once been the center of the world's marijuana production. With the help of the U.S. government, the Colombian government had sprayed the fields with a chemical defoliant and tried to kill off all the marijuana fields. It was effective, though quite obviously it also killed a bunch of good crops, food crops, as well. After that came the cultivation of coca for cocaine production, and now Colombia was the center of that illegal trade. The cocaine comes from the flower of the coca plant, Ramon explained, but the local people, the indigenous Indians, also chew on the leaves. The flower is the narcotic, but the leaves are a mild stimulant. "Coca leaves were the original stimulant in Coca-Cola, part of its original secret recipe," Ramon said. Further up the trail he pointed out a few coca plants and later some marijuana plants growing wild alongside the path.

"The big fields of cocaine, even marijuana, are usually on the hillsides, hidden by the trees, out of sight. You don't want to come close to those, even by accident. The government is always trying to find them and destroy them, and the paramilitary is always trying to protect them. You don't want to be caught in the crossfire! And that's exactly what's happened to the indigenous peoples here. This is all their land, has been since way before the Spanish arrived, and they just want to be left alone. They grow different crops for food, but then others come in and clear the fields and plant their coca, their cocaine, and then shoot and kill anyone who comes near. There are a lot of innocent victims in the drug wars, of course, but probably the most unfortunate are the indigenous peoples of la Sierra. They're a very gentle, simple, peace-loving people."

We saw some of their villages, with their round thatch roof huts, in the valleys off in the distance as we hiked.

Later in this second day of climbing the trail began to be marked with large stepping stones, obviously carefully placed on the path a very long time ago. Ramon said that at the height of the Tayrona civilization this would have been a very busy highway for the villagers coming and going from the main city. The improved path made the hike a little easier, but it was still very steep. In the steepest portions, there were steps, ancient stone terraces that formed steps up the side of the mountain. Ramon said there were more than a thousand hand-chiseled stone steps leading toward the entrance to the city. They helped.

The trail closely paralleled a small river most of the time. We were never far from the sounds of the water tumbling down the hills, and we passed several beautiful waterfalls, stopping once to dip in the stream and cool down. The jungle was very hot, easily in the nineties, and very humid and it felt good to rinse off in the icy-cold mountain waters, sparkling clear water that I guessed had been glacial snow only hours earlier. Perhaps these sparkling waters were among the many my mother had told me to watch.

We spent a second night in the tent, and continued our hike at daybreak. Just as the sun was rising over the mountains I caught my first glimpse of the Lost City.

The clouds were hanging over the hills, shrouding everything in a morning mist that only occasionally revealed the ancient remains on the distant hilltop. The stone foundations were covered in moss and surrounded with vegetation that made the entire site nearly disappear into its surroundings. Little wonder it had remained undiscovered for five hundred years.

We continued our trek, down this hill then up the final set of broad chiseled stone steps climbing steeply up the mountainside toward what must have been, once upon a time, the magnificent entry to an enchanted city. Today it was a silent monument to a vanished civilization. In this peaceful natural setting, where there was no obvious distinction between what was city and what was its natural setting - its environment, if you will - I couldn't help wondering whether the ancient civilization may have been more civilized than our modern ones, whether what had been lost was, in fact, our true nature.

We slowly walked around the ruins, almost silently, reverently, as though were visiting a cemetery, which in a way we were. The only sounds were the ever-present birds and the rush of the river in the valley just below. From time to time Ramon would point something out to me and explain it, but still with a gentle respectful voice.

"The Indians, the natives, they knew about this place all along, of course, even after the culture had disappeared. They used to call it by a name that meant "Green Hell." It can get cold at night, but it gets awfully hot up here in the middle of the day."

There were more than a hundred stepped terraces carved into the mountainside and a whole network of tiled pathways connecting everything to the several circular plazas that must have once been the center of community life and ritual. As I gazed at the terraces that were once the foundations for the city's structures, I tried to imagine what the long-gone wooden buildings might have looked like in their day. This was the capital of a proud nation of peoples, very advanced for their time, and the city was probably most impressive.

Many of the large stones appeared to have another function beyond merely being the foundation of a city. Some were positioned as monuments, aligned in relation to one another it seemed, almost like a small Stonehenge. Many of the large stones had patterns of lines inscribed on their face, which Ramon explained archeologists believed were a map of the city and of the maze of trails surrounding the city. Others surmised they might actually be a representation of the whole universe and the earth's place in it. The truth is no one really knew the hidden secrets of the Lost City.

We continued to quietly climb the terraces and explore the ruins, often pausing to sit for a while and just contemplate, to take it all in. Ramon took the burro to a clearing just below the city where he would set up camp for the night. I continued to explore and to ponder. I found myself thinking that this place was an important reminder of Colombia's past, but that perhaps in some way it was a part of my past as well. A part of me was Colombia, and a part of Colombia was this place. How much of me, how much of my connectedness with my natural surroundings, were born right here? Was it possible that some of the peoples who once laid out this city in the mountains were the forefathers of my father's forefathers? Was I in some very small way a child of this city, were the souls entombed beneath these stones my ancient cousins, my brothers and my sisters? Could they help me in my quest to reclaim my roots, to discover who I really was?

69

As I sat on a stone reflecting, I became aware of a pair of orange butterflies dancing together through the grasses and wildflowers below. How many butterfly lifetimes had come and gone through the centuries of this place, I wondered. How many caterpillars had crawled among these moss-covered stone markers before spreading their new-found wings and taking flight, discovering their former home through new eyes, from a whole new perspective?

As I played with these thoughts in my head, another Owl Butterfly passed by. I was no longer startled to see one but I still watched intently as she flapped her large wings and flitted her way back into the jungle branches at the edge of the city stones. I also saw a very colorful bird soaring in the clouds above, a large bird that for a moment I imagined might be the parrot, the guacamaya, of my earlier dream. She also flew into the high jungle canopy and disappeared. I thought about those dreams, about the about the butterfly, the parrot, the jungle, the sparkling water and the snowy mountains, and about how the dreams had seemingly all pointed to this place and led me to this moment.

And then they returned. The Owl Butterfly emerged from the jungle flowers and floated in circles in front of me, and the parrot swooped in from the trees, soared in a broad circle, and then landed on a stone perch just a few feet away. The Owl Butterfly flew toward the macaw – yes, it was a red and yellow and blue Guacamaya – and then toward me. It flew around me and then above me, once again circling overhead three times. But this was no dream. I was wide awake, albeit in something of a state of disbelief at what was occurring. I was sure I heard the Owl Butterfly say, "Hold out your hand," before she gently landed on my finger. The parrot, Guacamaya, started flapping his broad wings and came at me, startling me by taking up a new perch on my shoulder. I'm not certain which of them spoke to me next, maybe both, but again I clearly heard the words, "Follow me." I stood and started walking after the butterfly, with Guaca still sitting on my shoulder. She squawked gently into my ear, "We will lead you to your Mother and your Brother. They're waiting for you. Follow us." The Owl Butterfly made her way toward the far side of the Lost City, toward a path of flat stones that led back into the jungle. I followed, but then hesitated.

'I can't follow now, I can't just up and leave Ramon, I can't have Carlos and Sophia worrying about me disappearing in the jungle,' I thought. Before I could speak the Owl Butterfly answered, "They know you are following us. They have always known you were following us." I pinched myself, and followed. It was not a dream.

The Owl Butterfly led the two of us - me, and Guaca riding on my shoulder - along the path down the hillside and toward the forest at the edge of the Lost City, into what seemed almost like a dark tunnel through the dense jungle trees and foliage. The Owl Butterfly kept flitting back and forth among the plants and flowers alongside the path, alighting for a moment here and there, but always silently calling me on, until we emerged from the thick jungle in a clearing where we could see the river valley below and the snowy mountain peaks towering above the mist in the distance.

There was a rustling sound in the jungle leaves on the other side of the clearing, and a figure emerged, a young man, dressed all in white. He was a boy, younger than me I surmised. He was leading a mule. The Owl Butterfly flew toward him and Guaca left my shoulder and circled him as well. It was as though they knew this young man, this boy in white, as though they had been expecting him. Guaca landed on his shoulder. I swear it was

71

the mule who said, "Climb on my back. I will carry you up the steep and narrow path to where you must go. I will bring you to your Mother and your Brother."

The Owl Butterfly flitted off, way ahead of us, and Guaca soared into the jungle trees and disappeared in the distance. Without a word, the young man gave me a hand climbing onto the mule and led us back into the jungle and onto the narrow path that lay ahead.

Again I pinched myself. Again I confirmed this was not just another dream.

"So if it's not a dream," I said aloud to myself, "what is it? What's going on? Where am I going? What's with this talk of my mother and my brother? Are these the birds and the skies and the waters my mother had spoken of? Am I headed toward the snowy mountains of my dreams?"

"All your questions will be answered," said the young man, the first words he had uttered.

I believed him. So for the moment I answered my own questions, sort of, by letting go of them and just trusting they'd be answered in time. I came to a realization that all of this had been predicted by my mother and foretold in my dreams. I settled into a calm belief that I was somehow in the right place at the right time doing what I was supposed to be doing, and that I was being led in the right direction, led on a journey toward wherever it was that I needed to be going. Maybe I *was* being called.

We climbed the mountain trail for several more hours, clearly advancing higher and higher with every step of the sure-footed mule. Sometimes we were passing through the dense jungle, other times climbing a steep rocky hillside, and still other times winding our way through tall meadow grasses. From time to time I would see Guaca and the Owl Butterfly showing the way ahead of us, but clearly the young man and the mule already knew the way. No one spoke a word during the entire journey – not the boy, not the mule, not Guaca nor the Owl Butterfly.

After some hours we arrived at the edge of a deep gorge with a powerful river surging more than a hundred feet below us. It was a sheer drop down the vertical rock walls of the gorge to the rushing waters below. It would have been impossible to cross the chasm were it not for a massive bridge that had been laid across the gorge at its most narrow point. The bridge was constructed of entire trees, long thick tree trunks, tied together with vines. The bridge was held in place by upright trees that also supported a wall of tree branches that lined the two sides of the span. It looked like it was alive, green branches and plants and moss all over it, as though it was just another cluster of trees and intertwined vines anywhere in the jungle. The bridge appeared wide enough and sturdy enough to carry me and the mule across the deep gorge, but our way was blocked by a heavy gate. A line of thick vertical branches with pointed tips were strung together across the entrance and behind them two large logs were crossed in a big "X" to hold the gate securely in place - and securely closed. It was clear that someone did not want anyone crossing the river. The living bridge was silently but loudly proclaiming we were not welcome beyond this point.

The young man led us up to the gate, and just stood silently and waited. Then, as if they had been magically summoned, two men dressed in white came walking briskly toward us from the other side of the bridge and proceeded to lift the two heavy logs and then swing back the gate. They nodded in recognition to the young man and eyed me suspiciously as we passed. It was more than a little scary crossing the raging river below our feet as the planks and branches of the bridge creaked and shook under every step of the mule. As we slowly made our way across the span, the two men swung the gate back into position and secured it with the two logs. The way was once again blocked.

Safely on the other side, I saw that the landscape had changed. It was as though I crossed the gorge, crossed the bridge, and entered another world. The jungle had given way to a less dense more grassy forest and rolling hills. The sky that had been obscured by the jungle canopy was now clear and blue above us, and we could see the mountains stretching in front of us to the horizon, with a glimpse of the snowy mountains beyond them. In the sky there were occasional eagles or hawks gliding on the wind, flirting with the clouds, and I again heard my mother's voice, "Watch the water, watch the birds, watch the sky."

We continued on and soon climbed one particularly steep hill, arriving at the top of a broad ridge. What an amazing view! Spread below us was a spectacular valley, with a blue ribbon of a river meandering through the center, and what appeared to be a village, several clusters of round thatched huts. I could see cows and goats and sheep grazing, and a few Indians, some in the fields, others walking about, some on mules. A misty haze hung over the entire valley, giving the scene a mystical enchanted feel. Nothing was said, but I knew in my heart we had arrived at our destination.

We carefully navigated the steep trail down the side of the ridge toward the valley floor, toward the river. For the first time we were actually walking on level ground as we followed the river into the village. The first people we saw seemed to be afraid of me or at least very suspicious. And no wonder. I must have been an odd sight, riding on the mule with the parrot on my shoulder, the only white guy among all these dark-skinned natives, and the only one wearing an I♥ NY t-shirt! Children came out of their huts for a peek and eyed me suspiciously. The men and women would look me over briefly and then look down, apparently not wanting to make eye contact with this stranger. There were no greetings, no hellos, not a word. If it had not been for the fact that the young man was leading the mule, the young man in white who I guessed was one of them, I probably would not have been welcome at all.

The Owl Butterfly was leading the little caravan, the young man leading the mule and me with Guaca perched on my shoulder, and children were now following us, joining the procession a safe distance behind, and giggling at this strange sight. We came to a bridge across the river where we stopped and the young man motioned for me to dismount. He helped me off the mule, I stretched my stiff back, and he and the Owl Butterfly led me across the bridge. The bridge was a smaller version of the earlier one, made of entire tree trunks and blending into the surroundings as though the bridge was planted there, as though it was alive. We crossed the bridge, walked past a few more clusters of huts, and then made our way up a gentle hill at the edge of the valley.

The young man led me through a gate into another cluster of round huts where a small crowd of villagers was gathered. Again they all eyed me suspiciously. All except for one. A very short elf of a man stepped forward, the other villagers watching him, and me, intently. All of the villagers were short, but this one was the shortest of all. He looked to be a hundred years old. Big brown eyes and a large nose in the middle of a dark leathery face with character lines and wrinkles that spoke of wisdom, of years of living on the mountain. I couldn't help thinking he looked like a Hobbit. He too was dressed all in white. He was barefoot. He was clutching what looked like a gourd. His face was serious and almost expressionless as he moved toward me, appearing to be looking me over from head to toe as well, concentrating his gaze upon me, sizing me up. But there was no look of suspicion as with the others. There was almost a look of recognition. Then he greeted me. He reached out his hand and touched my shoulder and said something that sounded like "*azi mazari*," but all I heard and understood was "Welcome." There was an obvious reaction from the others, children giggled and the men and women smiled approvingly. This short man welcoming me was clearly a respected leader and his interaction with me was being watched very carefully.

He began to speak. He spoke slowly, deliberately, as though he was weighing every word before saying anything. Looking directly into my eyes he uttered words that I had never heard before but that I somehow understood perfectly. It was not unlike when the Owl Butterfly spoke to me – I never knew how she was speaking to me, but she was. I understood what she was saying even though I didn't understand how. So it was now. The individual words he spoke were unfamiliar, but I understood. I have come to understand that I was listening to the voice of his spirit, unencumbered by the distractions of language.

"Adam, welcome. Welcome to the Mountain. We have been waiting for you to come. We have been expecting you. The Elders have been expecting you. The Mountain has been expecting you. We all welcome you."

It was all so unbelievable. He knew my name. He was speaking a language I had never heard before and yet I understood him perfectly. And he knew I was coming. How did he know that when I didn't know that? In fact, I didn't even know where I was. It was so surreal I again wondered if I might be having another dream, but no, I was wide awake. This was no dream. This was real - not a new dream, a new reality.

As he continued speaking the Guacamaya flew off my shoulder and onto his. The Owl Butterfly flew around us both, then around the whole crowd, and then appeared to circle above us all – three times.

"Our friends have led you here, Adam. We sent Búho and Guacamaya to find you and bring you to us. You have heard our call in their voice. You have come, as we knew you would. You trusted your heart and you followed them. We thank you. Your Mother and your Elder Brother thank you."

I started to ask what he meant about my elder brother and my mother, but I held that thought as he took my arm and led me away from the crowd of villagers toward a nearby hillside. Three others walked with us as we left the villagers behind. The hillside was terraced, with wide steps carved into the slope, and the men motioned for me to take a seat. The hillside had a sacred-space feeling about it, like an intimate outdoor amphitheater where a Sophocles would have taught.

The four figures stood before me on the hill. There were two men and two women. The men were dressed in white tunics and pants, the women in white dresses and wearing many long strands of colorful beads about their neck. Their ages ranged from very old to younger, and their skin from dark to lighter.

The short one stepped forward and began answering my questions without my ever having asked them.

"We are the Elders. We are your Elder Brother, Adam, and the Mountain is your Mother, the heart of your Earth Mother. You are the Younger Brother. We have searched the world for you, for the younger brother who would understand, the one who would care. We have found you, and we have called you to come to us. We have a message for you, an urgent message for the Younger Brother. We have much to tell and much to share with you. We will give you a message for you to share with the younger brother everywhere. Your Mother is in danger, Adam. Our Earth Mother is gravely ill, and if the Younger Brother does not get the message, does not change his ways, she will surely die."

I was beginning to understand. So this was my elder brother, and the Earth was my Mother, and she was dying. He had answered a bunch of my questions, but raised many more. So they searched for me and found me, heaven knows how, and they sent for me and they have a message for me and I have to deliver it to the younger brother everywhere. That's a pretty big responsibility for a kid from the Catskills, I thought. Why me?

"Why you?"

Again he was answering my question before I could ask.

"Why not you? And if not you, who? Who cares enough about their Mother to listen? Who is listening to the rhythms of the world, to the heartbeat of his Earth Mother, trying to understand his purpose in life? Who has his whole life ahead of him, a lifetime to share the message and make a difference? You do. You're the one."

78

Silence. He played with the gourd he was holding, like it was helping him focus his thoughts, and he gave me time to consider what he had just said. I was the one. And why not? It would take a long while for the weight of that to sink in.

Still I wondered how they found me. If they never left the mountain how did they know about me, how did they find me?

"How did we find you, Adam?" He was doing it again — reading my mind. "How did you find us? The birds and the animals, the plants and the trees, the waters and the clouds. We never left the Mountain. We watched the water, we watched the birds, we watched the sky. Before you ever left your home they were speaking to us of you, and then speaking to you of us.

"If you create a ripple on the shore it will eventually cross the sea. Most people on the other side will never notice it wash up on their shore, but it is there nevertheless. Every ripple you have ever generated in your life has made its way to this mountain, Adam. And we've noticed. And without your knowing it, you've become aware of us in the same way.

"We called you, it's true, but you came to us because you were seeking us, not just because we called. You found us not because you were looking for us, but because you were open to seeing, to finding, to discovering. Because most others are not open to discovering they don't listen, they don't hear, they don't see. Those people would never find us.

"You are not a prisoner here. You came of your own will and you can leave, return home, anytime you wish, any time you want to walk away. But if you stay, we are offering you a gift. You will discover your real purpose in life. And if you know your purpose and follow your calling you will know true happiness, a happiness that is greater than any momentary pleasure, happiness that will last your lifetime, many lifetimes."

I knew I could leave, and my new teacher already knew I would not. It's a bit absurd, actually, but from the very first dream, when the Owl Butterfly called me to follow, I had never once hesitated, never thought for a moment about not following. And when she called me to leave Ramon, leave everything behind and follow her to this place for real, it had never occurred to me to say no. I had come to find my roots, to discover who I was, to begin to understand my real purpose in life. I was not leaving now.

"We are the people of the Mountain, the sons and daughters of our ancestors, the original peoples of the Mountain. And we are the Elders. We have consulted the ancestors and sought their guidance and have divined understanding from them. We know who you are and we understand why you have come. We understand what you want to ask. We understand what you need to know, what you need to learn. And we understand how you can help the younger brother to understand as well."

The Elders, whoever they were, had big plans for me. As for me, a lot of questions and a lot of uncertainty. It still didn't make a whole lot of sense.

"We are ready to help you with your work. You will have many teachers. We are ready to teach you and guide you in your learning. Some will speak of the past, our history. Others will share the secrets of what is written in the rock, on the stones. Still others will teach you how we are all connected, and how to listen to the plants and the animals. You will learn how to heal, because our Earth Mother is gravely ill. We will show you how to watch the water, watch the birds, watch the sky - how to discern what is happening to your Mother. We will teach you many things, but it is going to be a long process and you will have to work very hard. You will not learn about *things*. You will learn about your Earth Mother, and you will discover your self. We are going to lead you on a journey - a journey to the heart of the world. You are going to discover much. It will be a journey to your heart. You will discover your purpose in life.

"We will need to meet many times. And when we teach you, you need to chew on the teachings like we chew on the coca leaves – take it in, absorb its energy, let it expand your thinking."

He put his gourd into his mochilla and pulled from the bag a length of colored string. He took my hand and tied the string around my wrist, knotting it securely like a simple bracelet. Then he placed his hands on my shoulders and touched his forehead to mine. I had just been given a powerful blessing. The other three Elders proceeded to offer their blessing in the same manner, each securing a green cotton cord to my wrist and touching his or her forehead to mine.

"You have journeyed a long way, and now you have a very long journey ahead of you. You need to rest. Bunkey will show you to where you will sleep and the women will feed you. Chew on everything I have said, everything you have seen, all the questions that are arising. Take a little siesta in the hammock, and when the sun sets we will all gather to welcome you, to welcome you to the Mountain.

The young man who had brought me on the mule stepped forward and led me toward the cluster of thatched huts. Everywhere children were peering nervously out their doorways to see this strange outsider, and to giggle.

81

"I am Bunkey. The Elders will answer all your questions in time, but if there is ever anything you need, you just ask Bunkey."

He led me through the village and introduced me to the women. They showed me to what would be my bedroom. The inside of the round mud hut was bare, except for a hammock which was strung from wall to wall. This would be my bed. I had managed to grab my backpack as I was leaving Ramon to follow the butterfly and that was a good thing. A change of clothes and a toothbrush were now pretty much my only worldly possessions. I tossed the pack on the dirt floor as one of the women brought me a wooden bowl, a gourd cup actually, with a hot drink. It smelled like coffee, but tasted like sweet milk. "This is delicious. What is it?"

"It is coffee, raw coffee, not roasted in the fire. Very good for you."

Sure enough, there were small pieces of raw coffee bean, almost yellow like corn, not dark like roast coffee. Hot, sweet and delicious.

We stepped outside the hut and again women and children were watching us from the doorways of the cluster of other thatched huts. They brought me a larger wooden bowl filled with a hearty soup of meat and potatoes, even whole pieces of an ear of corn. And a wooden spoon.

"You have journeyed a long way. You must eat and drink. When the sun sets there will be a gathering in the *nuhue*, a ceremony to welcome you to the Mountain, with flutes and drums and sacred dance. When you have eaten you should rest. It may be a long night for you."

I sat for a while on a tree stump of a chair and I listened to the sounds. There weren't any. The entire valley was silent. There was no electricity, no motor vehicles, none of the usual sounds I was used to. Only the birds. I was in another world, another place and time. Not only was this valley, this village, like a strange and unfamiliar world, it was also as though I had traveled back in time, back to some ancient past. It felt like a storybook: "a long time ago, in a place far away."

Somehow, though, it also felt comfortable. I was not afraid. I had never been afraid, not from the first time the Owl Butterfly called me to follow. It felt right, like I was supposed to be here. The Elder was right - I wasn't forced to come here and I wasn't being held here against my will. But why was I here? Why this place and time? Oh, the questions. My head was full of them. Where was I, exactly, and why was I here? Who was this strange elder brother and what did he want to teach me? Was it the Earth Mother he spoke of who had wanted to talk to me in my dreams? And what did he mean she was dying? And how did that involve me, anyway? How long would I be here, when would I go home?

I climbed into the hammock and soon fell asleep pondering all these thoughts.

I was awakened from my brief siesta by a voice calling out. "Mister. Mister." I awoke a bit startled, disoriented, for a brief moment not remembering where I was. It was Bunkey calling me to the gathering: "Follow me."

It was only a short walk to the very large hut they called the *nuhue,* where a large crowd of curious villagers had gathered. The circular *nuhue* was much larger than the other huts, like a grand meeting hall. The sun was setting behind the mountains that surrounded the valley, and heavy clouds had come down and dropped so low that they, too, were touching the tops of the mountains. Darkness was settling in.

The Elder greeted me and led me in. It was totally dark inside except for the glow of four fires, one in each quarter of the circular dirt floor. In the flickering light I could see a few men seated around the fires, tending them, while others were lying in hammocks hung along the circular walls. But most of the men, and there were many, were seated on long benches arranged around the center, with a broad aisle connecting a front and a back door. The smoke of the fires filled the dome of the thatched roof. It was other-worldly, like being inside an ancient cave.

In fact, as the Elder explained it, it was more like returning to the womb. "The *nuhue* is like the Mother's womb, a sacred space where creation takes place. The roof above and the ground below represent the universe, with creation, life and death, cradled in between, the valley surrounded by the Mountain. It is the world-house, a place of this world and also the spirit worlds of the past and the creative imagination of the future."

And I had seen it as just a big mud hut. Silly me.

"The *nuhue* is constructed according to a plan given to the people of the Mountain by the Mother herself. It is the home of the Law of the Mother, the Law of Origin. It is the law of rhythm and balance and harmony. The four fires honor the four directions and the four forces of creation - earth, wind, fire and water. They create everything, they sustain everything. It is here that we speak of what we have discerned in the waters. It is here that we come to agreement on how it is we are to carry out the Law of the Mother."

There were only men in the *nuhue*. I wanted to ask about that, but for now it was time for introductions and ceremony.

Through the cloud of smoke I could make out a great crowd of villagers seated around the world-house. Many more were gathered outside the doorways.

"This is Adam, the younger brother."

There was a great buzz of chatter and a lot of nodding of heads.

"You know of him already. Together we searched for him, we found him, and we sent word for him to come."

Still more buzz. It reminded me of scenes I had seen of the Parliament in England where everyone loudly expresses their approval or disapproval as the speaker speaks. The members of this parliament seemed to be voicing approval, one and all.

"He has followed our call. He has come to us. He has come to the Mountain." The buzz continued.

"He is prepared to listen, to learn, and to share with the Younger Brother." Still more buzz.

"Let us welcome him to the Mountain, to the Heart of the World."

With that the buzz and nods of agreement were joined by the sound of flutes and drums. It seemed the party had begun, or maybe the ceremony. I think it was both.

The celebration was soon bigger than the world-house could contain. Inside the *nuhue* the men continued to discuss among themselves while also sizing me up. Slowly they began moving outside where the women had assembled a grand buffet of more hearty soup, rice, beans, vegetables and all sorts of fruit.

Some of the men and women had joined hands and were now dancing in one big circle to the rhythm of flutes and drums. Some were wearing elaborate headdresses with colorful feathers. It was not a gyrating sexual type of dance, but a very subdued and pulsating dance, the entire circle seeming to flow as one, first in one direction and then in the other. It was not a salsa rhythm at all. It was more like the beating of the heart.

"The people are happy, but they are serious as well," said the Elder. "They celebrate your coming and they ask the Mountain and the Mothers to bless what we will do here. Our Earth Mother is gravely ill. She is in pain. If the younger brother does not hear her cry and does not join us in helping to care for her health, she will surely die. We have hope. If we did not we would never plant another seed with the hope of it one day blossoming and bearing fruit. We have hope that the younger brother can change his ways, can stop destroying and begin healing. We know we need to share our message with the younger brother. That is our job if we are to continue to care for our Earth Mother. But we cannot do it alone. We need a messenger, a younger brother who will learn and teach and lead. Our Earth Mother needs that kind of messenger. We hope it is you."

I didn't know what to think. I had never thought of myself as any kind of leader. I was just a kid from New York, trying to stay out of trouble and doing what I enjoyed doing. I had my hopes, too - hope that I could learn a little more about myself, who I was and what my roots were. I wasn't here to save the world.

"Join the dance, find yourself in the rhythm." The Elder was once again speaking to my thoughts.

So dance I did. They took me by the hand and brought me into the circle. It was a simple rhythm, simple steps. Soon I was dancing as one with the group. They loved it! I was worried that this was a sacred dance and that my participation might not be respectful, but they invited me and encouraged me, and soon we were all moving together, in harmony with the same gentle rhythm. And there was singing. I couldn't understand a word of it, of course, but that didn't matter. It was more like a chant, more like sounds than words. Soon I was haltingly chanting the syllables in concert with everyone else. It was a global chorus to be sure. I felt the rhythm. I felt the words. I felt connected.

Then they handed me a drum. I was hoping they would. They all smiled broadly as I started banging out the rhythm, becoming one with the beat of everyone else. In this part of the world the drummer is king, and when they saw I knew how to play I became one of them for sure.

The music, the dancing and the chanting continued well into the night. There was more food and even a little home brew of some sort that appeared out of nowhere.

But I was exhausted, and the Elders knew it.

"Perhaps you should get some sleep. This is your home. Our people say this valley is the land where the sun is born. Return to us in the morning, when the sun is born again, and we will begin to show you all that your Earth Mother is waiting to teach you."

Chapter 4

In the Beginning

Just as promised, the sun rose in the mountains above the valley, the morning light shining through the open hole of a window of my hut. The night had been cool, but the first rays of the sun were already warm. One of the women brought me a hot cup of coffee served up in a small wooden bowl.

"Mister Adam." It was Bunkey. "When we get to the place where the Elders will be you must remove your shoes. The Elders will be offering you their sacred teachings in a most sacred site. It is important that your feet be in touch with the land, connected - connected with *la madre tierra*."

Soon we were off to see my new teachers.

They were waiting for me on the hillside. I slipped off my shoes as the Elders greeted me with something that again sounded like *azi mazari*. The Elder pulled something from his bag, his mochilla, and said, "When we meet, we offer each other the coca leaves. I give some to you, and you give some to me. It is a practice in giving and receiving. The leaves of the coca plant are a gift, a gift of energy. Whenever we receive a gift we must always give back something in return." He then retrieved a small mochilla from his larger one and handed it to me. "These are your leaves. Put some in your mouth, in your cheek, and chew on them. Keep the others to give back later."

I put a generous pinch of the dry leaves into my mouth and chewed on them. They had very little flavor, but soon there was a slight tingling sensation on my tongue and cheek. I did as the others were doing; I chewed on them as I would chew gum or maybe chewing tobacco. It didn't seem to be giving me any kind of a high or anything like that.

The Elder held up his gourd and explained, "When a boy becomes a man he receives the coca leaves." He pulled the stick from the gourd, the stick he was constantly dipping in the gourd then pulling out and rubbing against the outside of the gourd. He placed the stick in his mouth, licking the white substance from its tip.

"We mix the coca leaves with the calc from the seashells. It releases the energy of the leaves. The younger brother is not ready for that yet."

The Elders kept working their gourds, constantly dipping the stick in the gourd, dipping it in their mouth, and seeming to paint the sides of the gourd with it. Me, I just kept chewing my coca leaves.

"When a young boy is recognized by the Elders as a future Elder, he is brought to a place away from the others, to his own hut, where he is hidden from all distractions and carefully taught by the elder Elders. He learns how it was in the beginning, and the long story of our people, the original peoples of the Mountain. He discovers the spirit world, how to enter into her world, how to divine what she's revealing to us. He learns how we are called to care for our Earth Mother. He learns how to heal. He discovers everything that has been passed on to the Elders before him, in time it is all revealed to him, so that one day he can be a leader and can pass on all that has been revealed to him, so he can show

89

the way to those who will follow. This teaching takes many years for the young Elder.

"We have called you to come to the Mountain, to leave your world behind, to be alone in this place, free of all distraction, to receive the teachings. We will teach you. But with you we do not have many years as we do with a young Elder. Our Earth Mother is suffering. She is in need of healing. Every day we see the changes, we see the disease spreading. Every day we do our job, we do our work, we care for our Earth Mother. But it is no longer enough. We have seen what is happening to the Mountain and what is happening beyond our world. We can no longer ignore what the younger brother is doing. If the younger brother does not awaken and change his ways, if he does not become the healer instead of the one spreading the disease, then our Earth Mother will surely die."

He looked deep into my eyes as he delivered his solemn warning directly to my heart.

"It is said that near the time, when the world is very weak, one of the Younger Brother will come to help us. We have searched for you. Now we must teach you."

His eyes were almost tearful as he made it clear this was serious business. We were about to begin the teachings that he fervently hoped would change my life and begin to change the world.

"In the beginning, the natural law was given to the original people. It is written in the colors – it is written on the stone and in the water, in the colors of the rocks and the land, the colors of the oceans and the rivers and the snows, the colors of the plants and the trees, the colors of the birds and the animals and the fishes, and the colors of the people - the brown people, the white people and the black people, the red people and the yellow people and the peoples of all colors in between. The younger brother can learn to read the colors - with much spiritual work and effort."

I felt like I felt when my mother taught me something new. With her I always felt I was being given the gift of knowledge, not just facts to memorize; revelation that would pique my natural curiosity, knowledge that would inform my experience and grow into wisdom. She always told me the Earth was our best teacher, and I felt as though she was speaking to me now.

"In the beginning there was nothing – no land, no water, no plants or animals, no people. Nothing. Only *aluna*. Only the fertile sea of thought that is *aluna*. *Aluna* is the creative imagination, the mind, the consciousness. Everything is created in *aluna*; everything is created in the imagination. Nothing comes into being until it is imagined. When it is imagined it comes into being. So it was with *aluna*, in the beginning. All that is was first imagined, imagined in *aluna*. Everything was born in the imagining. *Aluna* is the ultimate reality, the source of our being. *Aluna* is everything that is, everything that was or ever will be. We - you and I, the elder brother and the younger brother - we were all given birth in the creative imagination of *aluna*."

He motioned for me to rise and follow him to a point on the hill where we could view the entire valley and the mountains beyond. With a sweeping wave of his arm he pointed to the broad horizon.

91

"All that you see in this world was first imagined in *aluna*. Nothing was ever created that was not first imagined. Everything that has ever been created was born first in the imagination. The creative imagination has given birth to all that has ever come into being. Everything. The beginning of all things lies in the beyond in the form of thoughts that have yet to become real."

I was looking out at the world from my new vantage point. I was watching the water, watching the birds, watching the sky, and already starting to see things in a new way. It was as if I was seeing it all for the very first time. It was as if my new teacher was holding the world in his hand and rotating it, turning it around and around and saying to me, look at it in a different way, from a different angle. Look at it from here. Look at it this way. All of this, everything, was created in the imagination.

"Everything was created in the imagination of *aluna*. First she imagined the sky and the sun and the moon and the stars. She imagined them into being. Then she imagined the land and the mountains, the oceans and the rivers, and then she imagined the plants and the animals and the birds into being.

"Finally she imagined the people into becoming, the people she imagined would care for all she had created, the people who would nurture it, protect it. The people who would be the living heart of the world she had imagined into being."

He explained that the Elders knew all the details of how everything was created but that it would take nine years to explain it all to me, and the details were not something I needed to know anyway. The process of creating, of bringing that which was imagined into being, was like spinning thread on a spindle, like the men weaving their clothing on the loom, like the women weaving the mochilla with their hands.

"The Mother stuck her spindle in the fertile ground of her imagination and spun it, turning the world of her imagining on its axis, spinning out a thread which is both time and space, creating first a heap of thread that is the Mountain, and then more and more, spiraling ever outward, eventually weaving the fabric that is the whole of the world. All the patterns and all the colors she had imagined are carefully woven into place, and finally the complex tapestry emerges. *Aluna* created all this that you see with her spindle and loom. She created and is still creating. We remember this whenever the men weave the clothes and when the women weave the mochilla. Our clothes, our mochilla, everything, may be helped into this world by our hands, may be shaped on our loom, but they were first born in the Mother's imagining. Everything that is or has been existed first in the world of *aluna* before it came into being in our world."

He motioned again at the world that was spread out before our eyes, and then reached down and took hold of a yellow flower growing at his feet.

"Everything is from *aluna*, everything is one with *aluna*. All the plants and animals, the mountains and waters, the sky and the birds – and all the people – were one in *aluna* and all are still one with *aluna*."

A butterfly landed on the flower he was holding, not an owl butterfly but a bright yellow one, the color of the flower. The Elder extended his hand toward the butterfly who fearlessly came to rest on his finger.

"Since everything is from *aluna*, we are all a part of the same One. You are the sun and the rain, the water and the plants, the birds and the animals. There is no such thing as 'nature,' apart from you and me. You are nature, I am nature, just as you are me and I am you."

Now it was the other Elders' turn. As we walked along the ridge, looking at the view of the valley, they explained to me that the energy of *aluna*, the creative energy, had been woven into the Mountain. One of them used a branch to inscribe a triangle in the dirt, saying the Mountain was a pyramid, a pyramid of energy. It was the job of the Elders to maintain the balance and harmony of the Mountain's energy. "Everyone has a job to do, every plant and animal has a job to do. The Elders' job is to care for the Mountain, the heart of the world. If the heart is healthy, if she is beating in harmony with the natural rhythms of the earth, then the earth is healthy. If the Mountain is not healthy, if the energy of the Mountain is out of balance, then the whole world is out of balance."

Another of the four Elders stepped forward and continued the teaching:

"The Mountain is the heart of the world, and those of us who care for her are the heart of the world as well. There is no difference, no separation – we are one, the Mountain, the people, the heart of the world. The Mother created the people, created them from her offspring, from her first born. She created the first peoples to look after her creation, to care for it, to be the caretakers of the world, to be the heart of the world here in the very Heart of the World. The plants and the trees, the animals and the birds were placed in the people's care, not for the people to dominate and exploit but for the people to care for. The people were created in the imagination of *aluna*, and the people have a spark of that creative imagination within them. The plants and the animals do not. The people can dream, can imagine a future, the plants and animals cannot. The people were created with a compassionate heart, a loving kindness that was given to them so that they would understand their purpose is to care for all the others. The plants and the animals do not have that kind of compassionate heart, do not have a creative imagination. The plants and animals only know their one small job in life, and they only know how to do it. It is the people's job to protect them so that they can continue to do their job. That is the people's only job, their purpose on this mountain, on all the Earth – to care for and protect all the others."

The fourth Elder took another branch in hand and again drew a line on the ground.

"After the Mother created the original peoples, the Elder Brother, she created a second people, the Younger Brother. These second people also had a creative imagination, the ability to envision things and bring them into being. In fact, that was to be their job, their only job – imagining and making things. But their creative mind was like that of the monkey - they never evolved, always jumping about, jumping from this branch to that, this idea to that, always wanting new things. They wouldn't stay still long enough to listen to the Mother, they paid no attention to the Mother's teaching, they ignored the Natural Law. They only paid attention to their monkey mind, never listening to their compassionate heart. They consumed all their energy making and using things and never developed their capacity to care for the things that were already around them. They developed their brain, but never developed their heart. They came to believe it was their job to conquer new worlds and ignored their responsibility to show loving kindness toward the world the Mother had created."

She pointed to the line she had drawn in the dirt. "It is for this reason that the Younger Brother was expelled from the Mountain. He was driven from the Mountain and cast into exile across the sea. He was sent to a harsh land where it was cold and where the fruits did not grow and where the animals did not abound, and here he was free to occupy his time making and acquiring things in order to survive. The elder brother would continue to care for the Mountain and the earth and leave the younger brother to follow his own pursuits on the other side of the ocean, in another part of the world."

The four Elders motioned for me to follow, and we made our way down the hillside toward the river and eventually to a collection of large boulders at the edge of the water. They pointed to strange markings on the stone, lines that were not unlike those on the rocks in the Lost City.

"We did not mark this stone. The people did not mark the rock. It was marked by wind and water, inscribed in *aluna*. It is a map of the Mountain, and beyond. All the universe is inscribed here. A map of the past and a map of the future. The Elders can read the map, can read the Mountain. We can see the place of the Mountain, the heart of the world, and we can see the places beyond, the lands beyond the Mountain, beyond this valley, beyond the sea, the lands where the younger brother has been using all his energy making things. We can read the changes. We watch the water. We watch the birds. We watch the sky. We can see in them what is happening beyond the Mountain. We can see the changes."

They led me across the river, not across the bridge this time, but by wading through the shallow water. The Elders don't wear shoes or sandals, they explained, because they want to feel the land, feel the water. They are always connected to the earth in this way. Sandals on their feet would create a disconnect, an unhealthy separation just as Bunkey had said. Touching the land with the soles of their feet is a constant reminder that they are one with the earth. They must have very strong soles since they're constantly walking the trails and climbing the hills and crossing the river in their bare feet. I removed my shoes again and waded into the river. The sun was already very warm and the icy cold waters were invigorating.

We crossed the river and walked toward the hills on the opposite side of the valley and began following the trail upward. There were clusters of huts and the villagers would peer at me through the open doors, the children peeking from behind the safety of their mother. I was the pale-faced curiosity, for sure. We continued walking for a considerable distance, at times climbing very steeply up the mountain. The Elders walk very briskly and it was often a challenge for me to keep up. As we got higher and higher I could occasionally catch a glimpse of the snow-capped peaks in the distance, barely visible through the clouds just above the nearer mountains.

We climbed to the top of a ridge and started down the other side when I heard the sound of rushing water. The river water back on the floor of the valley had been very calm, but this was a loud and powerful sound. As we made our way down the steep hillside I could see a deep canyon below with the waters tumbling through it and down the mountain. And above the waters was a giant stream of water cascading down the entire height of the mountain before us. The waters fell hundreds of feet into the pool below before continuing over the edge into the canyon stream below. I have seen many waterfalls, before and since, but this may have been the most beautiful of all.

For some time we all stood silently, reverently gazing at the majesty of the water. It was a moment of meditation, of prayer. For a teenager like me it could easily have been a time to jump into the blue pool and frolic under the cascading waters, but that is not what this particular time called for. The Elders quietly watched the waters fall and offered blessings with their gourds. I followed their lead and my mother's advice - I watched the water, watched the water in awe and deep respect. It was clear the Elders had brought me here for a reason, for another important lesson.

"In the beginning all was water. The water was the Mother, the water was *aluna*. Where there is water there is life, there is memory of the past and potential for the future. It is in the water that everything can be imagined into being. Without the water, nothing can be imagined. Without water the plants would die, the people would die, the Mother herself would die. That is the most basic law. Without water there is no life. Take away the water and everything will die. That is the Law. The people cannot change the Law, not the King, not the President, not the Congress or the Parliament. The Natural Law is constant, forever, unchangeable. Without water there can be no life. If we are to care for the Earth, first we must care for the water."

I knew that, of course, but with the backdrop of the magnificent waterfall the message of the Elders was powerful. In the beginning was the water. Water is life. Take away the water and you take away life. End of story.

"In the beginning we were formed in the water. The Mother formed us there. The waters are like the Mother's milk, they give life to the new creation, to the child of her womb. We were all conceived in the waters of *aluna*, in the creative

98

imagination of the sea of *aluna*. When you were conceived, it was known first in *aluna*, it was known in the water. Your future was known in *aluna* before you were born. You were conceived in the waters of *aluna* before you were born in the life-giving waters of all the oceans and rivers of this earth."

"You were born upon that sea. Everything we would ever remember was first in the waters, in the ocean of *aluna*. It always was. It was before it was. In the Mother's knowing. All the worlds beyond all the waters of all the rivers and seas have always been in the Mother's knowing. It always was, from the beginning. As long as there is water giving life to the plants and the trees, as long as there are clouds and rains and snow, the trees and skies will always hold all it is that we will ever remember."

I was hearing the words of my mother: "From the moment you were born, I have always known you were destined to live an adventure and make your mark on the world, to make a difference. The Earth is calling you, Adam. Listen to her. Follow her call. Watch the water…" I had played the words over and over in my head, in my heart, but now it was as if I was hearing them for the first time - what it was she had been trying to tell me, what it was that had always been in her heart.

The teacher waded into the water at the base of the waterfall and beckoned for us all to follow. He held a gourd in both hands for a moment, lifting it toward the waterfall, offering a blessing. He returned the gourd to his mochilla, and with his bare hands he scooped up the water.

"When you touch the water you touch everything. When you hold the water in your hands you hold the whole world in your hands."

Several times he scooped up the water and let it fall through his fingers, the waters sparkling in the sun, the bubbles dancing on the pond. He lifted a handful of water and held it out toward me, for me to look into.

"All that ever was or ever will be is in the water, in the memory of the water, the memory of the sea of *aluna*. Everything that ever was or ever will be has been born in the waters and nurtured by the waters. The water is *aluna*, the water is life. If we watch the bubbles we can see the memory of all that was, a vision of all that will be. All we should remember can be found in the water."

He turned his back to the waterfall and looked out at the horizon ahead, at where the water flowed to the edge and over the rock, falling in another cascade to stream into the ravine below. From there, the water continued its journey down the mountain, joining the river below, and eventually making its way to the sea. Ahead we could see the whole valley and the mountains on the other side, and the snowy peaks above all.

"As far as you can see," he said with another broad wave of his hand, "everything is water. The plants and trees are water, the snows are water, the rivers and streams are water, of course. Even the mountains and hills, even the rocks and stones, are all water, filled with water, literally mountains of water. And you are water. There is nothing you can see that is not water. The water weaves everything together, all is alive, all is interwoven. And just as the waters are alive, everything of the waters is alive. The trees and the plants, the mountains and the rocks, the animals and the birds, even the sky and the clouds - all are alive, alive with water flowing through their veins. There is life in the smallest drop of water, and there is water flowing through the tallest mountain.

100

Everything was born of the same water - every animal, every plant, every person, every mountain. All have the same Mother, all have the same waters running through them. This is why every mountain is your brother, your sister, your mother and your grandmother. Every tree is your cousin. We are all a part of the same One."

I had never thought of water in this way before. I have to admit, I had probably pretty much taken water for granted. I had always known water in my life, plenty of water, enough for drinking, taking a shower, watering the plants – there was always water around me and always enough water. It never ran out. So I guess I just took it for granted. Sure, I enjoyed looking at a beautiful lake or watching the river as much as the next person, and I knew there was life in the water, the "little beasties" we had seen through the microscope in science class, but I had never seen water in this way before. I was seeing it in a different way, from a different perspective.

"When you look at the water, when you want to see deep inside the water, you must always look at it from the four directions."

Like the butterfly, the Elder seemed to know what I was thinking.

"Look at it from the north, from the south, from the east and from the west. Turn it around in your mind and view it from top to bottom, from left to right, then turn it upside-down and sideways and look at it again. You have to watch the water with both eyes wide open if you are to see the life within it. With the eyes of a child you must look deep into the colors of the bubbles. You must watch the water from all four directions if you are to also watch the sky, to watch the birds, to discover yourself."

I would never view water in the same way again, never again take it for granted.

"In the beginning there was the ocean of *aluna*, the waters of pure consciousness, of mind, of creation. It was in the beginning, it has always been, it is now. *Aluna* created all and is still creating. *Aluna* imagined all before time and is now imagining the future. We can enter into *aluna*, into her memory and into her vision, by watching the water, by looking deeply into the bubbles of the waters. It is in the bubbles that we can read the memory of all that ever was. It is in the bubbles that we can see a vision of our future. It is by entering into *aluna*, by concentrating on all that is revealed in the colors of the bubbles, that our consciousness becomes one with the mind of *aluna*. We were all born of *aluna*, we are one with her and anyone can return to *aluna* at any time. The Elders enter into *aluna* all the time. The younger brother has forgotten how. When the younger brother left the Mountain behind he also left behind his connection with *aluna*. The younger brother lives his life without any sense of oneness with *aluna*. The Elders are different; we have never lost our way, never left *aluna*. We return to the realm of *aluna* every day. It is in *aluna* that we first discovered the law of how things were and how things were to be. It is in *aluna* that we continue to discern what we are called to do, to discover our job, to learn the purpose of everything in life and to know our place and our purpose in the Mother's great plan, in her mind, in her vision for the future. And it is in *aluna* that we can see what is happening in the world beyond the Mountain. We can see what is happening, we can discern the changes, we can read the future."

I believed him. He could see the waters as I had never seen them. He could read my mind. He could surely see the past and read the future. He was like a magician, but I was beginning to realize he was simply seeing clearly what was already there - there for anyone to see. The Elders had never taken any of it for granted; they had never lost their ability to see with eyes wide open.

"In the beginning was the water, the sea of *aluna*. The oceans and the rivers were born in the creative imagining of *aluna*. Since the beginning of time, the waters have had a rhythm, the rhythm of life. The waters of the sea rise up to the sky, and the clouds are born. The clouds embrace the mountain, and the rains and the snow are born. The waters of the snow melt into the fertile earth and begin their journey down the mountain. They form the lakes that become the source of the rivers and streams that all flow back again to the sea. And then the cycle begins again, the circle of life. The waters have had a million lifetimes and will have a million more. Every lifetime is recorded in the memory of the water, in the memory of *aluna*. Every new lifetime of the water has the potential to create new life. In its many lifetimes, all of the water has lived in the plants, in the animals, in the mountains and the rivers, in you and in me. The water is the thread that binds us together. Every lifetime is interwoven. Every lifetime has been different and each one has been recorded in *aluna*. Every one has been remembered."

The Elder silently fondled his gourd, rubbing the stick on the shell of the gourd, seemingly looking into the memory that had been inscribed over the course of many meditations.

"We have seen the changes. We have seen the changes in the water. We look into the water with our eyes, with our listening, with our feeling, with all our senses, we enter into the sea of *aluna*, and we watch the water, we watch the birds, we watch the sky – and we see the changes. The waters are changing. The rain no longer comes as it used to. We have months with no rain at all, and months when the rain washes the earth into the sea. Every year the snows on the Mountain recede. When all the snows have melted there will be no waters for the lakes, the rivers, the streams. Water that used to be pure as the snow is now unclean. Plants that were green are now dry and brown. Places that used to be fertile valleys are now under water, and other places now have no water at all. We have seen the changes. In *aluna* we have seen the changes beyond the Mountain, beyond the sea. And we have seen the changes beyond the changes, the changes that are yet to come."

Each of the Elders in turn offered a blessing in the direction of the waterfall, and tossed offerings from their mochilla into the waters below.

"This is our offering, our *pagamento*, our payment for all that our Mother has given us. For everything received, something must be given back. The balance must be maintained."

Then they motioned for me to follow them down the mountain, pointing out plants and animals and special trees to me as we walked.

"We will show you the changes. We will climb the Mountain to the snows, we will go down to the sea, we will follow the river, follow the water, and you will start to see. Today we will return to the village, to our river, and you can chew on all we have shared. And you can start to watch the water. Watch the water and begin to see what you have not seen before. Begin to open your eyes to what the bubbles will reveal. The younger brother can learn to read the bubbles, not as the Elders can, but to read them nonetheless. There is no magic in it. It's like looking at the stars – you don't need to know the names of every star or which is bigger or farther away to learn something about your place in the universe just by looking at them. You don't need to know how the bubbles work; you just have to be open to learning from them. You only need to let go of all that is keeping you from seeing clearly, all your old ways of perceiving, and let yourself be open to seeing the light in the bubbles, to see in a new way. Let go of thought and awaken yourself to knowing."

Another Elder added, "You can learn to see the changes, too. You can widen your vision and enter into *aluna*. If you don't learn to read the changes, they will happen without you being aware, and our Mother will die. The Mother will die if the younger brother does not open his eyes and awaken."

And another Elder: "Our mother is dying and the younger brother is sleeping. He needs to open his eyes and awaken. Our mother will not survive unless he opens his eyes, unless he is fully awakened to the reality of the world around him, the world he lives in."

And still another Elders said, "Over time we will show you more – we will wander the Mountain together and you will begin to see the changes for yourself. We will teach you how to see what you are not seeing now."

They took me back to the valley, to the river, and led me to a place by the water where I could see the rushing waters tumbling down the hill into a calm pool of water at my feet. I could sit on a broad flat rock and look at all the waters – the calm waters, the rushing waters, the sparkling waters and the bubbles.

"This is your work for the rest of the day. Watch the water. We will see you when the sun is born again in the morning."

Chapter 5

Spread Your Wings and Fly

It was as if I had stepped back in time, back to the beginning. As I walked along the side of the river there was not a sound, not a single sound that didn't belong. Nothing but nature. No cars on the road, no stereos blaring, no machines whirring. Only the sound of the birds and the occasional cow or lamb or goat. And the sounds of the river, the sound of the water. I found a large smooth boulder along the shore, half in the water, half out, and I sat upon it, and I watched the water.

"Watch the water. Watch the birds. Watch the sky."

I gazed into the waters. The words of my mother became one with the water, one with my thoughts, one with the reflection of the clouds on the ripples. I could see the colorful polished stones deep beneath the waters, and my mind dived even deeper. I imagined the world extending far below, and all of it a part of the water. My concentration flowed deep into the depths of the water's imagination, and soon I was lost in thought. The gentle flowing waters stilled my mind and seemed to transport me to another place and time, back to the beginning, back to when all was water and only water. My awareness became totally immersed in the water, I was aware of nothing else. I was soon oblivious to my surroundings, totally focused on the water, watching the water, listening to the water, even smelling the water and tasting the water in my concentration. It was as if I was floating, floating in the waters of my mind. I was trusting myself to the water, letting go of everything else. It was like when I first learned to swim. I couldn't grab hold of the water; if I did I would only sink. I had to learn to let go, to trust the water, to let myself float. That's what I was doing now, in my mind – floating on the water, floating in the water.

It was the Owl Butterfly who brought me back to the reality of where I was. Once again she circled me and called my name. And as I watched her I noticed something had changed. Where there had been quiet before, now there was total silence – no birds, no cows or goats, not a sound. And where there had been clusters of huts before, now there were none. And the plants and trees seemed to be different, too. There were fewer of them and they appeared to be smaller than they were before.

I called out to the Owl Butterfly. "What happened? Where am I?"

"In the beginning," was her only response.

I continued to look all around me, and everywhere was nothing. Maybe this was *in the beginning*, I began to think.

"Is this the past? Is this another dream? Have I gone back in time?" I asked aloud.

"We're never living in the past or the present or the future. We're only ever living in the now. The secret is in being present to the now."

I was certain that was an important thing to understand, but at the moment I was confused. Was I dreaming, or was this reality? And was this place, this place with no things, was it the past or the present or maybe even the future?

Once again, the Owl Butterfly was reading my mind.

"We are all living in the past, the present, and the future all in the same time. You and I. Just as there is no place where your 'self' ends and my 'self' begins, no place where the water ends and you begin – we are all connected, we are all one – so, too, is there no place where the past ends and the present starts, no place where the present ends and the future begins. Time and being are not a straight line from here to there; they are, if anything, a circle, an all-inclusive One."

I was continuing to discover that this was one wise Owl Butterfly. I'm not certain I understood fully what she was saying, but it somehow made sense nonetheless.

"Today you are in the beginning. It is always the beginning. All of life is a series of moments we call now, an endless thread of new beginnings."

The Owl Butterfly began flitting to and fro above my head, circling and flying higher and higher into the sky.

"Follow me. Follow me."

"Follow you? I can't follow you – you're flying!"

"Follow me. You can fly. Spread your wings and fly."

"I can't fly!"

"Of course you can fly – everyone can fly. But you can't fly until you choose to fly. You can't fly to the sky if you choose to stand where you're standing. You can never do something new if you continue to do what you're doing. The only way you can ever do something you've never done before is to change, choose to be different. You can't fly because you think you can't fly. That's your problem. You have to think different. In order to fly you have to let go of the world you're hanging on to. You can fly

109

when all your senses are alive. You can fly when you're not focused on what's keeping you down, keeping you tied to one little spot below your feet. To fly you have to let go of everything you're hanging on to. It's like learning to swim in the water. You have to trust the water to support you. You have to let go of all you're clinging to. We're all swimming in a sea of air - air that's full of water. Flying is nothing more than swimming in that sea."

"Yeah, right. Easy for you to say. You're a butterfly!"

"I wasn't always a butterfly, remember. I used to be a caterpillar crawling on the ground, stuck in the same place, just like you. Then one day I spread my wings and flew, I let go and soared into the sky. Today you're going to do the same. Follow me. Let go of where you are and fly."

And so it was that I was given my first flying lesson.

"You have to begin by imagining. Imagine you're flying. Imagine you're swimming in the sea of air and that you're using all your being, your mind and your body, your arms and your legs, even your breathing, to swim higher and higher, toward the surface above, toward the sky. Pull yourself up with your hands and arms, pull against the air, pull yourself free of what's holding you down, and then kick your legs, pedal your way up through the air. You have to give it your all – your entire mind and body need to be focused on lifting yourself off the ground and into the air."

"Like this?" I asked as I tried a little jump off the ground, with my hands flapping in the air. A little jump, and a quick kick of my feet, and I fell to the ground.

"You're going to fall. You'll fall plenty of times before you fly. Just get up and try again."

So I tried again. And again. And again. I didn't think I was having much luck at this flying thing until I started to notice that each time I tried, I got just a little bit better. I started thinking it was by flapping my arms like wings that I'd get the hang of it. But it turned out that what I did with my feet was more important. My arms are not wings, and waving them about in the air may look impressive, but it doesn't actually help you fly all that much. In fact, it's your feet that get you where you want to go. It's always been that way, I guess.

So I started sort of pedaling with my feet, a cross between pedaling a bike, and flipping my feet like I would do if I were under water. I pedaled faster and flipped the air harder, and I started staying aloft longer, moving higher. Oh, I fell to the ground a few times, of course - a lot of times, actually - but I kept trying, and kept getting better, kept going higher.

And then something sort of clicked. I don't know what exactly. Maybe it was just practice, maybe persistence, but all of a sudden it became almost effortless. My frantic pedaling and flipping and waving began to settle into much more of a glide. I was flying! It was like I had pushed my way up out of the water to the surface and now I was floating. All I needed now was an occasional flap of my arms, a brief gentle kick of my legs, and I could glide higher and farther with ease. I was really flying! All of a sudden it was easy. It was as though I had found my rhythm, as though I began to trust doing simply what felt natural.

Then I got a little carried away. I started doing broad turns, then rising higher then diving down, then soaring around in circles. All the time I was enjoying the view. The world looked so different from up here. I'm afraid I got so carried away with my acrobatic flying and the spectacular view that once again I crashed back onto the ground. It never hurt, though – I just picked myself up and got ready to fly again.

"OK, you're ready. You're ready to follow me, to watch the water, watch the birds, watch the clouds like you've never watched them before. The world is full of magical things that have been patiently waiting for your senses to grow sharper. Follow me. Spread your wings and fly. Open your eyes to a whole new way of looking at the world."

I lifted myself from where I had been stuck to the ground and I rose into the sky like a balloon, like a bird - like a butterfly. The Owl Butterfly led the way, and we began to follow the river. There were no huts, no people, no animals – only the river and the plants and the trees. Maybe I was looking down at the way it was in the beginning. Maybe. I was in an ocean of sky, looking down at the river of water, maybe just as it was in the beginning.

At first we were flying low, barely above the treetops, with a clear view of all that was below, all that was on the ground. And again there were no people, not even any signs of people. Just the raw beauty of the earth and the trees and the rivers and the streams. We flew slowly, gently, simply gliding, and I took it all in. At times we could see clouds of birds flying below us, at other times the waters of rivers and streams. I watched the waters, I watched the birds – I even watched the clouds as we flew among them.

The Owl Butterfly was well ahead of me, leading the way, when Guaca joined us from the trees below, her scarlet and yellow and blue wings looking beautiful against the green background of the earth below. Even as we flew, I could somehow clearly hear them both speaking to me, though I was never quite sure which one was doing the talking.

112

"You're flying, Adam. You've let go of your clinging and taken flight. If you can overcome what's holding you down, you can overcome anything. If you can see the world from above it, looking back at it, you can understand it. Taking flight is the first step toward understanding. Anytime you can see something from a different vantage point you gain a valuable new perspective. Things which were only seen before can now be understood. When you look at things up close, they seem distinct, different from the things around them. When you view the same object from afar it's hard to distinguish it from everything else; you start to view all things as connected, as an indivisible part of a much greater whole."

It was so true. Already I was no longer seeing trees, I was seeing forests. I was not seeing rivers and streams so much as seeing the Earth and its waters. And it was so beautiful from above.

Soon I could see a coastline ahead of the trees. I could see the sea. As we approached the beach Búho led me in a slow turn to the right and soon I was again looking at the land, and this time the snowy mountains were ahead of us, the snow-capped peaks as I had seen them in my dreams. The snow completely covered the peaks and looked like white frosting all the way down the sides of the mountains.

As we drew nearer to the mountains we were joined by what appeared to be two eagles. One had a white head, the other was mostly black and much larger.

"These are our brothers el águila and el cóndor, the Eagle from the north and the Condor from the south. They will take you higher and farther than we can go." And so higher and higher we went, still skimming the trees as we climbed the mountain

113

heights. The trees gave way to a more stark landscape and finally to fingers of glacial ice and then the snowy mountain peaks. The Eagle and the Condor led me in slow circles above the high mountain, higher and higher with every circle, until we were so high the snowy mountains were nothing more than a white speck on the geography laid out below me. I could clearly see the snows surrounded by a network of streams and then rivers all flowing toward the ocean and sparking in the sun. And in the distance, the sea.

Again I could hear voices, this time the voices of Águila and Cóndor: "Follow us, Adam, and we will show you the beauty of your Earth Mother."

We rose higher and higher, to what seemed to be almost outer space. I could see the arc of a dark blue horizon in the distance, and very clearly see the curve of the earth. As we moved beyond the snowy peaks of la Sierra we followed what appeared to be the three ranges of the Andes. We were high above them now and they looked like something from a geography book. Way off in the distance was the sea. Between the mountains and the sea was every other type of geography imaginable – rivers and streams meandering through forests, jungles, deserts and plains. Most everywhere things were growing. The earth looked very much alive.

Águila and Cóndor led me higher and then at times we descended, we made broad sweeping turns, looking at this and that from differing angles. Soon I was disoriented completely. I believed we were still above South America but I was no longer sure of what was north and what was south, east or west. At times South America was upside down, appearing to be 'above' Central and North America in the distance. I called out to the Eagle and the Condor: "What country is this below us?"

Now I don't know if eagles and condors can laugh, but if they can that's what they did. They looked at each other and laughed, I'm almost certain of that.

"What country? What difference does it make what country? Do you see any countries down there?"

Now it was me who was laughing – flying and laughing. Of course they were right. It was so true it was silly. There were no countries below me any longer. No borders except rivers and mountains dividing the earth into natural blocks of green and brown and yellow and amber, hills and valleys, forests and fields - one Earth wearing a quilt of colors and textures. But no borders, no countries. And still no sign of people – no cities or towns, no highways, no smokestacks.

I called out to the eagle and the condor: "I don't see any people or any cities. Are we in the past?"

The condor or the eagle, I don't know which, responded, "There is no place called 'the past,' no place where the past ends and the present or the future begins." It seems everyone knew this but me.

We were once again very high and flying toward the coast. We left what I believed was the coast of South America and headed out over what I think was the Pacific Ocean. Then we turned north and followed the coast up what I am now certain was Central America, and then toward North America.

We climbed still higher and as we continued up the west coast of North America I could see the North Pole, the Arctic ice,

115

on the horizon. As we approached what I think was Alaska I could see that the polar ice cap was much larger than I remembered it from maps and geography books. It extended all the way down the sea to the land. It was impossible to tell where Alaska ended and the ice began. We followed the ice sheet across to the other side, to Russia, I think.

Climbing still higher we continued circling the globe. The dark blue horizon was now a big arc, with the entire blue marble of the earth below us. We crossed whole continents – Russia, Asia and Europe – and then we turned south, toward Africa.

We descended as we flew over Africa and soon I could clearly see the beauty of the plains and the jungles, even a snow-covered mountain that I thought was probably Kilimanjaro. And as we dropped even lower I could see animals – great herds of elephants and zebras and wildebeests and more. And massive swarms of birds like clouds of pink and white below us.

But still no sign of people. No cities or towns.

Águila and Cóndor led me down the length of Africa and then we began climbing once again. As we rose high enough to see the whole earth below us we made our way across the sea. As we approached land, we descended and soon I recognized the snowy peaks of la Sierra Nevada in the distance, towering above the shoreline.

We drew closer to the snowy mountains and for the first time I became aware of people below us. There were the now familiar clay huts with their thatch roofs, and there were people moving about. The villagers spotted me flying above them. They smiled and waved.

And I also noticed that the snowy mountains were not so snowy as before. There was only a patch of snow on the very highest of the peaks.

But the Eagle and Condor didn't give me any time to dwell on this observation before we turned right and headed north once again, this time up the Atlantic coast, once again toward North America. The coastline was to our left as we made our way north, and this time I could see fingers of smoke rising from smokestacks and clouds of haze above what appeared to be cities. Clearly we were in a different place and time.

I was unsure of exactly where we were but I knew it was the east coast of the United States that was on the horizon over my shoulder. We descended still lower and soon a familiar skyline could be seen through the clouds. We were approaching New York City and she looked just the way I remembered her. We were apparently no longer in the past, whatever the past is – or was.

It was hazy over New York, the first time I had been aware of a man-made haze since I started flying. But even through the haze I could see the brilliant sparkle of the skyscrapers thrusting themselves upward toward the sky. The City is a beautiful monument to the ingenuity of man, but this time, and for the first time, I found myself feeling it was somehow out of place. Having looked at the beauty of the whole earth from above, a man-made city below now looked more like a blemish on the planet than a thing of beauty.

I was feeling like my own pilot now, and I boldly broke from the flight plan. I veered away from the Eagle and Condor and headed myself directly up the Hudson toward the Catskills, toward home. I dropped down low and followed a familiar road to our farm in the hills. It was beautiful seeing it for the first time from the sky - the house, the farm with its neat rows of plants, the farm stand.

And there was Mary! I couldn't believe it. There she was, walking up the walk to the farm. I dropped down still lower and began showing off, soaring in broad circles above her.

"Mary! Mary! Look. It's me. Adam. I can fly!"

She looked skyward, shading her eyes with her hand, but didn't seem so surprised to see me.

"Adam Rivera, I always knew you would soar with the eagles one day!"

That was Mary, alright.

With that the Eagle and the Condor caught up with me and re-took the lead. Back up to altitude, we continued west, beyond New York to more cities and towns and then the open countryside. There were signs of people everywhere. Buildings, highways, power plants sending great plumes of smoke into the air. And again there was water – rivers and streams and lakes – but even here in the vast countryside of America there were constant signs of the presence of people. Coal barges on the river, dams and power plants and factories, bridges teeming with traffic. Beyond the water there were other signs of humanity, and in particular people's use of the land to satisfy their hunger – hunger for food, to be sure, but more striking their hunger for energy. There were vast fields of cultivated crops – the proverbial amber waves of grain – but also deep scars on the land where coal and copper and other minerals were being dug out of the earth. And everywhere there were smokestacks spewing smoke as though they were vents releasing the earth's energy into the air. Just as there were puffy white clouds below us, there were constant plumes of grey smoke rising toward us as well. And every city, large or small, stuck out from the green and amber that surrounded it because of its man-made construction and a cloud of haze hanging over it.

After only a brief time living in the natural beauty of the mountain jungle of Colombia the cities didn't look all that attractive to me anymore. They looked very much as though they didn't belong, in fact. They were something out of place. If the earth were a living being, I would have thought she had a bunch of sores all over her face. She no longer looked healthy to me.

That being said, there was still much natural beauty as we continued to soar above North America. Over the Mississippi, over the Great Plains we flew, the Grand Canyon, and we rose above the majestic Rocky Mountains. We were high enough now that from above the Rockies I could see all the way to the Pacific coast. And even from this altitude the beautiful vistas were punctuated by clouds of gray smoke rising from hundreds of smokestacks seemingly everywhere. As we approached the coast there was an obvious haze hanging over every city and town.

We flew up the coast and ever higher. Soon I could again see the North Pole, but this time I could also see that there was significantly less polar ice than we saw the first time. The ice that had connected Alaska with the land to the west was gone.

Again we traveled down the coast of Siberia, then over China and India and on to Africa and then across the sea to South America once again. My geography lessons were coming to life before my eyes. Everywhere this time there were signs of people and their industry. Highways and cars and trucks. Broad swaths of forest that had been stripped of trees. Coal mines carving up the mountains. And as we approached the now familiar pyramid-shaped mountain I noticed that the snows were receding. The snow cap on the high Sierra was as I had seen it when I first arrived, but much smaller than what I had seen on my first flight around the world – an obvious look at what it must have been like in the past.

Águila and Cóndor weren't about to let me rest just because we had arrived again at 'home.' We kept on flying, turning north again. My first exercise in flying had become very natural-feeling, more gliding than hard work, and I discovered I was not tired at all, even after having circled the globe twice now.

So it was back up Central America - I could easily make out the Panama Canal connecting the Atlantic and Pacific – then out over the Caribbean toward what I thought would be Florida. We were high enough now that I could see the southern part of the East Coast on the horizon, but as I followed it down with my eye there was no Florida at the bottom, not where it was supposed to be. The Florida that should have been there was now under water.

I called out to Águila and Cóndor again: "Are we looking at the future?"

"We're always looking at our future. When you look at the future all you're really doing is looking at now from a different perspective."

We continued northward and descended a little so that eventually I could make out my familiar home again, the island of Manhattan. It, too, was partially underwater now. It had shrunk, with water having replaced where land used to be, where streets and buildings and parks and cars and buses used to be. Even the

Statue of Liberty was under water at its base, still thrusting her torch to the sky, but now seeming to proclaim she couldn't be drowned.

I realized I was seeing a glimpse of my future. But I also realized once again the meaning in my mother's words and in the Elder's teaching: watch the water. How did I know this was the future? Because I was watching the water. The ice on the mountain tops, the ice on the North Pole, the waters of the ocean and now the waters of the New York, rivers and shorelines, all had changed. In fact they were talking to me. Just as the Owl Butterfly had said in my very first dream, just as the Elder had taught: "All the birds and the plants and the trees can speak to you, even the waters and the clouds. If you will listen." At this moment the waters were speaking to me of my future, the future of my home, the future of the planet.

I didn't have much time to dwell on these thoughts before we were joined in the air by another bird, this time a pelican - in fact several pelicans. They came together in a wedge before me and once again I heard a voice cry out, "Follow me."

Unlike the Eagle and the Condor, the pelicans flew very low, very close to the surface of the water. I followed. Soon we were gliding silently just above the surface of the ripples and the waves, rising and falling as the sea rose and fell.

Then the lead Pelican abruptly dove headlong into the water and disappeared. When he emerged from the water he rose back into the air and called to me again: "Follow me." Again he plunged into the sea. I gathered he wanted me to follow him into the water. I had trusted the Owl Butterfly and had learned how to soar, but I was not so sure about flying into the ocean.

121

Again the Pelican emerged from the water and called for me to follow. I wasn't at all sure about this. But after a little hesitation, I swallowed my fear, and chose to follow. Lowering my head and pointing myself toward the water I let out a loud "Oh shit!" and fell headfirst into the sea. Splash!

After the initial shock, the water was actually warm, and I discovered that swimming underwater was just like swimming in the air above. Soon I was gliding through the water just as I had been gliding through the air. I was flying underwater!

And fly we did - skimming over the bottom of the ocean just as we had been gliding over the land. The water was clear and I could make out hills and mountains and canyons below, just as if we were still flying over the earth. The truth is we were still flying over the earth, of course. It was just a little wet here, that's all. And instead of flocks of birds we were surrounded by schools of fish - thousands of colorful fish! The Pelican called me to follow (yes, I could "hear" him underwater!) and we began to glide over the bottom of the sea. The seascape was every bit as spectacular as the landscape had been above water, maybe more so. And just as on land, all the hills and peaks and valleys and ocean canyons were covered in green. The plants were much different than the land plants, but just as lush. And everywhere there were fish and other sea creatures darting about while huge schools of fish surrounded us, seemingly oblivious to this stranger in their aquatic domain.

It was an otherworldly experience. It was completely silent, an eerily silent world down here. And I was breathing somehow, even though I was many feet underwater. I don't know how I was breathing, but I was, and after having experienced flying I was beginning to learn to simply accept new experiences I didn't fully understand. From time to time the Pelican led me back up to the surface and we did take a quick breath of fresh air - the Pelican had to breathe, too - but then we would dive underwater again. Apparently we were both simply holding our breath for an unbelievably long period of time. In any case it all felt very normal, whatever my new normal was now. I was just enjoying it all.

There were a few scary moments, though. There were several huge stingrays gliding across our path from time to time, and some very large octopuses (octopi?) that were a bit frightening. And sharks - lots of sharks. Most of them were small, but occasionally a very large shark would glide into view and appear to be checking me out. But each time I encountered one, or more properly when a shark encountered me, it apparently decided I belonged in his watery world and didn't represent his next dinner.

Some of the fish were unbelievably large - bigger than me by far. And there were dolphins, very playful dolphins, and they were seemingly the most curious of all, swimming round and around me, looking me over and appearing to encourage me to join in their play.

But the most spectacular of all were the whales. Several huge whales were gliding above us - yes, above us - just below the surface of the ocean, and the sunlight from above sparkled through the water and revealed the whales' gigantic silhouette. At times a whale would rise to the surface and with a thrust of its tail that churned the water all around us it would leap into the air and flop back down into the sea. At other times they would dive elegantly very deep to the depths below. The whales seemed to rule to ocean, dominating the watery universe I was now a very small part of. With the whales that were surrounding me I became aware of just how small and fragile I really am.

Once again I returned to thoughts of the water. It was water that was supporting this giant of a mammal, this massive whale, as it glided effortlessly above me on the surface of the sea. It was water that was supporting me, for that matter. And the water was teeming with every kind of life imaginable - plants and fish and eels and octopus and squid and starfish and sea anemones and coral and crabs and lobsters - everywhere there was life. Everywhere there was water giving it all life.

Even as beautiful as all the marine plants and animals were, it was the landscape - the seascape - that grabbed my attention. The bottom of the ocean is not flat! There are rolling flat plains, to be sure, but then there are deep canyons, many where I couldn't even see the bottom, and then equally high mountains rising up from the ocean floor. And everywhere there were rocky hills and coral reefs topped with plant life that swayed gently to and fro in the ocean currents. The land forms and the plant life left me feeling as though I was exploring a whole new planet for the very first time.

Again I was experiencing water in a whole new way. I was watching the water intimately. I had become one with the water, just as the Elder had said.

For the first time I had no idea where on the planet we were. I think we had entered the water near South America, near Colombia, and the water had been warm and clear so we were probably in the Caribbean, but I really didn't have any way of knowing exactly where I was.

I was awakened to that fact when the water began to feel cooler, and then much colder. Wherever we had been in the world, we were now somewhere else. The plants on the ocean floor seemed to have changed. I can't say exactly how, but they were different. And the fish were different, too - bigger and not quite as colorful as the ones in the warmer waters. And soon there were more whales - more and different.

The water became colder and colder as the Pelican led me on. I was aware of the cold, but somehow my body had adjusted and it didn't seem to bother me. I just kept gliding along underwater, taking in the ever-changing view.

In an instant the geography changed dramatically. Ice! The green seascape now included massive mountains of ice. Some appeared to be floating silently on the sea; others seemed to rise dramatically all the way from the ocean bottom. What had been a colorful but mostly green seascape was now becoming a monochromatic blue-gray and white - lots of white.

We were surrounded by even more whales now, and soon many seals and walrus and otters. But the sight that revealed exactly where we must be on earth was the sight of a polar bear and her two cubs swimming in the cold waters alongside us!

I was in the water, but my head was above water. I scanned the horizon and all I could see was water and massive islands of ice floating in the sea. Other than the ice and the water the polar bear family was the only sign of life. Even the Pelican had disappeared. I was alone, alone in the eerie silence. The only sound was the lapping of the water against the ice sheets and a creaking sound in the distance that I presumed to be the breaking up of the ice.

I pulled myself out of the water and climbed up onto one of the islands of ice. I sat there for a while, just looking at the dramatic starkness, the blue, white and gray all around me. I asked myself whether I was observing this icy world in the past or the present or the future, but I guess I was beginning to learn from my many teachers because I instantly realized it didn't matter. As I gazed out across the vast Arctic ice and water I understood I was looking at the past and the present and the future all at the same time.

I was alone. I was at the top of the world. I could see forever. But in the whole world spread out before me, the only life I could observe was a family of polar bears. Just then a kayak with a lone Eskimo silently paddled into view. He waved, not at all surprised to see me, and he continued on.

I wondered what I should do next. How was I going to get home? Should I return to the water, or should I try to fly? I sensed the polar bears were asking the same question.

As I pondered these existential quandaries, the Pelican burst from the water and into the air.

"Follow me," he seemed to say as he plunged himself head first back into the water. I did the same.

I immersed myself in the water again and was immediately surrounded by bubbles - millions of bubbles. That's all I could see - bubbles, bubbles and more bubbles. Tiny bubbles, all around me, shimmering with color, every color imaginable. I couldn't see fish, couldn't see the bottom of the ocean. I couldn't see anything but millions of tiny bubbles. I was immersed, not in the sea, but in the colorful bubbles.

Again the Pelican came darting through the bubbles in front of me, turned upward, and broke through the surface and into the air. Again I heard, "Follow me."

We were flying, once again skimming low, just above the surface of the sea, when I noticed there was no longer any ice. The blue sea stretched before us all the way to the horizon where I thought I could make out the snowy peaks in the distance. It seemed we were headed 'home.'

As we approached the broad sandy beaches of what I'm pretty sure was the Caribbean shore, we crossed a lagoon where a river met the sea. The Pelican led me up the river. It was a beautiful river valley, with palm trees to the left and the right of the river banks. Birds were singing and screeching and flying to and fro before us. As we followed the river higher and higher, the plants and trees changed, and soon I began to recognize this as the river of my new home, the mountain valley of my new friends, my new teachers. We had returned to the Mountain.

The river tumbled over the rocks, cascading as a waterfall into a broad pool below. The Pelican plunged into the crystal blue waters, just as the waterfall was doing, and I followed. Splash! Again I was surrounded by millions of bubbles. I couldn't see anything but bubbles. I was totally disoriented, unable to discern what was up or down, left or right. I was being embraced by the bubbles and being tossed and turned around and around in the waters.

The bubbles seemed to be carrying me now, carrying me effortlessly to the shore. I emerged from the water and looked back at the waterfall and at the millions of bubbles dancing on the water where the cascade met the waters below. I had returned home.

I reached my hands into the water and scooped up some water - some bubbles. I looked into the bubbles, deep into the bubbles. They were like a kaleidoscope - a kaleidoscope of images, past present and future - each bubble revealing a clear and colorful image of some place I had just seen on my whirlwind flight around the world. In one bubble there was all of New York City, in another the farm in the Catskills. Still another bubble clearly revealed a Florida under water, another an image of the Arctic ice adrift. There were what appeared to be Amazonian natives, waving happily from the river. And African natives, looking for all the world exactly like the Amazonians. Then a bubble with what I think was a Native American Indian in a canoe on a river. He waved as well. There were bubbles with the earth looking as beautiful as the day it was born, and others where the landscape was scarred by smokestacks and freeways. And in one bubble I swear I saw my mother. She was gently saying, "Watch the water, watch the birds, watch the sky."

I turned to see exactly where I was. I was startled to find the Elders standing silently behind me.

"You're all wet," said one. "It seems you've been watching the water."

"I saw the whole world! I saw the past. I saw the future. I must have been dreaming!"

"It wasn't a dream. It was *aluna*."

Chapter 6

As If It Were Yesterday

In the land where the sun is born the day begins before the dawn. I was still waking and stretching when the woman who was my host offered me a gourd cup with hot coffee. When I reached out my hand to take it she gently waved me off and lovingly scolded me. She was apparently the wife of one of the Elders, and as I would learn was also an Elder herself.

"You must receive with both hands open. If you reach for something, if you take something with only one hand, you are doing just that - taking. Reaching, grabbing, grasping, taking. Receiving is something else altogether. When something is offered, you should receive it, not take it. There is a difference. Extend your two open hands and receive that which is offered. It is impossible to take something from another with two hands open."

That would be the first of many teachings on this new day. Then came the next:

"The Elders will be coming to fetch you soon. They will come bearing gifts - gifts of their most sacred teachings. They will offer them freely to you, for you to share with the younger brother. You should receive them with both hands open; with both eyes open, with both ears open. With your mind and your heart open. And when you are offered a gift, you should respond with a gift in return. For the people of the Mountain it is the tradition to offer a gift of coca leaves."

She handed me another very small mochilla, this one again filled with dried coca leaves. I received it with both hands open. Just as the Elder had done yesterday, she gave me a lesson in the etiquette of the coca leaves.

"These are your coca leaves. You will offer a handful of them to the Elders when you greet them, and they in return will offer some to you. You will put some leaves in your mouth, between your cheek and gum, and gently chew on them. They will help keep you awake, awake to the reality of what you will learn. Awake to the reality that is all around you. Much will be revealed to you in your dreams, but you will only understand if you are fully awake."

OK. I think I will need to chew on that one for a while.

The Elders arrived at the hut. We greeted each other and exchanged our gifts of coca leaves. Then the Elders beckoned me with a now familiar, "Follow me." I followed as they walked briskly up the hillside to a ridge that offered another sweeping panoramic view of the hills and valleys below – a vista that extended all the way to the sea on the distant horizon. I could watch the water, watch the birds and watch the sky, all at the same time.

"You have been watching the water. You have entered into *aluna*. You have experienced how it was in the beginning. From the Mountain, the mountain that is born in the waters of the ocean and that rises to the waters of the snows, you can see all the worlds beyond all the waters of all the rivers and seas."

"After the Mother had spun her thread, after she had woven the fabric that is her creation, she drew a line in the ground, inscribed a line on the stone, and separated the younger brother from the elder brother. When it became clear that the younger brother was destined to use his creative imagination for making things, not for caring for his Earth Mother, the younger brother was cast across the sea. There he lived, in a land where the weather was harsh and the mangoes and the papaya and the bananas did not grow. For thousands of years the elder brother did his work, did his job, cared for our Earth Mother, and the younger brother was forgotten.

"One day, a day not unlike this day, a day that seems like yesterday in the memory of the ancestors but that was in truth five hundred years ago, giant birds, floating birds with wings of cloth, appeared on the shores. They carried on their backs the return of the younger brother.

"The younger brother had heard of the riches of the Mountain - the abundance of the fruits and the spices, the stories of the gold - and had returned to take what he believed belonged to him.

"We speak of this invasion by the younger brother as "Columbus." For us Columbus was not a person but an event, an event that continues to this day. Columbus was the return of the younger brother and the beginning of the rape and killing of our Earth Mother."

With the emotion of a son recounting the death of his own mother, the Elder shared the details of the Columbus event. Apparently the peoples of the mountain have never had a written language, never used cave paintings or hieroglyphics. The history of the mountain and its peoples is recorded in the collective memory of the Elders, passed from ancestor to ancestor through the ages. It is from this memory that the Elder spoke as if Columbus had happened only yesterday.

"Before Columbus the many peoples of the Mountain lived in harmony with their Earth Mother, with *la madre tierra*. We fished the sea and we tilled the soil. From the beaches at the base of the mountain to the high ground just below the snows we raised our cows and sheep and goats, planted our beans and picked our fruits. And we cared for our Earth Mother. When we received the gifts of the Earth, we gave something back, always living in harmony, always protecting the delicate balance that is the living planet. The Mountain is the heart of the world and we are the heart of the world, the loving, compassionate, caring heart of the world. That is our job. That has always been our job.

"But Columbus came with a heavy heart. He came to drive us from the land, to take from *la madre tierra* without ever giving anything back. He came to take, to grab, to possess, and to rob our Earth Mother of the life she had been sharing with us and with our ancestors through all the ages of time. Since the beginning of time our Mother had been creating. Every day, when the sun was born anew, this land became again a beautiful new creation. Columbus came only to destroy.

"When Columbus and his Spanish conquerors arrived, the Mountain was a garden in perfect balance. The Mountain rose straight out of the burning sands of the sea to the eternal snow of its twin peaks, and in between were every kind of landscape and climate known on Earth. There were deserts, coastal jungle, tropical rain forests, cloud forests, open woods, alpine meadows, even high tundra. All of that was teeming with life - bears, monkeys, jaguars, deer, turkeys - and many, many more. In the waters were fishes of every description plus alligators, frogs, turtles. And in the sky and in the trees were every kind of bird imaginable - condors and eagles, pelicans and storks, macaws, parrots, toucans, hummingbirds and hawks.

132

"The Mother created the Mountain to be the heart of the world and to be home for all of her creation. The heart of the world is the heart of a living planet, and at the time that Columbus arrived the heart of the world was beating in harmony, all life was thriving in the balance. And the original peoples of the Mountain, our ancestors, were carefully tending the garden, carefully working to maintain that balance, living in harmony with the natural rhythms of the Mountain."

The Elder's voice was shaking and his eyes were moist with tears. He paused and returned his gaze to the horizon. He surveyed all the land that was spread before him, seeming to ponder what was then, and what was now.

"Columbus destroyed that world. Yes, the land is still here, and we are here, but the heart of the world that Columbus found is no more. The heartbeat is weaker, the Earth is out of balance, much of her energy has been depleted."

With a blank stare he peered silently into the horizon of the past.

"Christoforo Columbus never came to the Mountain. But for the peoples of the Mountain every conquistador was Columbus. Every ship that ever crossed the ocean bearing a cross on its wings of cloth was manned by Columbus. Every priest, every soldier, everyone hungry for gold was Columbus.

"After centuries and centuries of living on the other side of the sea, the younger brother returned to this land. He saw the riches the Mother had bestowed upon the land and he began to take all that he desired. He killed, shot, many of our ancestors. He took the gold which had been here, sacred gold, our golden

Mothers, all kinds of gold. They took everything, took so much, so much.

"The original peoples who lived close to the shore, they climbed higher, high above, fleeing for their lives. They left behind the energy of their gold, climbed even higher. Almost weak, where there was no food, they climbed up. They tried to live in the higher ground, never felling trees but always taking only what was freely given, the little branches that were on the ground. And they planted new seeds.

"But the younger brother climbed, too. With his guns and his fierce dogs he continued to hunt down the elder brothers. The younger brother felled the trees, built their homes, cleared the land of that which was living. And they forced the elder brothers to climb still higher where there were no crops to sustain them. Many died of hunger and weakness.

"But the Elders never forgot that it was their job to care for our Earth Mother. Even when they had nothing to eat, even when there was no help from those below, even when they had been robbed of the energy of their gold they never forgot. Always they said, 'Let us keep the customs, keep the traditions. Let us continue to respect our Mother Earth, *la madre tierra*, and continue to care for her.'

"It is in continuing to care for the Earth that we actually saved ourselves. It has always been that way."

I was being given a profound lesson in history - and much more.

"The younger brother continued to arrive and multiply. They felled the trees, they took from the Earth without ever giving anything back. They raped our mothers and our daughters and killed our young men. They spread their disease.

"In the beginning the Mother taught us how to live together like brothers. And we lived together like brothers. We, the elder brother, lived right down to the sea, we lived everywhere here, and we didn't destroy or do harm to anything. The Mother taught us how to live and make our fields in peace.

"We lived peacefully, but when Columbus came it changed. They started to say to us, 'This land here is mine, that land there is mine, this over here that's mine, too.' If we make a field and plant it and then sell it or someone takes it away it's like cutting off one of the Mother's breasts or her legs or her arms. When Columbus came the younger brother started to say, 'This here is mine, that there is mine, it's mine, it's mine.' People cannot live in peace when they are saying, 'This is mine, this is mine, and it's no longer yours.' The land was meant to be shared and cared for by all."

What a simple principle, one that seems to have been lost with the advent of 'civilization,' I found myself thinking. These simple people have actually found the secret to living together in peace. These simple people are the ones who are truly civilized, I thought.

"The elder brother understands that the Mountain is his ancestor. The younger brother believes that the Mountain is a pile of rocks waiting to be taken away.

"When Columbus came they took away the things that were ours. They took away our gold. They took away all our sacred gold. They set dogs on us and we had to flee. We ran in fear, and as we ran we left everything behind us. We had sacred figures of gold when they set the dogs on us. We lost them. They took our soul. They took everything."

Silence. Each of the Elders held back a tear and sat for a moment in stony silence.

The Elder rose and continued his teaching by walking us up the hill and then down the other side toward a muddy marsh.

"This used to be a sacred lake. Today the water is drying up. There is no longer sufficient water. Plants and animals have disappeared. Who is at fault? The younger brother is at fault.

"We fled from the younger brother, moving always higher and higher. We crossed the deepest rivers and burned the bridges behind us. We cut ourselves off from the younger brother to save ourselves, to save the Mountain, to save the Earth.

"Finally the younger brother would come no higher. He retreated to the fertile valleys below and continued his futile search for more gold. And we continued to do our work, to care for our Earth Mother, to try to maintain the balance, to preserve the energy of the Mountain. For five hundred years we have tried to protect the Mountain from the ongoing invasion of the conquerors, the younger brother. We have never stopped caring for the Earth.

"But today our work alone is no longer enough. While many of our brothers and sisters, mothers and fathers have disappeared because of the younger brother's heartless actions, we have survived. We have continued to care for our Earth Mother. But the Mountain is changing. We hear her crying. She is in pain. And she tells us that all the world is changing, too. We are the heart of the world, but the entire body is gravely ill. She has infections that are spreading over her whole body. The spread of the disease must be stopped, and for that to happen there needs to be a healing of the heart.

"The younger brother must return to *aluna*, return to the way it was in the beginning, to recover his love of his Mother, to once again begin doing his job, to once again become the loving, caring compassionate heart of the world."

All of the Elders nodded in agreement. We sat together on the mountain and pondered this thought.

It was an interesting thought. I'm no student of history, but I knew the story of Columbus, of course. And being from New York I knew that Columbus was Italian and that the Italians of the U.S. claimed him as a hero. The Native Americans not so much. He sailed for the queen of Spain, under the Spanish flag, and he saw himself as one who was saving souls for Jesus Christ and also bringing vast amounts of gold back to the Queen and the Pope, mostly to finance their wars in Europe.

I knew that Columbus had been followed by the Portuguese and the Dutch and the English and the French explorers who also viewed the 'New World' as their own, their property to exploit as they saw fit.

And I knew that the conquests and the battles and the disease that followed the Europeans wherever they went throughout the Americas eventually resulted in the complete extinction of many of the original peoples - the Incas, the Aztecs, the Mayas, the Toltecs, even the Tayrona of Caribbean Colombia. Their entire populations and cultures were raped, pillaged and eventually completely destroyed. They all died.

But not the original peoples of the Mountain. Why? Why did these simple peace-loving people survive the conquest which killed so many of their brothers and sisters up and down the continent? The Elders believe they have the answer: they survived because they never stopped caring for the health of their Earth Mother. It was in their ceaseless commitment to caring for the planet that they, in fact, were caring for themselves. It was by striving to save the world that they ultimately saved themselves.

It was not bigger and more powerful weapons that saved them. It was not better military strategy that saved them, unless running away and hiding in the high mountains counts as a military strategy. It was certainly not by amassing vast amounts of wealth - not gold, not oil or anything else of so-called value - that saved them. It was reclaiming their oneness with their Earth Mother and rededicating themselves to caring for her that saved them.

The Elders were not being at all subtle with their story. There just might be a lesson here - a lesson for me, a lesson for today. Their teaching was working. Once again, I was seeing things from a new perspective, with new eyes.

If the people of the mountain had chosen to spend their lives acquiring things and accumulating wealth they would have perished. Instead they chose to live simple lives, creating a sustainable culture where the people cared for each other and cared for their Earth Mother. And they survived. They thrived.

Columbus also survived. Columbus is alive and well and living in Colombia today, at least as the Elders understand the Columbus event. It has never ended.

"Columbus and those who followed have never stopped taking from our Earth Mother. To this day they cut deep scars into the Mountain and take her life-giving energy. They take the minerals that are the heart of the Mountain and they put them on boats and carry them away by sea, just as the first Columbus did. Then they burn them and heat up the earth. They are burning their own home. This Columbus never learns.

"They took all our gold. The gold figures, each one shaped by loving hands, each one different, each one a living figure of our Mother. Most were melted down and taken across the sea. The few that survived are now hidden away in museums. Today these mothers are dying, trapped in glass cages in the museum, with no one caring for them, no one feeding them, no one nurturing them as our Mother has always done for us. Many more mothers were melted in hot fire, turned into worthless rocks of metal to be carried across the sea. The gold of the earth is our Mother's blood, the monthly blood of her fertility. The Mother gave up her golden blood with the same rhythm that every mother gives up the blood of her womb. We made our figures from the blood that was shared, never cutting into our Mother's veins, never taking from the Mountain, always receiving with open hands only that which was freely offered in the clear waters of the rivers and the streams. Columbus and the younger brother took her blood, they took our Mother's blood. And they have never given anything back.

"There is no longer any gold in the Mountain. The younger brother took it all. The younger brother has all the gold, in his museums, in his vaults. But what good will it be to him when he takes everything else from the Mountain?"

As he spoke it occurred to me that this would be the right time to return the golden figurine I was wearing about my neck. My little chance to give back.

I took the cord and the golden figurine from around my neck and offered it to the Elder.

"I want to give this back. I want to do my little part to return the gold to the Mountain."

"We know how it is that you received this gold, Adam. Like you, it was born of the earth. It was shaped by the original peoples of the land. It was taken from our land, it is true, but this Mother found its way to your mother. It was offered as a gift to your mother. She cared for it, protected it, and it protected her. When it was time, this golden figure of our Mothers was passed on to you, offered to you freely by your mother. It is yours now. It was always meant to be yours. The gold we are meant to receive should never be taken, it should always come freely offered from our Mother. This golden figurine has come freely offered from your Mother. You were meant to care for it. If you care for it, it will help you find your way, as it has always done for your mother. For now, it is in your care." And with that the Elder held it over my head and returned to my neck.

He then reached down and took a small plant, perhaps the shoot of a new tree, in his hand and pulled it up from the mound of earth in which it was growing. Then he scooped up some of the soil from the mound of earth. And then some more, and then some more, and then some more. Soon there was no longer a mound of earth at all. There was no longer a little mountain of earth. Only a hole in the ground and an uprooted tree lying silently beside it.

"Columbus continues to take and to take, all the while never giving anything back in return. Always taking, always taking. One day there will be nothing left to take. The Mountain will be gone. The Mother will die."

Then he carefully, lovingly, replaced the young tree, replanting it again in the fertile soil.

Chapter 7

Strangers on the Shore

I again found myself gazing toward the sea as I walked the hills in the afternoon, pondering my history lesson from the Elders. Columbus and the conquistadores had been just another impersonal footnote in the history of the world I had been spoon fed in school. But for these people, the people of the Mountain, my new friends, it was very real - and still embedded clearly in their 'memory.' In a very real way it had represented the end of the world for them. The calm peaceful life they had been living in harmony with all things was suddenly turned upside down and nearly destroyed. Their old world was, in fact, destroyed. They survived by adapting, by adopting a whole new way of living, leaving the coast and taking refuge on higher ground. They came together as a community, a sustainable community, in which everyone cared for the planet and for each other. Why did that sound so radical?

And I thought about the gold. I toyed with the golden figurine I was once again wearing around my neck. As I held the gold in my fingers I appreciated for the first time that this golden figurine was my ancestor, one of my mothers. I felt life in the gold, life I had never felt in gold or any other stone or metal before. For the first time the shine of the gold, the reflected sunlight off the golden figure, struck me like a ray of life, not just a ray of light. I'm sure I didn't yet appreciate fully how this little piece of gold was my living ancestor, but I was starting to get there.

Suddenly I became aware of a great commotion below the ridge, a chorus of excited voices. A group of ten or so children, teenagers and younger, were rushing up the hill toward me, clearly agitated about something. As they got closer I could see Bunkey appearing to lead the charge as they raced toward me yelling loudly, words I didn't understand but which clearly sounded like danger.

The danger soon became clear. My pondering the lessons of the Elders had caused me to lose sight of where I was wandering and I now found myself practically on the beach, on a rise at least, with a clear view of the beach not far below. And there on the horizon, some considerable distance from shore, was what appeared to my uneducated eye to be a Spanish galleon, with huge white sails and the large mark of an "X" which I took to be a Christian cross. Alongside the galleon men were scurrying down the side of the ship by rope and into wooden longboats, several of which had already carried what appeared to be Spanish sailors to the shore.

It looked like a scene from an old movie or maybe from that novel I had read so many times, Treasure Island.

But these were not pirates, at least not in the Treasure Island sense. These were the Spanish conquerors, the ones who would change history and not in a good way, and the children had been right to sense that they spelled danger.

There were also adults on the shore who knew the danger. I saw maybe a hundred or more Indians hurrying up the hills into the dense jungle. The soldiers were yelling at them as they pursued, and the Indians were screaming in fear. And there were dogs. Growling, snarling dogs were biting at the heels of the Indians as they fled for their lives.

The children who had sought me out were yelling, too. They seemed to be saying, "Follow me," as I had now heard so many times, but they were also crying out to me, "You must help. You have to save our brothers and sisters, save our mothers."

Damn! Why does everyone keep thinking I'm the one who can make a difference? The Spanish armada, as well as the tide of history, is attacking the New World and I'm supposed to stop it!

Bang! Bang! Gunfire rang out and echoed back from the mountain. I heard screams, screams from the women. And I heard excited shouts from the would-be conquerors: "El oro! El oro!" - Gold! Gold! I could see the men attacking the women and holding them down on the ground struggling. The men ripped the shiny gold from around their necks and from their arms and ears and hair, raising the golden figures in the air like they were sports trophies.

What is it with these guys that they think everything they 'discover' somehow belongs to them? I thought.

No time for such thoughts now, however. Longboats of sailors and snarling dogs were still unloading on the shore and all racing toward the peoples of the Mountain. It seemed I needed to do something and do something quickly. But what? I had a rag-tag band of indigenous teenagers and I was sure they could easily recruit more, but we were facing the Royal Navy, so to speak, and they were armed. The kids had only some bows and arrows, which I trusted they could use very well, but still the odds were certainly not stacked in our favor.

I found small comfort in the fact that my band of warriors were actually all a bit older than the young Jim Hawkins of Treasure Island fame, and he managed to overcome the pirates of

Long John Silver. Perhaps if we were clever enough we might have a chance to rescue some of the gold as well as some Indian souls from this army of Spanish zealots - and change a little history in the process. Or, perhaps more likely, we could be completely overrun.

"Bunkey. You need to warn the others to stay away, to run high up the mountain. But then you need to get us some more men. We're going to need some of your strongest friends to help."

"Aye, Capt'n," said Bunkey, already starting to sound like a young Jim Hawkins, "but I don't understand. Why does the younger brother want our gold? Why does he take what is not offered to him? If he doesn't understand the gold is his mother, of what value is gold to him?"

"They will melt down the gold and use it as money, to buy things, Bunkey."

"I don't understand this word, 'to buy things.' The Mountain gives us everything, if we care for her. Why does anyone need to buy things?"

I had no good answer.

Bunkey scurried off and I began to get a grip on my thoughts and started to work up a plan. We couldn't overpower them, that was obvious, so we would have to outsmart them. Meanwhile I was afraid women were being raped and many more were being killed. We had no time to lose.

As I was sorting out the options for some sort of plan, a young sailor from one of the longboats began running away from his boat, across the beach and toward our lookout on the hillside. We had been discovered!

"Come on boys, follow me!" I cried and we started up the hill toward higher ground and a more secure hiding place. But the young sailor was quicker afoot than we were, and as he drew closer he called out, "Amigo! Amigo!" - friend, friend. I turned and observed that he was as scared as we were but was also indicating he was no threat. "Amigos! Amigos!"

As he drew closer it was clear he was no older than Bunkey, a cabin hand I presumed.

"I can help you," he called out, and he lifted his hat in something of a salute, and as he did so a great bundle of long dark hair fell out and about his shoulders. He was not a "he," at all, but appeared to all eyes to be a she.

"I'm Maria - and yes, I'm a girl. I was a stowaway on this galleon for some many days and nights, weeks as it were. I know what these less-than-honorable men have plotted against you, and I can help you save yourselves and the others."

"How is it you came running in our direction?" I asked.

"I've a keen eye, I do, and I spotted you straight away on the hill, above the rest. You don't look like an Indian, if I might say so, sir, and by your clothes I knew you wasn't a man of the crew. It was a moment's instinct that told me you were the one who could help save the others."

As she spoke I was immediately struck by how much she looked like my Mary back home - the spitting image, I dare say. And then I was struck by what it was she next had to say:

"I came aboard this sturdy galleon, the Santa Marta by name, in Palos, my mother and father having passed away, and myself in dire circumstances. I was determined to make my way to the New World. I made myself to look like a boy, and hid among the canvas of the sails 'til we was well out to sea. As would be expected I was discovered one day as I foraged among the scraps for some food. I confessed to having stowed away, and asked forgiveness of the Captain, and offered myself in service to Her Majesty's galleon from that day forward. I've been an honest cabin boy these several weeks since, and a right good'un I hasten to add. But to this day it has been known to none that I was a girl doin' a man's work. To all the crew I was José Maria."

It was a tale straight out of Robert Lewis Stevenson, I thought.

"Now, just after sundown, this being only last evenin' of which I now speak, when all my work was over and I was on my way to my berth, it occurred to me that I should like an apple. I ran on deck. The watch was all forward looking out for any sign of land. The man at the helm was watching the luff of the sail and whistling away gently to himself, and that was the only sound excepting the swish of the sea against the bow and around the sides of the ship. In I got bodily into the apple barrel, and found there was scarce an apple left; but sitting down there in the dark, what with the sound of the waters and the rocking movement of the ship, I had either fallen asleep or was on the point of doing so when a heavy man sat down with rather a clash close by. The barrel shook as he leaned his shoulders against it, and I was just about to jump up when the man began to speak. It was the first mate´s voice to be sure, and before I had heard a dozen words, I would not have shown myself for all the world, but lay there, trembling and listening, in the extreme of fear and curiosity, for from these dozen words I understood that the lives of all the honest men aboard, and the lives of all the Indians we were to meet on their own land, depended upon me alone.

"What I heard was the mates confessing to one another that the Captain, an honest man by their account and loyal to the Queen and to the Pope, was seeking to save the Indian souls for Jesus Christ, to be sure, but that the others had no interest in other than the gold. The wishes of the Captain for a peaceful account with the Indians were to be ignored, and the crew would kill all the Indians they was able, as if it were sport, and would gather up all the gold they might possibly rip from their dead bodies. With the ship's hold filled to the line with treasure, she'd be set a-sail for Spain, leaving the poor Captain and his few loyal men behind.

"That, my new friends, is the scenario you see unfolding before your very eyes even as we speak."

This was the worst possible news, but it came as no surprise.

"The mate I overheard was tellin' the others the Indians were un-civilized and our peaceful overtures would only be met by a strike with poison arrows. We had no choice but to kill the lot of 'em. 'Dead men don't bite,' said he."

I could scarcely believe that the ones who openly thought themselves to be the 'civilized' ones could be so brazenly cowardly and brutal and greedy and unabashedly un-civilized.

"The mate finished his oratory to the men, then broke into a kind of sing-song: 'Here's to ourselves, young and old, plenty of prizes and plenty of gold.'"

Maria continued her story:

"As the mates sang of their gold, a sort of brightness fell upon me in the barrel, and looking up, I found the moon had risen and was silvering the mizzen-top and shining white on the luff of the fore-sail; and almost at the same time the voice of the lookout shouted, "Land ho!"

"Next I knew we was droppin' anchor, and with the crew all on the bow I made like a river rat out of that apple barrel and ran swiftly into the first longboat I was able, and that's what brung me here to you. I doubt the others saw you, what with their greedy eyes only on the treasure and all, but I spotted you boys right away, you not belongin' in the picture, as it were, and I was immediately of a mind to flee the motley crew and perhaps earn a little favor beyond them pearly gates by helpin' to save the lives of a few innocent souls, them ones that aren't of a mind to hurt nary a soul themselves, I venture to guess."

The young lad, who was in fact the young gal, Maria, turns to me and continues, "So now you knows all what I know. What be your plan, Capt'n?"

I had already spied what appeared to be a pair of pistols in her belt and a musket over her shoulder. "Do you know how to use those arms, young lady?" says I.

"Course I do, Capt'n. But I'm afraid I have little 'munition and scant dry powder, does I."

"That's OK," I replied. "We're not out to kill anyone, only to scare them into thinking they've run into a serious defense of this beach. A single volley into their ranks from our side should do the trick, I'm thinkin'."

Damn! I was already starting to think and talk like a pirate! But these were no pirates, at least not in the Jolly Roger sense. The pirates of old attacked the ships of those who had stolen from the new lands in the New World, galleons that were

149

loaded to the gill with treasure like this galleon would soon be if we didn't put a stop to it. And so it was that we began to set in motion a plan to stop the piracy of the Mountain before this sorry ship ever set sail to fall victim to the real pirates on the high seas.

Once again it was I, a most unlikely Capt'n, as it were, who was being asked to come up with a plan that would save the world, or at least the little world of my new friends on the shore of the Mountain.

It seemed to me that we had two concerns, and we needed to be about addressing them forthwith. First we needed to stop the men who were attacking the women and men and children on the shore and up the mountain. My gentle friends were being raped and killed and robbed of their gold even as we plotted our response. And we were sore outnumbered.

Second, we needed a plan to reclaim the gold the conquerors had already taken and that they were still ripping from women's bodies even now. This was the sailors' treasure, to be sure, but to my new friends it was so very much more - it was the fertile blood of their mothers, the energy of the Mountain. We needed to return it to the land, to the people, to *la madre tierra*.

But how?

As I started to draw together a plan in my head, I heard a rustling in the jungle behind us.   "Bunkey, is that you?"

Yes Capt'n, 'tiz I. With a company of sturdy men, I am, sir."

I shook my head. Now even the Indians were talking like pirates!

I looked over the company of sturdy men - and women - that we had thus assembled: Bunkey, Mary, I mean Maria, and maybe ten or twelve others, all young and strong, but a little on the short and thin side. So it would surely take cunning rather than brawn if we were to save the day.

First we needed to find a way to scare the ship's crew into believing that there was an army waiting for them up the hill. That would be with a couple of volleys from the pistols and musket.

"Bunkey and Mary - I mean Maria - you take the men around that hill so you're facing them down, square in front of them - but at a safe distance up the mountain, of course. Maria, you're going to need to divide the three arms among three of the men, each a bit of a distance from each other, so when the volley is fired it seems to come from several directions, from several soldiers. Then the men will need to return to you for new powder and balls. Show the men how to fire the guns. Mary - I mean Maria - I know you're the only decent marksman among us, but we don't need accuracy here, only shots fired in the general direction to give the men a scare. You'll be best employed reloading the arms"

Meanwhile, I had a little plan of my own.

"While you men are scaring the bejezus out of the sailors - and they will retreat, I'm telling you, as they know they're about a filthy dirty business and any sign that their God is against them and they'll run back down the mountain like scared rabbits. While you're firing your volleys I'm gonna set about gettin' the Captain to come over to our side. He'll be on the ship. In the confusion on the shore of the mountain, I'll slip aboard and scare the bejeezus out of this Captain What's-His-Name. He's not gonna know what

151

to make of me, dressed as I am, and I'll be telling him, in a very
ominous tone, I'm the ghost of his future and that his men have
mutinied and he is to be left aground to die a slow death on this
forsaken piece of beach, with nothing but coconuts and bananas
all the rest of his days. Trust me, we'll have him on our side in no
time. You guys just fire the volleys 'til the men are runnin'. Oh,
and it wouldn't hurt to shout up your loudest and scariest war
cries, either. You're not trying to kill anyone, but you can sure as
hell scare the life out of them."

"Capt'n, you should take this." It was Maria, and she held
out a short but stout saber, a cutlass I think they'd have called it.
"I lifted it from the first mate. And you should take one of the
pistols. The Captain may have wanted to save the Indians' souls
and let them live a proper life to the end, but he's not a gentle
man. He won't give up his command easily, trust me on that."

"No," said I. "I'm not much good with a flintlock pistol,
and you'll be needin' all them that you've got. Though I'll be
thankin' you for the saber. But I plan to take the Captain with
cunning and surprise. You can trust me on that."

"The Captain's on board the Santa Marta, sir, along with
the Mate. Capt'n came ashore and read a proclymashun to the few
gentle Indians what approached him, claiming the land and all she
holds for the Queen and claiming all the poor souls for Jesus
Christ. Can you imagine that? What does ya' suppose the Indians
made of all that gibberish, and in the Spanish tongue no less? Ha!
Then the Capt'n unleashed the crew to have their way with the
women on shore and to scoop all the gold they could carry, then
he hid hizself away back on the ship. I suppose him and the Mate
to be full of the rum by now, savoring their conquest. They
should be easy pickins if you can get to them before the men

return, but take care, Capt'n. As I said, they won't be givin' up easy."

OK, so I was now Captain Adam, and I had a plan, and I was sticking to it. This was Phase One: scare the bloodthirsty sailors on the mountain into fleeing the Indians and running tail back to the ship, while I snuck aboard and won the Captain over to our side. Phase Two, the return of the gold. That would be coming soon thereafter, but more on that in its time. Truth is I was still trying to figure out exactly what Phase Two of the plan was!

I found myself fondling the gold figurine. Maybe it would help me find a way.

Before I could sort out my plan, one of the vicious attack dogs burst through the bushes and appeared to charge toward Bunkey. Then he stopped. He just sort of sat down in front of us, appearing to be looking into Bunkey's eyes. He looked like a pet dog at the foot of its owner. He cocked his head a bit, like he was greeting a friend. And then Bunkey looked directly into his eyes and spoke to him. I couldn't understand a word, but the dog appeared to be listening attentively. And the dog barked back in what seemed to be a dialog with Bunkey. They were having a conversation! Why was I not surprised?

Bunkey turned to me: "The dogs are like you and me. They do what they've been taught to do. They've been taught to attack anyone the sailors attacked. But that's not their nature. Their nature is to live in harmony with all others. This one understands that we are his brothers. He wants to help us."

Then the dog turned to me, and this time I could understand him: "I will tell the others to follow me. We are not naturally mean. We do as we have been taught to do. It is the same with people, it seems. And we can change. It is clear that the people of this land are our brothers and sisters, not the 'enemy' as we had been taught. We will help you. These men are also not naturally mean. They, too, are only doing as they have been taught. We will help you chase these intruders from your land."

Then he seemed to bark out to each of us in turn, "Follow me!"

I barked out my own orders: "Bunkey. Maria. Take your men and get to it. It'll take you some time to get up the hill, to get well ahead of the sailors. You need to be well above them and spread out, so they think there's a bunch of you. While you're getting into position, I'll hurry down the hill with the rest of the lads and take the ship from the captain. When you startle the men with your gunshots, we'll be ready for them as they come running scared towards the ship. After you've fired your volleys, double back and join us at the ship. But take care - we may be in a precarious situation when you find us.

"OK, now. Get going and fire as you're ready."

The odds were beginning to turn in our favor. We now had a few arms plus the dogs on our side. If we could also get the captain to switch sides, maybe we could pull this off.

I took the few remaining men with me and we headed down the hill toward the longboats beached on the shore. The tide was going out and the beached boats were now a bit up the shore, some distance from the water. I could see no one on the ship, nor did I hear a sound coming from her deck. In almost a whisper I began to lay out the plan:

"OK, men. Cut these boats from their ropes and let them loose to drift away with the tide. Push them into the sea."

Some of the longboats already had gold tossed into them, making them heavy, but we cut the ropes and pushed them almost silently into the receding tide. The beach is actually the side of the mountain and it is very steep. The waves come in slowly, rolling up hill as it were, and then fall back very strong and fast. So as soon as the longboats were shoved back into the tide, they immediately washed out toward the sea.

Bang! Bang! Bang! The first gunshots rang out from the hill, accompanied by a fierce chorus of shouts from Maria and Bunkey and the others. They were followed by obviously confused and frightened shouts from the Spaniards, this time with the dogs nipping at their heels! I gathered from the sound of their voices that they were soon in full retreat.

And then I couldn't believe my eyes! Charging down the hill came Bunkey astride a most magnificent white horse. In his tunic, with his long black hair flowing behind him, he waved his pistol in the air and let out a fierce war cry. He was the perfect picture of an Indian warrior to be sure. In fact it appeared he was even wearing war paint! If the Spaniards weren't scared to death before, they were now, and they tripped over themselves as they scrambled to flee down the mountain.

That was good, but it meant they'd be heading in our direction soon. It was time for Phase Two of my plan. The problem was, I had no real clue as to exactly what that Phase Two plan was going to be!

"OK, men. Get into the last boat. We're gonna take the ship."

155

How a half dozen Indians and a kid from New York were gonna get up the side of a Spanish galleon and take her from her Captain, I had no idea. But I had come to the realization that this was obviously just another dream and anything was possible. If I could fly around the world I could surely take command of a little wooden boat, right?

We pushed our longboat into the water, and I looked back at the beach to see the Spanish sailors running down the hill. They were discovering there were no longer any of their longboats on the beach.

The boys had no problem grabbing the oars and paddling us toward the galleon. As we approached, I could see a dozen or more heavy ropes hanging down her side, the ones the sailors had used to climb down into the longboats earlier. We would have to climb up the ropes and into the galleon, and do so quietly and in secret. I had no worry about the Indians - I'm sure they climb up vines all the time. But me? I was no Tarzan, no expert at rope or vine climbing. But again, this was my dream - I could do anything!

We pulled up alongside and without a word the boys started climbing up the ropes like monkeys. As for me, I was a bit slower, but no problem!

As we pulled ourselves up over the rail, I could see no one on the deck. I motioned for the boys to be silent and to follow me. We laid low, almost crawling, and made our way toward what appeared to be the main cabin, all the while watching for any sign of the Captain or others. No sign of anyone.

I confess I was very scared. The captain or one of his mates could be anywhere, and they wouldn't be at all happy to see us. We tried to be as quiet as we could, but in the silence even the slightest sound seemed loud. We inched up to what I thought was the main cabin and I carefully peered through a window. The cabin seemed to be empty - not a soul.

From that vantage point I could see that the largest cabin was actually at the rear of the ship. From the elaborate woodwork I guessed this was actually the captain's quarters. Again I motioned for the boys to follow me, and we stooped over and stealthily tip-toed along the edge of the deck toward the aft cabin.

Again I peered through a window and this time I saw two bodies. I say bodies because they was slumped over the chairs and the floor, looking as though they was passed out. I figured Maria had been right - they was drunk on rum, they were!

I could hear the sounds of the Spanish sailors back on shore, crying out as they fled what they thought was a band of armed Indians and their own dogs that were now chasing them back to the boat. I didn't have much time to do whatever I was going to do.

I figured that rum or no rum, the captain and his mate were going to wake up when we advanced on them. I had my sword, but the boys had no weapons at all. Through the window I scoured the cabin for any guns or knives or swords. I didn't see anything. It seemed that if there were any, they would be on the men themselves. We would have to disarm them.

I pushed open the cabin door as quietly as I could. It was a big heavy wooden door, and it creaked mightily as I opened it. But still no movement from the men on the floor. With the boys on their hands and knees behind me we inched toward the bodies. Sure enough, there were knives and cutlasses on their belts. By the cut of their clothes it was easy enough to guess which was the captain and which was the mate. The captain was nearer our position, and there was at least one knife on his belt. I approached as quietly as I could and reached over his belly for the knife. That was enough to cause him to stir. I think I wet my pants! But still he was not awakened. I slipped the knife out of its sheath, then spied another. When I had both knives in hand I retreated a bit and handed the knives to the boys.

Then I made my way toward the mate. He also had a short knife and a broad cutlass on his belt. As I inched closer I spotted a pistol lying on the floor beside him. I was hoping I could grab all the arms before the men awakened, but by now my knees were trembling. I don't think I was cut out to be a pirate.

Scared or not, I slid the pistol toward me and passed it to the boys. Then I lifted the cutlass, then the knife that was in his belt. That was the final straw. The mate leaped up, and the captain after him. A scuffle ensued, but by then I had somehow managed to relieve the mate of his knives and had tossed them to the boys.

I was so frightened I can't recall exactly how it happened, but with the captain and his mate visibly frightened of us - not to mention still being drunk with rum - the boys and I quickly managed to take control of the two men, and I found myself standing behind the captain, my arms around him, holding my cutlass to his throat as If I had been doing this sort of thing all my life! The boys had the mate pinned to the floor with their knives and one of them proudly holding the pistol to his chest. In a matter of seconds the brief scuffle had ended with us firmly in control.

As frightened as I had been, it was now clear that the captain was far more frightened of us. I can only imagine what he thought of this band of Indians and a teenager from New York dressed like a Colombian tourist!

I turned the captain around, my cutlass still pressed firmly against his throat, and I looked him square in the eyes.

"I am the ghost of your future."

I have no idea how that came out of my mouth, but it did. Now I was sounding like a cross between Robert Louis Stevenson and Charles Dickens!

"I have seen your future and it is bleak indeed. You and your like have defiled the Lord's Creation. Your God placed before you a veritable Garden of Eden and you crossed the seas only to rape and pillage her. And much you did in the name of your own Lord and savior, Jesus Christ. Your judgment will be heaped upon you."

Damn! I was laying it on thick! And it was working. Shiver me timbers, he was shakin' in his boots!

"Spare me, oh apparition! Have mercy on this poor Christian soul!"

"I'm a Christian, I am - Adam Joseph Rivera, by name - and I swear an oath no harm will come to you at the hands of me or these Indians should you choose to come ashore this fair land as one of them.

"You'll not be claiming this land for Spain. This mountain is home to folk far wiser than you, what's been livin' here since before the first year of your Lord. Our mother Earth ain't the property of no one soul, but if it were t'would belong to these

159

people of this here mountain, and you'd be a better man to learn a thing or two from them.

"I am a messenger, 'tis my job to warn you. The world as you have known it is about to come to an end. You can listen to me, or not - as you choose. You have unleashed your men on this land, and they are about to turn on you as they have turned on the fair people of this mountain. They smell only gold. But the gold is not your gold. In fact, it is not even the gold of the Indians. It is the gold of the land, the gold of the Mountain. It's the living energy of our Earth Mother. What value is the gold to the younger brother from across the sea when he doesn't even understand that the gold is his Mother? If you keep taking from the Mountain, soon there will be no mountain. If you keep taking, taking, taking without ever giving anything back soon there will be no land, no life. You will have killed your Mother. And you will pay the price for all eternity, I swear to you."

OK, just as planned I had thoroughly scared the bejezus out of him now!

"You have a choice: continue destroying as you have been destroying, and then be destroyed yourself. Or you can change. You can join the people who have given their lives to caring for this land. You can be a part of returning the gold to the land where it belongs. And you can change your heart. You can follow the mandate of your Jesus Christ and you can start to truly love your neighbor as yourself.

"When your Lord taught you to love your neighbor, he meant first to love your closest neighbor, your Earth Mother herself. And then to love your brothers and sisters - all of them - and to love your neighbors the mountains and the rivers, your neighbors the plants and the animals, and to love all your

160

neighbors as yourself. You have bandied about the name of Jesus Christ but have blasphemed his teaching with the very actions of your life.

"I am come from the future. I know well that many more will follow you to this coast carrying their Bibles and the flags of their kings and queens. They will plant the colors of Spain on these shores and will even build a city to be named after your fair ship, I would venture to predict. But you, Capt'n, if you're a smarter man than I think you is, will spend the rest of your days living in this paradise, living here on the Mountain.

"One way or another, you'll not be captain of the Santa Marta when she sets sail. You have two choices, as I sees it: either you join up with us and start making friends of the Indians what's lived on this mountain for some hundreds of years before you 'discovered' it, or you let the crew toss you overboard to survive on your own. Either way, this is your new home for whatever time you have left before you makes amends with your maker."

I was just finishing my impromptu sermon when Maria and Bunkey burst through the door, waving their pistols.

"Capt'n we're here! Are you O.K?" It was Maria, with Bunkey right behind her.

"How did you guys get here so fast?"

"Actually, it seems we're a bit late, Capt'n. But you appear to have things pretty much under control. Good on ya'! "

"And Bunkey, how did you get that horse?"

"Well, Capt'n, remember I told you if ever you was needin' somethin' you should just ask Bunkey? Well, I thought I was hearin' your voice in my head, sayin' you was needin' a Warrior

161

on a White Horse! Oh, and that war paint? That was your idea, too!"

I just shook my head. "Well I don't know how you did it, but yes, it was exactly what we was needing."

"As soon as I charged down the hill on Blanco, once we'd set the men to fleein', we all ran after 'em fast as we could. We ran behind the bushes and came up around the other side of 'em so's they couldn't see us, and then we swam to the ship. We was hopin' we could get here in time to be of some help."

"We'll be needin' your help, for sure. But the captain here knows his choices."

I turned to the captain and said, "What say ye, sir? Will you side with us and start making amends? Or will you take your chances with the Indians and your own mutineers? Which'll it be?"

The captain was a sight. His face was white as a sheet, his lips quivering as his bloodshot eyes met mine: "Seems there's no choice as I sees it. I'm not the evil man you seems to think I am, and neither are my men. It's true the gold has brought out our lesser nature. But it's also true that we serve our Lord first, and killing these gentle souls is not our mission. You are right. We will be judged harshly if we continue to forsake the Lord's teachings. We wish to save souls, not kill them. It seems we must start by savin' our own. I am at your service, Capt'n."

"OK. I'll take you at your word. Now we have work to do. We'll need your help getting the men to give up the gold. And I'm sure that won't be easy. I'll need you to issue orders from the ship that they're to lay down their gold on the shore if they're ever to see Spain again."

162

"Capt'n, I have an idea." It was Maria speaking. "I can fire a cannon round to stop the men in their tracks on shore and put the fear of God in 'em. Then you bring the captain to the bow to speak to the men. They'll listen then, I'm sure of it!"

"Sounds like the plan I was already workin' on," says I with a smile. "Let's get on with it."

The first mate seemed to be half still drunk and half agreeing with the captain, but I had Bunkey tie him up just in case. We walked the mate and the captain toward the bow, as Maria and the others readied the cannon.

The men were standing on the beach, gazing at the longboats well out in the water, and looking confused. Some were in the water, trying to swim with their heavy shoulder bags weighing them down, their greed sinking them before they would give up their grasp of the dead weight. Others were still scurrying down the hill, trying to outrun the dogs at their feet. They, too, looked almost silly as their heavily-laden shoulder bags threatened to trip them up.

Boom! A thunderous cannon shot roared out, and echoed back from the mountain. Maria had purposely missed the men, but the ball whizzed darn close to them - close enough to scare the bejezus out of them! To a man they stopped in their tracks or stood up straight in the water. They were all staring at the ship.

I had led the captain to the bow where he mounted the highest portion of the deck and addressed the crew on shore:

"Men. Listen to me and listen close. Our future is in the hands of our Lord. A messenger from God, a messenger from the future, has spoken to me. We have defiled the Lord with our actions. This is not our land - it is God's land. And these Indians

163

are not our enemy, they are God's people, too - our brothers and sisters. And the gold is not our gold. It, too, is God's gold, it is the Mountain's gold. If any of us is to ever set foot in Spain again, we must make an offering of the gold we have taken, lay it on the altar of this Mountain, and make peace with our brothers."

Needless to say, this was not met with unanimous approval from the crew on shore. There was a great deal of shouting and arguing and raised voices. The voice of reason turned out to come from the dogs. They began to bare their teeth and tongues menacingly at the men, and those who clung to the mochillas they had snatched and their other bags of gold were soon relieved of them by the growling dogs. That was enough to scare the others into shedding their bags as well. Soon the beach looked like a playground of boys who had just been told by the teacher to give up their toys. Pouting faces, and bags of gold and shiny gold pieces all strewn along the sand.

"Capt'n, tell the men to leave the gold on the beach and to enter the water, retrieve their longboats." The captain shouted the orders as he was told.

"Bunkey - you go ashore and tell the others they can retrieve the gold the men are leaving behind. Some of you guys go with him. Tell them it is the men's *pagamento*, their payment, that the men wish to help heal the land, to restore the energy of the Mountain. Tell them that the younger brother can change his ways."

"But Bunkey, be careful," said Maria. "The men still have guns."

As Bunkey and the others dived into the water, I led the captain to the deck from the bow.   "What be your wish,

164

captain? Stay aboard the ship to be at the mercy of your crew, or return to shore with us?"

"I serve at the mercy of the Lord. I will remain with my ship, and with my men. If I can succeed in changing their hearts, it will be the Lord's work, not mine. If not, so be it. I may be tossed into Davy Jones' Locker with little chance of ever seeing dry land again, if that be God's will."

"OK, boys. The sailors will be fetching their boats and quickly making it to the side of the ship to board. We need to get out of here.

"Capt'n - we should get rid of the powder. We can't have them firing back at us again." It was Maria and that sounded like good advice. She always seemed to say the right thing at the right time, did this Maria. "You guys help me toss the barrels of powder overboard." And that's what was done.

With the powder safely in the sea, it was our turn. As the men began climbing up the ropes on the windward side of the galleon, we dove overboard on the leeward side. Our heads and arms were barely visible from the beach as we made our way secretly to shore.

Some of the sailors were still on the beach, torn between rushing to the boat safely or clinging to their gold. Bunkey was leading the Indians back to the shore to retrieve what belonged to them. He was shouting in his language, apparently telling the Indians to gather up the gold and, at the same time, shouting at the Spaniards to drop their gold and leave. It was working. The Indians were now more excited than frightened, and the sailors were scared and retreating - down to the last man.

Bang!

A shot rang out, and Bunkey fell to the ground.

"Bunkey!"

Out of the corner of my eye I spotted what appeared to be the last of the sailors, racing toward the boats - and waving a pistol. But my attention was on Bunkey. I ran toward him and found him laying face down in the sand. His friends were racing toward him as well and were gathering around him, visibly shaken. He seemed to be breathing, though, and I couldn't see any blood. Then he moved. He slowly lifted himself up and shook himself off. And he started to laugh! In whatever language he was speaking I understood him to say that the ball had hit his mochilla, the thick strap of his mochilla. It had knocked the wind out of him, but other than that he was fine. Over and over he said it was his mother's mochilla, the one she had woven just for him, that had saved his life. We exchanged a big hug to the cheers of his indigenous friends.

I turned to survey the scene. All the sailors had left the beach and were swimming toward the lifeboats, some were already climbing up the ropes to the deck. The beach was strewn with bags of gold - mochillas and other leather sacks. A few dogs remained, wandering the shore.

The Indians began gathering up the gold. While I was sure that many of the pirates, as I now thought of them, had pocketed a good deal of gold for themselves, it seemed the dogs had talked them out of most of it.

I gathered Bunkey and Maria and we walked among the bags of gold arm in arm. All in all, our adventure had been a success.

"Hey, we didn't change the world," said I. "but we did what we were able and maybe we made a difference." Again, I hugged them both.

A great shout arose from the galleon. A body dived or fell - I'm not sure which - from the deck to the sea below.

I turned to Bunkey and Maria, but they were gone. The mochillas of gold were gone. In their place were the Elders, standing silently on the shore.

"I was dreaming again, wasn't I?"

"Perhaps. But you were doing what you could do. And you were discovering that you could make a difference. That may have been your dream, but it is likely also your reality."

"I wanted to save the gold," I said, as my fingers held up the golden figurine that hung from my neck. "I wanted to save the Mothers."

"We know."

I lifted the string necklace with the golden figurine from around my neck. I held it in my hands for a moment - my two open hands - contemplating it.

I reached out my hands to the Elder.

"I want to return this to you."

Once again I was offering my mother's golden figure to the Elders.

"Now I believe you should have it," I continued. "It's true I was meant to receive it, to receive it from my Mother, but only so that I might one day return it to you."

167

This time the Elder received it, warmly clutching my two hands as he did so.

"This time we accept. You have learned how to give and how to receive. On behalf of *la madre tierra* we receive with open hands this precious gift from your mother, from our Mother."

I had done it. I had returned the gold. From the Mountain to New York and back to the Mountain it had gone full circle. I had cared for it, it had protected me in battle, and now I was returning it.

The Elder clutched the golden figurine tightly in his hands and pressed them to his forehead. He quietly uttered a blessing, maybe a thanksgiving. Then he passed it to the next Elder who did the same. And then the next, and the next. When each had offered his blessing, they repeated the blessings with me. Each in turn pressed the golden figurine to my forehead and pressed his forehead to mine.

"Like you, this golden Mother was born of the earth. Like you, it has been shaped by the original peoples of the land. Today we have shaped it still again. It has been born anew, just as you have been shaped by the peoples of the Mountain and made new."

Then he ceremoniously returned it once again to my neck.

"It has helped you find your way. It has always been meant for you."

Chapter 8

The Energy of the Mountain

"Nothing should go un-noticed."

The sun was just beginning to appear over the mountain. The Elders had gathered to greet it, and to offer me still another lesson in how things really are.

"The sun rises every morning, whether here in the land where the sun is born or elsewhere, and most people don't notice. Nothing should go un-noticed."

The Elders speak with a profound economy of words. Nothing should go un-noticed. I could probably unpack that little bit of wisdom for hours, for days, for a lifetime. How much have I missed simply because it went un-noticed?

"When you really pay attention, when you let nothing go un-noticed, everything is your teacher. Listen to the birds. They never let the sun rise un-noticed. And the trees. They spend their lives thrusting themselves upwards toward the sun. They never let a sunrise go un-noticed. Even the water. Every morning the first rays of sunlight strike the top of the high mountain, and the waters respond. The snows are warmed and begin to melt, releasing the waters to start their long journey down the mountain toward the sea. In nature, nothing goes un-noticed. Certainly not a sunrise."

In a few short days this may have already been my greatest lesson. Everything should be noticed. Watch the water, watch the birds, watch the sky. The real lessons in life don't come from words, they come from paying attention, from observing. The Elders with their profound wisdom were doing little more than helping me open my eyes, to see, to notice what was all around me.

"As the world turns and the sun comes up, notice the Mountain. The Mountain is alive. The Mountain is a being, just like you and me. The Mountain is our ancestor. The Earth and the moon are our mothers. The sun and the snows of the Mountain are our fathers. Just as all that is or ever was or ever will be was first imagined in the water, so it is that all that is or ever was or ever will be was born in the energy of the sun. The Mountain was born of the sun. The Mountain is the living energy of the sun. There is no other energy. Just as without water there is no life, without the sun there is no energy. The gold, the coal, the oil - all the things the younger brother believes are energy - were first the sun. All the energy, all the life-giving energy that is the Mountain was first the sun. When the sun returns in the morning and pours her life-giving energy freely down upon the Mountain, it should not go un-noticed.

"Follow me. Let us experience the sunrise, and take time to notice how the energy of the sun and the moon and the Mountain can be felt all around us. You can feel the sun on your face, no?"

"Of course I can."

The morning air was cool and crisp, but the first rays of the rising sun were already warm upon my face.

"That warmth - the energy of the sun - is millions of miles away, but you can feel the heat, feel the energy. I can feel the same energy. The Mountain, the birds and the plants, all are feeling

170

that very same energy even as we walk. We are all connected, you me, the Mountain, the birds and the plants and animals, we are all connected, all interwoven within the same cloth of energy, threads of energy running through us all and tying us all together. And empowering us, giving us life.

"Life is energy. Everything on the planet is alive - the plants and animals, of course, but also the Mountain and the rocks, the rivers and the oceans. All are alive with energy. And where does that energy come from? It comes from the sun. We are all connected, all interwoven with the energy of the sun. I am the sun and you are the sun. All the plants and the animals are the sun.

"Just as there is no life without water, so too is there no life without the energy of the sun. That is the law. That is the original law.

"Every action and behavior is informed by what we call the 'Law of Origin,' the spiritual and environmental law that governs the relationships between everything in the natural world - the mountains, the plants, the animals, the water, the weather, even the cycles of the sun and the moon, the planets and stars. When the great Mother gave birth to the peoples of the Mountain she gave us the mandate to uphold her Original Law: that all creation must be protected and nurtured. We were not given the earth, air, water or the sun. It is all part of us, and we part of it all. We must care for it as we would care for ourselves."

The Elders motioned me to follow and we walked along the ridge and then into the jungle forest and down the mountain toward the sea. As we walked the Elders would stop and point out something to me, something I would otherwise have let go un-noticed.

"Look at the trees. Perhaps the greatest source of energy on the earth after the sun itself. They spend their entire lives reaching for the sun, growing ever higher and higher. And as they do, they are all about giving and receiving. All day long they soak up the energy of the sun, freely offered, and turn it into new growth - leaves that breathe in the air and then give back. The trees breathe out the oxygen that sustains the planet. Without the trees there is no life. Why? Because without trees there is no energy from the sun nor water from the rains providing oxygen to the air. And as with the water and the sun, without oxygen there is no life. That, too, is the law."

I admit I had been guilty of perceiving the Elders as being somewhat backward, uneducated, not having a 'modern' scientific knowledge. I was obviously wrong.

Again, the Elder knew what I was thinking:

"The younger brother thinks he is the only one who understands how things work, who knows about the science of things, the way things are. We have known all these things since the dawn of the first sunrise. How did we learn about oxygen, for example? We opened our eyes and observed. We never let anything go un-noticed."

I was discovering a new way of understanding 'science.'

"The younger brother thinks energy is something he digs out of the mountain, to make his electricity, to power his cars. Yes, we know about electricity and cars, too. Just as the world changed with the arrival of Columbus, so, too, did everything change with the younger brother burning the energy of the Mountain in his many cars and electric power plants and building his cities of steel. We have observed all this in *aluna*, and we have

seen the younger brother drive his cars and trucks up the
Mountain and his heavy machinery cut the rock out of the
Mountain. We have read the stones, the waters, the clouds and
have come to know what is happening beyond the Mountain. In
the bubbles we have seen the images of coal mines and copper
mines, of huge dams, of power plants spewing smoke, of polluted
cities, of sprawling freeways and housing developments, of mega-
farming operations with insecticides being sprayed, oil spills on
the shores –we have seen it all. We have seen this disease that the
younger brother is spreading throughout the living planet. The
younger brother believes the Mountain is nothing more than a
pile of rocks waiting to be dug up and hauled away to give energy
to his things. For us the Mountain is our ancestor and it has life
and energy, energy that is part of a delicate natural balance,
energy that is meant to be left alone, to be left where it is - in the
land, in the living Mountain. The younger brother thinks he
needs the energy of the Mountain to put in his things so he can go
faster and farther. Go where? To his death and destruction?"

The Elder's voice was trembling. Death and destruction
were very real for him. As was the apparent stupidity of the
young brother as he observed it. Certainly that had not gone un-
noticed.

"Energy is not in the coal and other rocks that are cut out
of the Mountain. Energy is everywhere, everywhere the sun
shines. It is in the air, in the water, and yes in the Mountain and
the rocks. At this very moment, you and I are communicating
with one another in a sea of energy. You don't understand my
words and I don't understand yours, but we understand each
other. That is because we are transmitting energy to one another,
not mere words. Your energy is touching mine and mine is

touching yours. Everything on the planet communicates with everything else through the threads of energy."

As the Elder shared his teaching, I noticed something had changed. The Elder's lips were no longer moving. He was speaking no words. I was hearing no sound. But I was understanding everything he was somehow saying.

"The Mountain and the rocks, the water and the plants and the animals – maybe you don't hear them like you hear your mother. But they are constantly talking to you nonetheless. And communication is more about listening than about ordinary speaking. If you are paying attention, if you're truly listening, you will hear them speak to you.

"The Mountain speaks without words. The mountain touches us with his energy, communicates with us. The mountain also listens. With the Mountain, nothing goes un-noticed. The younger brother can learn to listen. The younger brother must learn that nothing goes un-noticed."

I could only imagine how much I had let go un-noticed in my life. Could I really learn to observe everything as the Elders observe it? I don't know. I'm not a shaman from the Mountain, I'm just a kid from the Catskills.

"Energy is like nature. In fact what we call nature is just another way of speaking of what we call energy. There is no place where energy ends and we begin, no place where we end and energy begins. I am energy, you are energy - the Mountain, the plants, the animals are all energy. And it all comes from the sun. We are all connected to the sun, to the Mountain, to each other."

The Elder bent over and dug up a bit of earth with his hand.

"When the younger brother cuts into our Earth Mother and takes out the coal or the oil or the gold it is like he is taking away her arms or legs. We move with the energy of our arms and legs. If we think we need to move farther or faster we could say we need more energy, we need more arms and legs. And we could rip off the arms or legs of another. But that would be silly, wouldn't it? Yet every day the younger brother is doing just that – he is stealing the energy from the body of his Mother and then burning it to make his things go farther and faster. He is removing the energy from his Mother. Eventually his Mother will die, and the younger brother will die along with her. In the end he will have gone no farther nor any faster."

I was beginning to feel a little embarrassed about being the younger brother myself.

"The Mountain is the eyes, the ears, the lungs, the arms of nature. Everything in nature is a Being; a mother or father or brother or sister who is alive and has a spirit. Our rivers are like the veins that run from the head in the glacier peaks thru the body of the Mountain. If these things are destroyed, it will bring an end to our indigenous culture, it will destroy us as a people. The Mountain is our sacred abode. It is a natural pyramid, with its water sources, mountain ranges, minerals, and plants and animals forming a living body that is the heart of our Earth Mother herself.

"That is why we say this is the Heart of the World - it mirrors all that is happening in the rest of the world, and if the Mountain dies, if the heart stops beating in rhythm, our Earth Mother will die. Our territory, the Mountain and our sacred sites are like temples where the memories and our ancestral knowledge are kept. If the younger brother were to destroy the Mountain it

175

would mean that the Mountain would lose its energy and our people would lose their knowledge. Who we are is written in the earth, in the trees, in the snow peaks, in the lagoons, in the wetlands. The rocks that are carved by the water and the wind are our books, our law, and our agreements with nature."

As we continued walking and talking, the Elder continued to make certain that nothing went un-noticed. We passed a garden where carefully tended fruits and vegetable were growing.

"The sun pours out its energy on the land and on the plants. It is all the energy we need. These bean stalks grow tall and straight because they are reaching for the sun."

It's true - these were the tallest, healthiest bean plants I had ever seen, and I was raised on a farm! They could easily have been the inspiration for "Jack and the Beanstalk."

"It is their calling, their essence, to become the bean plant they were meant to become. If they are unable to realize their calling, to become what the Creator meant them to become, they will perish. It is the same with people. We all have a calling, a job to do, and ours is to care for our Earth Mother. If we fail, we, too, will perish.

"The plants take in the air and the water and the natural goodness of the land, but they get their energy from the sun. Everything we need - our fruits and vegetables, our water - all this comes to us because of the energy of the sun. And it is all we need. Everything we need for life - everything we need in order to do our job in life - is provided by the land and the water and the air and by the energy of the sun. We don't need to destroy the Mountain to power our things. The younger brother doesn't need to take the Mountain's energy and hoard it for himself. What will he gain from that?

"All spiritual and physical energies of the Earth are mirrored in the Mountain, in the heart of the world. It is our task to maintain the balance of the energies of the Earth by caring for and protecting the energies in the Mountain. The younger brother does not understand energy, does not understand the ways of harmony and balance. The younger brother is greedy and takes more than he needs, destroying the Mother in the process, without any feeling of gratitude. The sun and the earth give the younger brother all that he needs, and it goes un-noticed.

"We, the people of the Mountain, do not take more than we need. We, too, need energy - to cook our food, to heat our huts at night. But we burn only the branches we need and we plant seeds that new branches might grow. We use the energy of the sun that has been stored in the branches of the trees. We tend the trees, and we mend the ones that are broken. We have all we need and we will always have all we need. We do not understand why the younger brother is never happy and always wants more. We give thanks to Mother Earth for everything with our sacred offerings, our *pagamentos*, through giving back to balance what we have taken. We give thanks for everything, and for everything we receive we give something back. That is the way it must be."

"When we plant the seeds, we do it together, a man and a woman plant together. The mother did not only create the physical world, but she shaped and peopled *aluna*, creating a Mother and a Father for everything that exists. Life is meaningless without a creative energy. Whatever is alive must have a Mother and a Father. Men and women are not simply people, they are the embodiment of creative energy. The harmony

177

and balance of the world is constructed out of the creative partnership of the masculine and the feminine, the dynamic process of weaving on the loom of life."

I had not thought of beans as energy before. And I had certainly never thought of them as having a masculine and a feminine nature before. I had so much to learn.

From the beanstalk garden we continued our walk deeper into the dense foliage of the costal jungle. I saw a non-stop mind-boggling array of fruit trees and other plants and finally had to ask what they all were.

"In the high mountain we grow potatoes, onions, cabbages, lettuce, strawberries and raspberries and blueberries, tamarilloes, pumpkins, garlic, wheat and more. On the lower mountain we care for the corn and the beans, rice, yuca, sugar cane, arracacha, malanga, coca, cotton, pineapple, papaya, guava, passion fruit, sweet granadilla, mangoes, oranges, lemons and limes. And of course we grow coffee. We have the water and the sun - and the energy of the Mountain. Everything grows here if it is cared for."

So many of these things I had never heard of! This kid from the Catskills had a lot to learn.

The birds and the animals liked the fruits as well. As we continued our walk the monkeys were chattering in the trees and the birds were flitting from mango to juicy mango. We were walking a path that made its way through a canopy of trees and plants, and soon we emerged at the base of a hill and a stream with still another beautiful waterfall. This truly had the feel of a veritable Garden of Eden.

We gathered together at the bank of the stream, and the Elders stepped into the waters in their bare feet.

"The waters of the Mountain begin as the snows on the high peaks. They provide their energy to all the plants and animals as they roll down the mountain toward the sea. In the ocean they join all the waters that ever were and that ever will be. They become one with the creative energy of *aluna*. There the energy of the sun lifts the waters to the clouds to begin the whole cycle again. It is the cycle of life, maintaining the balance. Energy is always flowing, always moving, from one place to another, always seeking balance. Yes, the Elders know these things.

"But now the younger brother is taking the energy from the waters. Many dams are being built to block the waters and fill the valleys so they can generate electricity to power their things. The blocked water floods the lands, even our most sacred sites, and forces our people to flee their ancestral homes. The younger brother says this is better than taking the coal and the oil from the Mountain and burning it. We say the Mountain is our home, and the waters are also a part of the mountain and should be left alone. The water was meant to flow where the water was meant to flow. If the course of the waters is changed by the younger brother, the balance is changed, the energy is changed. What the younger brother does with the water does not go un-noticed."

One of the Elders began lifting stones from the water and placing them one on top of the other until he had dammed up a little portion of the stream. Water began building up behind the stones until it found a new way to continue flowing down the hill.

"Moving even a few stones can change the energy of the Mountain, can upset the balance," he graphically taught.

179

He then carefully dismantled his little dam and gently returned the stones to their place in the stream.

An eagle was soaring overhead. It did not go un-noticed.

"Our brother the eagle understands balance. He balances himself in the sky, suspended in a sea of water we call air. He notices the wind, always making little adjustments to maintain the balance, to remain in tune with the rhythm of the air, the wind, the sky. When he loses a feather from one wing, he intentionally drops a feather from the other wing. He makes a minor but very important correction to the balance. He makes a *pagamento*. Maintaining the balance is important, and it's everyone's job."

We continued our walk until we were on another ridge and could see the coast in the distance and the hills and a valley before us. The hills were scarred, the tops having been flattened, and black coal was piled all around. It was a sharp contrast to the green jungle we had just been enjoying. I knew what I was being shown.

"Every mountain has a job, an energy. Now, see this mountain over here? This mountain is dead. This mountain was also our ancestor; this mountain also had energy and a job to do. Then they cut into the mountain, they opened her up and took the energy from her. They cut her into pieces and they took the pieces away. They took her life."

We walked to the now abandoned mine. The Elders walked upon the rocks of coal in their bare feet, providing an ethereal contrast to the black ground. The Elders again bent over and this time each picked up a piece of coal.

"This is the energy of the sun. For millions of years the sun nourished the plants and the animals that were born here, that thrived, and then died on this land. Then the sun powered the rain and the wind that buried all that life energy under the ground and baked it for centuries, storing the energy in the heart of the Mountain. It is part of the life force of nature, the continuous energy cycle of life, death, and rebirth which keeps all the world alive. Yes, the Elders know about these things, too."

I no longer had any doubt that the Elders knew pretty much everything that needed to be known.

"When the younger brother comes to the Mountain and takes the coal or the oil he takes the energy of the Mountain. When he takes the energy from the Mountain and burns the coal in his machines he destroys not only the Mountain, he destroys the balance. The coal energy is part of the Mountain. It is meant to be left alone, to be left in the earth. If it is taken from the Mountain, something must be given back. The younger brother never gives anything back. He only burns the coal, putting it into the air, blocking the sun. It does not belong in the air. It belongs in the Mountain. The coal energy has all been removed from this mountain. There is no energy, no mountain now. It is dead. Soon there will be no more mountains. No more balance or harmony. No more Earth Mother.

"The younger brother is destroying the land in search of a new gold, black gold, energy for his things. Soon he will have taken all the energy from his Earth Mother, and she will die. The younger brother will die, too. All this while he lives in a garden providing him with everything, and under a sun that gives him all the energy he could ever consume. The younger brother's destruction does not go un-noticed."

181

The Elders walked among the coals silently, sometimes picking up another piece and looking at it, turning it in his hand to see it in different ways, the sunlight playing on the shiny facets of the black crystal, revealing all the hidden colors of the rainbow. I'm certain in their mind's eye they were looking into *aluna*.

"It's not a problem of using too much energy. Do we say the trees and the plants are using too much energy? No, of course not. We could plant more trees instead of cutting them down and there would always be enough energy. Why? Because the trees don't take energy from the mountain, from the land. They receive energy from the sun. And they return to the air in fair measure more than they have received. Giving and receiving. The younger brother takes and takes from the mountain, from the land, and never gives anything back."

The Elders took their lumps of coal and together they slowly walked to a grassy spot on the hill that had not been disturbed. They climbed a short way up the hill to a very large smooth rock that protruded from the ground and which had a pattern of lines inscribed in it by centuries of wind and water. We walked to the rock and from the vantage point could see all of the beautiful valley below us. In contrast, the scarred mountain top looked like an ugly scar on the land.

"This is a sacred site to our people. It is part of the Black Line, an invisible energy line of sacred sites around the Mountain that mark the division between the land and the sea. It is from the energy of the sea that the original natural law was received. The younger brother forced our people off this land so they could cut into the Mountain and take away the coal, take away the energy of the land. On this day we give a little something back. It is not enough, but it is what we can do. We replace a little of what has been taken away. We do our part to restore balance to the Mountain, to the energy of the Earth."

With that the Elders each added his or her piece of coal to the many that had been placed at this sacred site before. Each Elder cupped the lump of coal in his hand and pressed it to his forehead before placing it on the stone altar: "We offer this pagamento to all our spiritual Mothers and Fathers."

We stood in reverent silence for some time. Then we slowly resumed our walk. And the Elders continued their lesson:

"We still continue to care for the world as we were taught by our Mother. For thousands of years we have lived in accord with the laws of nature. The younger brother is now living outside the laws of nature. It has not gone un-noticed. When once we lived in harmony with all of the natural world, nature is now turning against humanity and becoming the enemy. In fact, the younger brother has become his own enemy. The changes we see on the Mountain are the result of the younger brother living outside the laws of life and laws of nature, the natural law of the balance of the world. Our *pagamentos*, our payments for what has been taken, are no longer enough. The energy balance has been altered. This time it will take a change of heart by all people of the planet to restore the balance."

We could hear the sounds of the waves as we made our way down the hill toward the shore. There were fishermen in colorful wooden boats flinging their nets across the water, while the Elders negotiated with others on the beach for a few fresh fish.

As is typical of Colombia we were soon joined by friendly folk with flutes and drums. I could look over the shoulder of my ancient friends and see in the distance, beyond the coconut palms, the tall metal cranes of a new port facility. Off shore huge ships were lined up waiting to carry away the coal. Pelicans glided silently past, skimming the surface of the calm sea. The fishermen continued tossing their nets as dinner was cooked on the beach - over a wood fire.

Chapter 9

The Power of Imagining

I sat for a time on the beach, just watching the little fire that had cooked our lunch. I looked into the flames. So many times had I enjoyed watching a fire, and a fire on the beach was the best of all. But this time was different. The dancing flames were alive. The fire was alive, a living being. Like any living thing it needed heat and air and food - fuel - to live. Take any of the three away and the fire dies. The fire consumes energy, the branches it was devouring even as I gazed into its mesmerizing flickering flames, and it gives off energy, heat and light energy. Little branches from living trees heating and illuminating my little place on the beach. It was like camping, but this time nothing was going un-noticed. The more I watched this little fire the more alive it became. And the more oblivious I became to everything around me. I was in a trance, deep in my own meditation, meditating on the energy of the fire.

I was so lost in my thoughts that I hardly noticed the appearance of an Owl Butterfly. It seemed to be attracted by the flickering light of the fire. It looked like something out of a dream as the firelight illuminated its fluttering wings as it seemed to circle the fire.

"Follow me." I'm sure I heard her say, "Follow me."

So I stood up to follow and as I did so I thought I heard the sound of an automobile. Yes, here in the silence of the shores of la Sierra I was sure I heard a car engine, something I had not heard for days. Then I heard an awful crackling of wood, the crunch of metal…and splash!

I started to follow the butterfly's lead, toward the sounds, when I heard the screams of "Help! Help! Young man! Young man! Help us, help us please!"

As I looked around for the one calling out, I realized I was no longer on the shores of la Sierra at all. In fact, it looked as though I was back in the countryside of the Catskills. My little campfire was still flickering on the sand, but the beach was now alongside a country stream. Palm trees had been replaced by pine trees.

The butterfly led me toward a most unbelievable sight. An antique automobile, something like a Model T, had apparently crashed through a narrow wooden bridge and was now sitting nose down in a few feet of water. It actually appeared the bridge had split right down the middle and deposited them in the river. The one who was calling out for help was stumbling, half trying to swim, half trying to walk. "Help! Please help!" He was very well dressed and his heavy wet clothes were weighing him down. Three or four others were all struggling to get out of the half-submerged car.

In an instant I kicked off my shoes and jumped into the water, almost bumping my head on the bottom it was so shallow. I stood up in the waist-deep water and stumbled about to open the car doors and pull out the passengers. It was an almost comical sight as I helped each one to safety. The shallow water presented no danger at all to me, nor to them for that matter, but they were all dressed in heavy formal clothing, like they were headed for a wedding or a funeral or something, and now that they were soaked from head to toe they could barely walk, much less swim, to safety. They were all older men, in their sixties perhaps, who I suspect had no idea how to swim anyway.

I looked each one over for any injuries and they all looked fine.

"Thank you, thank you young man. You've saved our lives!"

It hardly seemed that dramatic to me, but so be it. That's how they saw it, and they were all over me, embracing me in their soaking wet formalwear and thanking me profusely.

They didn't look or talk like anyone I had ever met in the Catskills. They were a sight, with their out-of-place formal clothes all covered in chocolate brown mud. By the looks of it I was surmising they must be part of an antique car club, out for a dive in the country. And they talked funny.

"Allow me to introduce myself. I guess you don't know me but I'm Henry Ford. I made the car you see there stuck in the mud."

Yeah, right. Henry Ford. The Owl Butterfly was circling above. Either I was dreaming or this guy was hallucinating.

Another extended his hand saying, "And I'm Harvey Firestone, the man who made those tires."

Then he introduced two of the others: "Meet Thomas Edison, the man who invented the electric light - and this gentleman is Warren Harding, the President of the United States."

The last to shake my hand was the one who had been calling for help. "I guess you don't know me either?"

187

"Nope, can't say I do," said I, "but if you can tell tall tales like these other gentlemen, I wouldn't be surprised if you said you was Santa Claus."

As the others all laughed in mock embarrassment, he said, "No, not Santa Clause. I'm Luther Burbank. And we all owe you our deepest and heart-felt gratitude. By the grace of God you came from nowhere and surely saved our lives."

Yep, they talked funny. If I was dreaming once again, this one took the cake!

"And who might you be, lad?"

"Adam Rivera, sir."

"And you're from around here?"

"Hmmm. That depends. Where exactly is 'here?'"

Again, they all laughed.

"Why, we're in the Catskills, of course."

"In that case yes, I'm from around here!"

More laughter.

The one who had said he was Henry Ford continued: "We're camping just upstream. It's our practice to go camping together often. We would be honored if you would join us."

And so it was that I found myself in the company of Henry Ford, Thomas Edison, Harvey Firestone, Luther Burbank and President Warren Harding. Or so they said.

"I'll have my people get a horse and pull the car out. We'll have to walk back to the campground, I'm afraid, but it's not far. Follow me."

The Owl Butterfly was already in the lead, but I'm sure it went un-noticed by the others. And what was with this, "I'll have my people get a horse?" What people? And why a horse?

The camp was just a short walk up the dirt road. As we rounded a bend in the road I could see it was a most elaborate campground. Several large green canvas tents had been assembled and arranged in more or less a circle, with comfortable wooden chairs and tables scattered about. While there was a well-constructed rock fire pit in the center, there were also many attendants organizing something of a full-blown kitchen area off to the side. This was first-class catered camping - not like any camping I'd ever seen. Not surprisingly, they'd even hung a string of electric light bulbs! I was beginning to accept the preposterous notion that these gentlemen were, in fact, the famous men they were claiming to be.

Mister Ford seemed to be the host and he graciously offered me a comfortable Adirondack chair and asked the staff to bring me a cup of coffee. And he also asked them to round up a horse and fetch the automobile from the river. These must have been his 'people,' and they didn't seem to be the least bit surprised that the men had driven the car into the river.

"Please excuse us for a minute, but I think it necessary that I and the others get out of our soiled clothing. I'll see if I can round up a change of clothes for you, too, son. Someone here must be about your size," he said, looking at my dirty t-shirt and shorts. "Please, make yourself comfortable. We'll be ready for some lively conversation in a moment's time."

Yep. They talked funny.

I looked around the green valley with the river running through it. It was like the Elders' valley but with Catskills pine trees and oaks. And cars. There were several other handsome antique cars parked all around the camp.

A young lady approached. "Mister Adam?"

"Mary!" I swear it was Mary, all dressed up in her Sunday best with a long skirt and flouncy blouse - and a frilly bonnet.

"It's MaryAnn, sir. Mister Ford asked me to bring you these fresh clothes. You can change in that tent over there."

MaryAnn or not, I was sure she was Mary.

I ducked into the tent and put on the pants - trousers would better describe them - and a starched white shirt and a suit coat. What a perfect gentleman I was! They'd be laughing at me in New York, that's for sure! My shoes were wet and covered in mud, so I stepped out of the tent in my new formal attire - and bare feet. The Elders would have approved.

One by one the men returned, sporting clean clothes, again looking like they were going to a wedding, not a picnic by the river. And as each took a chair in the circle I couldn't help noticing that Mister Ford and Mister Edson certainly resembled the old history book photographs I remembered seeing of them.

I was perhaps being a bit rude, but nonetheless I blurted out the first of many questions I had: "Are you gentlemen really who you say you are, or is this just a car club tour, with you guys all dressed up in old-fashioned clothes and driving around the countryside in your antique cars?"

"Antique cars? Did you hear that men? An antique car."

The men enjoyed a hearty laugh over that one, as Mister Ford continued:

"Young man, this is a brand new automobile, the newest car on the road, the very first of the new Lincoln touring cars to come off the assembly line. I'm guessing that's why you didn't recognize it."

That pretty much confirmed what I had been thinking. Once again I had been transported to a different place and time.

"No sir. I didn't recognize it because I'm from a different place and time. What year is it here?"

"Why it's nineteen-twenty-three, lad - here and pretty much everywhere else, I suspect."

That was good for still another round of hearty laughter.

"You say you're from a different time. Please, tell us more."

"I'm from the future. It seems I've had had many lives, some in the past and some in the future. And for reasons I can't explain I now find myself revisiting them."

The men exchanged glances at one another, their laughter replaced with looks of puzzlement and disbelief. Fair enough. I couldn't really believe what I had just said, either.

Henry Ford again: "Interesting. I've been studying reincarnation, actually. I think I believe in it. It makes sense to me, in a very logical way. But you understand that it's not easy to believe someone who stands before us and says he's from the future, right?"

"Yes, sir. I understand. I'm not really sure I believe it myself."

"Well, then. We'll just suspend our disbelief for a bit, and you can tell us something about this future you say you're from. Alright?"

"Alright. I can tell you a little about what the future will look like in let's say, oh, fifty years from now. But first I have to tell you I'm just beginning to learn that we all shape the future we live in. And you men here today will have a lot to do with the shape of the future of the world, in fifty years and beyond. You could actually change the future, make it something different from the future I've seen."

A little murmuring and a lot of nods from the men.

"Mister Ford, in fifty years there will be more cars in America than there are people. For you, that may be good news. For the planet, I'm not so sure. The bad news for you is most of those cars will not be Fords!"

More murmurings. Mister Ford seemed both startled and amused.

"Mister Edison, in fifty years it will be an electric world, even more than it will be a world of cars. Nearly everyone, even the poorest households in Africa, will have electricity. Almost everything will be made using electricity and most things will be powered by electricity. And Mister Ford, in the future more and more automobiles will be powered by electricity, too. Again, that's the good news - at least if you're in the business of selling electricity. But again, that's not good news at all for the health of the planet. Coal-fired power plants, like the ones you designed, Mister Edison, will dot the landscape around the world. Massive dams will divert the waters of the rivers for hydro-electric power. Man will even harness the power of the atom, nuclear energy, and put it to work generating more and more electricity. But all of these power plants will cause the slow destruction of the planet, polluting the air and pouring toxic waste into the waters."

Edison piped up: "What about the sun? Will we get our power from the sun?"

"Yes, people will generate electricity from the sun. But not enough. The future of solar energy is still being written."

Edison then surprised me a bit with his grasp of the situation:

"I understand, son. We're like tenant farmers chopping down the fence around our house for fuel when we should be using nature's inexhaustible sources of energy - sun, wind and even the tides. I'd put my money on the sun and solar energy. What a source of power! I hope we don't have to wait until oil and coal run out before we tackle that."

"I hope so, too, Mister Edison. Don't stop dreaming, sir. You may not usher in a solar future in your lifetime, but it may well be your vision that sets it in motion. Nothing ever comes into being without first being imagined. And you gentlemen are certainly experts at imagining what can be. You can imagine solar energy into being. You can shape the future."

With those words I understood what was happening. The Elders had been teaching me about energy and about caring for the planet, ostensibly so I could be a messenger to others. And here I was - already sharing the message with Thomas Edison and Henry Ford! Ever since that first day on the Mountain I had been asking myself, "Why me?" How can one kid from the Catskills heal the world? How can I get others to listen? And now here I was - confidently sharing the Elders' message with Thomas Edison and Henry Ford - heck, with the President of the United States, himself! - telling them they can make a difference. Maybe there's hope for me after all.

"We can all shape our future," I continued, "Even me. But I can't imagine there are any others on the planet today, at this moment, who have a greater opportunity to re-write the course of history than each of you."

"Henry and I have talked about that at length," continued Edison. "We both believe automobiles and homes can get their power from the sun one day. With automobiles the problem is that electric cars wouldn't be able to go very far from home, from where they were plugged in. And even homes couldn't be located very far from where the solar electricity was produced."

"That's today, in nineteen-twenty-three," I responded. "But you gentlemen are creative geniuses. You can set in motion the research that will one day result in new and lighter storage batteries and solar panels that are small enough and efficient enough to be mounted on the roofs of homes. Anything is possible, right? Even horseless carriages! Don't stop dreaming."

I turned my attention to the others.

"Mister Burbank. I'm not as familiar with you as I am with some of the others, but I know of you, for sure. I lived on a farm, a farm right here in the Catskills, and my mother grew fruits and vegetables and herbs and spices and sold the plants and seeds. I'm sure many of those seeds owe a debt of gratitude to you, sir. And heaven knows I've eaten a ton of Burbank potatoes in my short lifetime! I would venture to guess that your influence on the future will be every bit as great as that of Mister Edison and Mister Ford, though it may not be noticed as much. I do know that in the next fifty years people will discover the harmful effects of using pesticides on plants, and more and more people will be growing foods pesticide-free and organically."

Burbank was obviously impressed that I was something of a farm boy and that I knew something of his work.

"I understand that fruits and vegetables and flowers may not seem as exciting as new cars and electric appliances," he said, "but it seems to me that as population grows and droughts and floods become more common we will need stronger and better plants to feed the world. In fact, I'm working now to find new ways that plants and trees can be trained to work better for all mankind."

"That sounds promising, Mister Burbank, but perhaps even more important will be finding ways that people can be trained - trained to care for the plants and trees, to care for the earth. What do you think?"

"I love humanity, which has been a constant delight to me during all my seventy years of life; and I love flowers, trees, animals, and all the works of nature as they pass before us in time and space. What a joy life is when you have made a close working partnership with nature, helping her to produce for the benefit of mankind new forms, colors, and perfumes in flowers which were never known before; fruits in form, size, and flavor never before seen on this globe; and grains of enormously increased

195

productiveness, whose kernels are filled with more and better nourishment, a veritable storehouse of perfect food, all produced naturally - new food for all the world's untold millions for all time to come."

"Mister Burbank, I am honored to make your acquaintance. If you can care for our Earth Mother in such a way, with such a passion, and also share your message with the world, you, sir, will have done much to re-write the future for the better. I thank my mother for introducing me to the joys of nature that you describe, and I hope I may humbly walk in your footsteps."

"Mister Firestone. I don't know all that much about you, either, but I can tell you that fifty years from now your tires will still be winning auto races. And all those cars I said would be on the highways all over America and the world - plenty of them will be sporting Firestone tires. But like the others, there is a down side to the planet. I believe it takes a lot of energy to turn rubber into tires. And I know for certain that old tires don't decompose naturally. The same countryside that will be dotted with power plants spewing smoke and cars polluting the air will also be littered with old rubber tires."

Firestone responded: "Young man, it's no coincidence that I sit before you today in the company of these enlightened gentlemen. It turns out that my friend Henry here has a vision for the future that takes all of that into consideration. Along with Mister Burbank we are looking at improved strains of rubber plants and new ways of cultivating them organically. In fact our vision is to encourage the development of an entire agricultural community in the jungles of the Amazon in South America, where the local people would be trained in newer and better methods of horticulture, and then the rubber would be made right there, with local labor - local people earning a proper wage and living in new homes made with local natural materials. We strongly believe that the automobile - and its rubber tires - can move the world while not destroying it, and do so in a genuine partnership with nature and with our workers, wherever they may live."

I vaguely recalled having read of Ford's and Firestone's attempt to create a utopian rubber production operation in the Amazon, and that it had failed. I didn't tell Mister Firestone that part.

"That sounds very commendable, sir. The future will be shaped by such vision, to be sure. In fact it is in the creative vision of your imagination that the electric bulb and the automobile were first imagined into being. So it is with the future. It is in the creative vision of your imagination that the future will be imagined into being. As I said to Mister Edison, never stop dreaming."

I was sounding like a parrot, reciting the words of my teachers the Elders, and the gentlemen were pondering them seriously when I turned my attention to Mister Harding:

"Now Mister President. Your turn. For a politician you've been remarkably quiet, conspicuously absent from the conversation so far." That was enough to return a smile to everyone's face. I couldn't believe I was talking to a President of the United States, and making a joke, no less!

"Young man, I'm still having difficulty bringing myself to believe that I'm speaking with someone who claims to have come to us from the future. That being said, I am most intrigued by all that has been spoken, by you and by my good friends."

I remembered very little from my history lessons about Warren Harding - little or nothing in fact. But as he spoke, he clearly had the commanding presence of one with presidential stature.

"Well, sir, the future that I come from is for certain a political place and time," I remarked. "The next fifty years will be filled with challenges - another World War and many other international conflicts, and strife and division and economic depression at home - but also some small victories. A young president will even lead the country to put a man on the moon."

"No - it can't be!"

"Yes, sir, it's true. Just as I can't believe I'm talking to a past President of the United States live and in person, I understand you can't believe what I'm telling you about the future. But I swear it's all true."

"And how is it that you believe that I, and those of us here, can somehow re-write the future, re-write our future for the better?"

The President was obviously an experienced Chief Executive, gathering the experts together and then asking the questions. And listening. I liked that.

"Mister President, I have been listening to some very wise teachers. Before there were fifty United States - I mean forty-eight United States - before there was politics or much of anything else, there were the original peoples of this land. I have been listening to them. I have been learning from my ancestors. I am learning there is no place or time where the present ends and the future begins. Our every thought, our every spoken word, our every action effects something somehow somewhere some time.

Every one of the thousands of choices we make today and every day shapes the future we will be living in tomorrow."

Wow! I wish my teachers on the Mountain could hear me now. I don't know how the words just kept coming, but they did. It's true, I have been listening to good teachers, and it's sinking in.

"I understand that, young man, and I believe it. But I'm a politician; I want answers now, not metaphysics."

"Fair enough. O.K, imagine if you will the America of fifty years from now. There will be automobiles and super-highways everywhere. There will be giant airplanes carrying passengers from New York to California in just hours, electric appliances will be making your life easier, entertaining you with images and music, and even cooking your meals in seconds. All these modern inventions will be demanding more and more energy to keep them running - more coal to burn in the power plants, more oil to burn in our cars. Populations will be growing, food and energy will become more and more scarce. There will be conflict and war over the scarcity of food, water and energy. Pollution in the air will begin to change weather patterns, droughts and floods will be more common."

In my newly discovered voice of authority I continued: "With all of this, what will be our biggest challenge in the future? What can we do to help shape a better future? Is the answer better cars from Mister Ford? Or better tires from Mister Firestone? Or is the answer new electric-powered conveniences and more electricity from Mister Edison? No, I don't think so. To this kid from the Catskills - and also from the future - it seems the answer is more likely to be found by Mister Burbank. We need to be paying attention to the plants and the trees, the water and the birds and the sky. Nothing in nature should go un-noticed. In the future we won't need more cars or more electricity, we will need clean water and clean air, we will need healthy plants and trees. We will need to care for the planet. That's our job. That's our job if we're politicians, that's our job if we're tending the garden. We will need to care for the world if we are to survive, if we are to leave any kind of future to our children and our children's children. That, Mister President, is your challenge if you want to re-write our future. Care for our Earth Mother. She is our future."

Wow. Maybe I could be the Elders' messenger after all.

The President continued: "It does sound as though you have some very good teachers, young man. So be more specific. Tell me what your teachers would tell me. How is it that I can care for the world? How can I lead the people of this country to better care for the world? You know, the people aren't demanding that I care for the world; they want me to help them get a better job and a new car. The post-war economy is recovering, people are starting to see a brighter future, and they want me to help bring it about. How do I balance that with caring for the health of the planet when what people want is more cars and more things that demand more electricity?"

As the President asked his question, the same question I had been asking myself, I again spotted the Owl Butterfly circling just above us. I held out my hand. Sure enough, it circled the entire group of us and then landed gently on my finger.

"Mister President, you should follow my friend the butterfly." I raised my hand and released the butterfly into the gentle breeze. She circled above the group three times and then widened her circles until she disappeared in the woods.

"Mister President," I continued. "Have you seen the country? Really seen the country, all of it, from sea to shining sea, purple mountains majesty, amber waves of grain - the whole thing? You should see it. You should follow the butterfly and explore it. Nothing should go un-noticed and you should fall in love with the country, with the earth, all over again. Have you ever seen Alaska, for example? One day Alaska will be a State, but for now it's still 'Seward's Folly,' an unspoiled wilderness of unparalleled beauty that sits atop one of the largest oil reserves in the world. That, Mister President, is the kind of challenge future presidents will have to deal with - balancing care of the earth with the energy needs of an expanding population. The answers will come to you more clearly and easily if you get out and see our beautiful country, all its awe-inspiring mountains and rivers, lakes and streams, the cities, and farms, and truly fall in love with America the beautiful. I have come from the future and I have come from the heart of the world. You have just fought a World War, defeating the enemies of Europe. In the future there will be another World War and many other enemies. But fifty years from now the real enemy will be those who would destroy the planet, who would attack the natural environment. In the future, we will all need to become the heart of the world. Camping in the Catskills is a great start. But it's not enough. We need a president today, and in the future, who loves this land and who loves the Earth."

"It's funny you should mention Alaska, young man. I already have oil men calling on me to open it up to drilling for oil. We could be free of our dependence on foreign oil if we did that. Maybe it makes sense."

"You haven't seen anything yet, Mister President. If you think oil men are pressuring you now, wait 'til you see the future!

That's why I'm saying go see it. I've recently been all around the world, and it opened my eyes. Do as I did and look at the world with new eyes, with eyes wide open. Fall in love again - with your country, with the land. Once you do, it will be much easier to discern what is right and wrong, what are the right choices.

"If you loved your Mother, loved your Earth Mother as your real mother, you would never allow oil interests or anyone else to harm her, would you? My teachers have taught me that caring for the planet requires little more than cultivating a conscious effort to do no harm. Get out of the White House and see America. Cultivate your compassion for the land."

Henry Ford addressed the President: "Warren, maybe you shouldn't be worrying so much about what you think the voters want. People don't really know what they want. If I had asked the people what they wanted when I was designing the automobile they would have told me they wanted a faster horse! I think what Mister Adam here is reminding us is that what the people really want is leaders who have a vision for the future."

"Mister Ford is on to something," I said. "In the future I come from there are very few leaders with the vision to look beyond the next election. The world will need leaders with vision and a willingness to take risks. We will need leaders who constantly ask the question, 'Am I doing my best for the long-term future of the planet?' All of you have that kind of vision. Are you willing to take the risks? What is each of you going to do the shape the future for the better?"

I don't know how or why I had been placed in the company of these leaders in this place and time, but somehow I was finding the courage to speak up and nudge each of them to make a difference. Without realizing it, I think I was again

202

learning to spread my wings, beginning to morph into the messenger butterfly the Elders believed I could become.

Mister Edison didn't hesitate. He nudged me right back, asking the question that woke me up:

"What about you, young man? What are you going to do to re-write the future? How are you going to change the world? If we were to pick up a history book a hundred years from now, what would it say about you? "

Chapter 10

The Rhythms of Nature

"Listen."

It was dark and still. The sun had not yet risen. There was only a hint of dawn on the horizon. The nearly full moon still hung in the sky above the Mountain

"Listen to the birds. Listen to the sky, to the wind, listen to the water."

The chatter of the earliest birds was the only sound breaking the morning silence.

"Listen to the rhythm. Listen to your Earth Mother."

I listened harder for the wind and the water. I could hear them.

"The sun rises every day and the moon begins a new cycle every month. They set in motion the rhythms of nature, the rhythms of life. The Mountain responds to the rhythm. Every plant and every tree, every bird and every animal responds to the rhythm."

I remembered my musician friends saying pretty much the same thing in the asphalt jungle of New York. I understood it then; it made even more sense to me now. Same rhythm, different jungle.

"The Mountain is the Heart of the World. It mirrors the rest of the world. It beats with a rhythm, as does the rest of the world. It has all the elements of life: earth, wind, water, fire. As does the rest of the world. All of life is connected, interwoven, all beating in harmony to the same rhythm, the rhythm of the sun and the moon and the stars, the rhythm of the Mountain."

Our early morning walk had already taken us higher up the mountain. In some places it was dense tropical jungle, in other places broad grassy valleys. The sun was rising now.

"The Mountain is a garden, as is the rest of the world."

There were long rows of vegetables and neatly pruned fruit trees scattered all about the valley. And many other plants and trees just growing natural and wild.

"Everything grows here."

It was true. There were so many plants and trees, so many different fruits and vegetables, so many I had never seen before. I didn't even know what most of them were. I wanted to learn.

As usual, the Elders knew what I was thinking.

"We don't have enough time to teach you the names of all the animals and plants and trees. You should have learned these things as a child. You did not. You were hidden away in a cave you called home, isolated from the reality of the world, removed from the mountains, the birds, the plants and trees. You seldom saw the sky, the sun and the moon and the stars. But it is never too late to step outside your cave, to get away from the city, to watch the water, watch the birds, to watch the sky - and to listen. Listen to the rhythm."

I probably spent more time outdoors than most, time in our own modest garden in the Catskills, but it's true - I didn't pay much attention to the sun and the moon and the stars, and I

205

certainly couldn't name all these plants and fruits and vegetables. I had been letting a lot go un-noticed. And most of my listening had been to music.

"You know the names of rock stars you'll never meet, but you don't know the names of the birds and the plants that are all around you every day."

How did he know about rock stars?

"The Elders pay attention to everything. As a young child, the future Elder is removed from all distraction and taught to pay attention to the things that are important. He learns about the plants and the animals and the birds and the trees, about the wind and the water. He learns how to listen, how to listen to all that his Earth Mother has to teach him."

Does he learn about rock stars? Never mind.

"We will teach you. We cannot teach you everything you should already know, but we can teach you how to listen, how to pay attention. We can awaken your curiosity. We aren't born with knowledge. We all have to learn things. But we are born with curiosity, the natural curiosity of a child. The younger brother has learned much about things, things that don't matter, but he has lost much of his natural curiosity. We cannot teach you everything, but we can help you become curiouser and curiouser. With that, over time you can learn everything that matters."

It was already working. Ever since the first moment I arrived on the mountain my head had been full of questions. Every day I was becoming curiouser and curiouser. With every teaching I received from the Elders I wanted to learn still more, to experience more. I was already feeling the energy of the Mountain, already responding to the rhythm.

"These simple beans are a good place to start," the Elder said as we continued our walk and began our day's lesson.

"All over the mountain you will see these beans growing tall. We have been planting the same beans for hundreds of years. The Mother gives us the beans, an almost perfect food. And when we receive, we give back. The beans are more than food, they are living seeds. We plant the seeds, we care for the plants. The plant grows, the flowers appear, the bees carry the life of the plant from flower to flower, from plant to plant, and soon there are more beans. We harvest the beans, they nourish us, sustain us, and we plant the beans anew. The cycle begins anew. The rhythm, the cycle of life, is repeated and repeated."

We grew beans on the farm back home. I didn't pay much attention to them. I'm afraid they went largely un-noticed.

"The beans are one of the 'three sisters.' The first sister is corn, she grows tall and strong and helps the second sister, the bean, by allowing her vines to climb up her stalk. In return, the bean vine gives corn the nutrients she needs to grow. Squash is the third sister and she grows low to the ground, throughout the corn field. Her large leaves help control the weeds and keep the soil moist.

"Everything is connected, interwoven. The people of the Mountain depend on the beans. We eat more beans than just about anything from the garden. And the beans depend on us. If we did not plant the seeds, if we did not bless the beans properly, if we did not place the poles and plant the corn to support the plants, if we did not plant the squash, if we did not care for them all properly, they would simply wither and die. If the bees did not come, if the rains did not come they would die. Everything depends on everything else."

The Elder reached out to one of the plants that had fallen from its pole. He lifted it back into place and retied a thread of a vine to hold it.

"What has been hurt must be tended. What has been broken must be mended."

We walked from the beans to the corn and the squash and the tomatoes, all growing in abundance. The Elder bent over and picked up a tomato that was rotting on the ground.

"The plant needs the earth to sustain it, it needs healthy soil. When the tomato falls, when the fruit dies, the sun and the rain, even the insects, break it down and return it to the soil, to the land, to the earth. Nothing ever truly dies. All is reborn. Everything is born of the Earth Mother, and everything returns. That's the cycle, that's the rhythm."

There was much more growing in the neatly-tended gardens, many vegetables I recognized from my own garden, many I did not. And there were herbs and spices, too. Again many I recognized, many I did not.

"The plants provide our food. They feed and sustain us. We must do the same for them."

Again the Elder bent down and picked some leaves from one of the herbs.

"The plants sustain us and they also heal us. The plants provide our food and our medicine. Our food is our medicine and our medicine is our food. And just as the plants heal us, we must be healers ourselves. It is our job to be constantly tending the garden, healing the garden that it may heal us."

The Elder pointed out the coffee plants and the coca and the cacao.

"The coffee and the chocolate and the coca provide food and medicine. The Elders chew the coca leaves to stimulate the mind, to awaken our mind. The cocoa gives us chocolate that is both food and medicine. The bark and the leaves and the seeds and the fruit - all are for healing. The coffee is also food and medicine. The Elders have been using these gifts from the Mother for hundreds of years, always with care, always with respect, always paying attention to how they heal and sustain us. The younger brother has all too often found ways to abuse the gifts he has been given. The sacred coca, for example, has been grown by the younger brother only for the pollen of its flower to make cocaine, a powerful medicine that can have many benefits when used properly. The younger brother has used it only for a fruitless escape from his reality. The same with the marijuana, the cannabis, the hemp. For years we grew the hemp. We smoke the hemp in our sacred rituals, like tobacco, as we have done for hundreds of years, but we also make thread from the hemp and use it in our weaving. The younger brother uses the marijuana like alcohol, and strips it from the land to sell it and get rich - false riches. The result has been wars and killings as the younger brother took away our coca plants and drove us from our land so they could grow more for themselves. Then the government came and sprayed poison on our gardens, killing the coca and the marijuana and everything else, poisoning the sacred land. We have no more marijuana, no more hemp. We are worried about our coca. The younger brother is always taking away, never giving back, destroying the balance, destroying the harmony. The younger brother does not dance in tune with the rhythm."

At the edge of the garden the Elder lifted leaves from the smaller herb and spice plants. He broke them and smelled and tasted them, offering them to me. I recognized the mint and the cilantro and a few of the others, but many were new to me. The herbs and spices we grew in the Catskills were not the same ones that thrived in the tropics, I guess.

"Every plant has a job to do. One plant helps with digestion, others calm the mind, and others heal injuries or relieve pain. Many are good when used in a tea, what we call *aromatica*, and drinking the tea of many of the plants that grow all around us helps maintain the balance and the harmony of the body - the rhythm."

From the gardens we walked the path toward the trees. As we walked the Elders pointed out many of the fruits, already knowing I didn't know the names of many of them. There were bananas, of course, but many different types of bananas, more than I ever knew existed - *bananitos*, or little bananas, and red and green bananas of all sizes. And some of what I thought were banana trees turned out to be *platanos*, plantains, which are not bananas at all. They look like big bananas, but they're more like sweet potatoes in texture and flavor. I had already learned they were very important in the Colombian diet. We saw many more trees I was familiar with, like oranges and lemons and limes, but many more I was not. The Elders introduced me to their names. There were mangoes and papaya that I was somewhat familiar with, and then lulo (a citrusy fruit), borojó, carambola that I recognized as Star Fruit, curuba, guanabana (that tastes a little like strawberry-banana custard!), guayaba (that we call Guava in the States), maracuyá (we call it Passion Fruit), and zapote (about the size of a softball with fruit that tastes like papaya). There were even tomatoes growing on trees - what they call 'tree tomatoes' -

that are not tomatoes at all but a delightfully sweet fruit. Avocados the size of footballs! And pineapples growing right out of the ground!

If all that sounds a bit overwhelming, it was. I tasted most of the fruits. I tried to remember most of their names, but with not much success I'm afraid.

"Everything grows here," the Elder said again. I believed him. My mother would have loved this place.

"But everything that grows depends on everything else that grows. The people depend on the fruits and vegetables to feed and heal them. The plants depend on the birds and the bees. Everything depends on the Earth, and the earth is renewed by the decaying of that which once grew in the same soil. And everything depends on the water. Nothing grows on its own. Not the plants, not the people."

We followed the path into the forest, into the jungle. Everything was growing everywhere. I was noticing things that had previously gone un-noticed. There were grasses of a hundred kinds growing right under my feet. Ferns and colorful leafy plants along the side of the path and the edge of the woods. There were flowering shrubs and fruit trees I didn't recognize. Giant bamboo. And trees - lots and lots of trees. The largest trees rose a hundred or more feet into the air, seeming to join hands with each other above us, forming a canopy that almost blocked the sun. Some were so big around I could only imagine they must be hundreds of years old.

"The trees are water. The waters of the Mountain are all constantly making their way down the mountain, always seeking to go lower and lower until they reach the sea. Not the waters in the trees. The water in the tiny capillaries of the trees defy gravity, they go upward. It's a property of the water. In the tiny veins of the trees the water goes higher and higher. If it did not, the tree would not survive. If the tree did not survive, it could not take the waters from the highest branches, the highest leaves, and turn them into clean air for all to breathe."

I remembered that. "Capillary action" they called it in science class. But I never realized it defied gravity, never realized it carried the water upward to the tops of the trees. I bet even my science teachers had never realized that. But the Elders had. For them nothing went un-noticed.

"The trees need the water, the air needs the trees, we need clean air and clean water. Nothing grows on its own."

Everywhere I looked it was covered in green. Not an inch of the ground was without at least something growing on it. As I looked even closer, trying to not let even the smallest plant go un-noticed, I discovered we were not alone. Just as there were grasses and plants and trees everywhere, the ground and the plants were teeming with insects and animals.

Ants - big ants and little ants, red ants and black ants - were most everywhere, all seeming to be marching in a line according to some plan, all doing their job, as the Elders would say.

I saw spiders and worms and caterpillars and lizards, butterflies and moths and flies and fleas - all living on or among the trees and the grasses and the plants. Monkeys were watching us from the high branches, and birds were everywhere - big birds and little birds, colorful birds and others that blended in, almost disappearing against their green and brown background.

There was so much life in this enchanted forest, this little patch of earth. I looked, and I listened. All the bugs and animals were busy, moving about doing I don't know exactly what, and the birds were chattering and flitting from branch to branch. The Elder was right, there was a rhythm. I listened. I could hear the rhythm in the song of the birds, in the movement of the leaves in the wind, even in the water that was running down the mountain everywhere. It was as if everything was engaged in a dance, moving to the rhythm, making their own music, contributing their little part to a grand jungle chorus.

"Everything is alive," continued the Elder, "and every living thing depends on every other living thing. Nothing exists alone, by itself. Every living thing was brought into the world by another living thing, was nurtured and sustained by many other living things. These giant trees need the smallest plants to give them life. The plants need the insects. The insects need the plants and the flowers. The plants and the flowers need the earth, they even need the rocks and the stones. And all need the water. Nothing exists on its own - not the plants and the trees, not the birds and the animals, not you and I."

The Elder pointed to a large grey rock, a boulder, granite I imagine, and to a little bit of yellow-green moss or lichen growing on it.

"Everything is alive. The rock is alive. Every living thing has a job to do. The rock has a job to do. There is water running through the rock. The water and the rock are feeding these tiny plants. The rock was born of the earth. Deep in the earth the plants and the animals died. Over many years they formed the rock. The rock forms the earth. The little plants draw the water and the earth from the rock. The plant thrives, and the rock is broken down to return to the earth and begin the cycle all over again."

Wow. All this going on with just one rock. I couldn't help thinking that all this was going on all around me, right under my feet in fact, every day, all over the world, and going largely unnoticed.

"If the rock were to run out of water, the little plants that grow on the rock would die. The deer and the other animals that depend on the little plants for their food, they would die. If the little plants did not break down the rock, there would be no new earth. No new earth, no new life. Every living thing has a job. Every living thing has another living thing that depends on it doing its job. If this one rock were to be removed from the Mountain the cycle would be broken, the rhythm disturbed. If the rocks were to be hauled away and crushed to dust to be used to make some new highway or modern building, these little plants would die; every living thing that depends on these tiny plants would die. Everything is connected, interwoven. The Mountain is not a pile of dead rocks. It is alive. And every living thing on earth depends on the Mountain. The Mountain is the heart of the world."

From plants on rocks to plants on plants, the lesson continued:

"Plants grow on rocks, plants grow in the earth. And they also grow on other plants." He reached out to a beautiful orchid that appeared to be growing on the side of a huge tree. "The people of the Mountain call these 'air plants' because they are not rooted in the ground. Most of them get their nourishment from the air and the water around them, not from the tree they are growing on. The plants provide a habitat for other insects and

214

birds and animals - even for other plants - that are beneficial to the trees they are living upon. Nothing lives alone. Every living thing has a job to do, a job that includes supporting every other living thing."

The Elder pointed out numerous other plants that were happily living on other plants and trees - mosses and lichens and vines and broad-leaf flowering plants. It was a symbiotic relationship that I would otherwise have let go un-noticed.

"Even the smallest ant has a job." He lifted an orchid-like flower to reveal a line of ants following each other up and down the long vine-like root of the plant, down the side of the tree. "Neither this flower nor this tree could survive without these ants."

Really? I thought ants were nothing more than a picnic nuisance - except to an ant-eater, of course.

"If you would look closely you would find hundreds, maybe thousands, of ants, dozens of different types of ants all busy doing their job right here under this canopy of trees. The ants recycle the leaves and other decaying plant materials, restoring the soil, enriching the earth."

He began turning over leaves and lifting branches to reveal exactly that - big ants and little ants, red ants and black ants - all totally ignoring us and racing up and down, back and forth to perform their job, whatever that was.

"These leaf-cutter ants cut sections of leaves off other plants and carry them to their underground nests. The ants chew the leaves into a pulp, mix it with a special fungus - still another plant - and fertilize it with their own fecal material. This rich fertilizer supports the life of the trees of the forest, it renews the earth."

Sure enough, hundreds of ants were all carrying their little green piece of a leaf and marching in a line down the tree and across the path.

"These big ants lead this other little insect to the tree. The insect sucks the sugar from the tree, sugar that the ants eat. In return, the fierce ants protect the tree by attacking other foragers and climbing vines which would otherwise cover the plant. Nothing lives alone. Every living thing has a job to do, a job that includes caring for every other living thing."

"Some of the plants contain natural chemicals that make them toxic, even poisonous. The toxic chemicals deter foraging insects that would harm the plants and the trees they live upon. These chemicals play an important role in the plant's defense. When used properly, these toxic chemicals also have important uses in our natural medicines as well."

He turned over a leaf to reveal a beautiful red and yellow and gold and black butterfly.

"These heliconia butterflies have developed mechanisms to exploit these chemicals to their advantage. They lay their eggs on passion flower vines. The young caterpillars emerge and feed upon the leaves. The adult butterflies produce and store chemicals in their bodies which make them poisonous to birds that would prey upon them. Birds have learned to recognize the color pattern of the heliconia butterflies and avoid them. Other butterflies - non-toxic ones - have learned to mimic the pattern of the poisonous butterfly, so they share in the same protection. No living thing survives alone. Every living thing depends on every other living thing. One protects and cares for the other."

I remembered how I had read that the Owl Butterfly had developed its owl eye pattern to fool predators. Nature was amazing!

There were many other colorful butterflies in this tropical forest, along with many beautiful hummingbirds, some with incredibly long tail feathers and long curved beaks. And bees - lots of bees around all these fragrant and colorful plants and flowers.

The Elder pointed to the hibiscus, red and pink and yellow hibiscus growing in profusion. There were bees and butterflies and hummingbirds all enjoying the flowers which the Elder said also had healing benefits in the tea.

"The plants and even the biggest of the trees could not survive without the birds and the butterflies and the bees. And the bees and the butterflies and the birds could not survive without the trees and the plants. And all the trees and the plants help sustain us as well."

The bees and the butterflies and the birds had been all around us the whole time, of course. But now they were not going un-noticed.

"The bees live on the nectar of the flower, and in turn they carry the life-giving pollen to the flower that will give birth to the new seed, the new plant. The bees are not the only ones who have this job. The bats are pollinators, and so are the birds - the hummingbirds and the sunbirds. Wasps are pollinators, and beetles. So are the butterflies and the moths. Even the flies carry pollen from flower to flower. And even the monkeys. That's right, the monkeys and other furry animals brush up against the long-stemmed flowers as they swing from branch to branch, and without even trying they pollinate the flowers along the way."

I was starting to get the picture. Everything has a job, and many have multiple jobs, ones I had no clue of before.

"The bees are helped by the flowers. The many colors of the flowers appeal to the bees, attracting them. Some of the colors and markings on the flowers can only be seen by the bees, they're invisible to you and me. The flower's sweet smell also helps guide the bees as they do their job, and some flowers even smell like the female bee, luring the male bees to the pollen. Even the shape of the flower helps, providing a landing pad, a perch for the feeding bees and butterflies and moths and hummingbirds."

Everything was dependent upon something else and supporting the life of another. I was getting the picture.

"Listen. Listen to the birds and the bees. Listen to the rhythm. Carrying life from flower to flower and back again to another. Carrying seeds and pollen, sustaining and renewing life. Everything has a job. And nothing survives alone."

We were deep into the jungle now, where the canopy of trees provided welcome shade from the warm sun that was now rising high in the morning sky. The Elder pointed out numerous mushrooms, big ones and small, black ones and white, and lots of very colorful ones. These were not the mushrooms of the Catskills!

"The mushrooms also provide food and healing medicine - for us and for the animals and birds and insects of the forest. But their most important job is to break down the dead wood in the forest. They also recycle the leaves and the bark of trees. Without

218

mushrooms the forest would be buried under dead trees. Without mushrooms the forest would die."

He picked several different mushrooms and bit off a piece of one and chewed it. He offered some to me.

"Some mushrooms can make you sick. These are good."

I chewed on the mushrooms and swallowed. They tasted like ordinary mushrooms to me.

"The ants eat the mushrooms and so do many other animals. We eat the mushrooms. They are good food and they are good medicine. But some are poison. Even the good mushrooms, the ones that can heal, can make you ill if you eat too many. The Elders know which mushrooms are helpful for which disease, we know which ones we should eat and which we should not. Some mushrooms are called magic mushrooms by the younger brother because they can cause colorful dreams. It is true that some mushrooms can open the mind and help one see and feel his connection to everything in nature. But the younger brother eats the magic mushrooms just for fun. The Elders use the mushrooms in their spiritual work, to help people whose understanding is blocked, to heal the mind and expand the consciousness. The Elders never use mushrooms or coca or anything else just for fun. They are a sacred gift from the Mother that can be beneficial when used wisely, and which can be toxic when abused. It's a matter of balance. Respecting the harmony, the rhythms of nature."

The Elder walked still further into the jungle, past many more clusters of colorful mushrooms, toward one of the largest trees, a twisted, gnarly tree with rough ancient-looking bark and broad branches reaching out in every direction. Long thick vines hung down from the branches, giving the tree a very jungle-like personality.

"The fig tree is totally dependent on one wasp and one wasp only doing its job. Each species of fig has a single species of wasp which pollinates it. The female, laden with pollen, enters the young fig to lay her eggs in the interior of the trunk, where the seeds form. Doing so, she pollinates the fig flowers. The young wasp larvae and the young fig seeds develop. When the young wasps emerge, they mate and the wingless males die. As the females crawl out of the fig, they are dusted with pollen which they carry to the next young fig where the cycle is repeated. The rhythm is repeated over and over. All dependent on one wasp. If the wasp does not do her job, the *ficus* disappears from the earth. One wasp makes the difference."

The teacher's lesson was not lost on this student. One makes a difference.

"The birds and the bees and the animals also disperse the seeds throughout the forest Some seeds may cling on the fur of monkeys or other mammals. Other seeds are swallowed and later dispersed unharmed through the droppings of birds, bats, fish, reptiles, monkeys and other animals."

He walked past a beautiful Bird of Paradise flower toward another tree, a big broad tree with large nuts or small fruits hanging from the branches.

"The nutmeg is used in our cooking and in our medicine practice. The fruits of this nutmeg tree are eaten by a bird, a large bird, the magnificent Bird of Paradise. The outer fruit is digested but the inner seed, the nutmeg, is protected by a thin hard shell. The large fruit passes through the large bird unharmed and is dispersed throughout the forest. No Bird of Paradise doing his job, no nutmeg tree."

"This is the Brazil nut. The Brazil nut is very rich in nutrients and also used in our medicine practice for good health. The flowers are pollinated by special bees, several large-bodied bees, and also by the *agouti*, a large forest rat. The *agouti* gnaws open the hard fruits and disperses the seeds. No bees and rats doing their job, no Brazil nut trees.

"Most of the seeds of plants are spread by the wind. But in the dense rainforest there is little wind to spread the seeds. The seeds are eaten by the birds and then passed through to land on the ground with a dropping of natural fertilizer and soon there is new life, a new plant or tree. And it is the trees themselves that provide the natural habitat for the birds. No trees, no birds. No birds, no trees."

The Elder led us to another ridge where again we could see the valleys below us and the hills and mountains beyond. There were blocks of land where large tracts of trees had been cultivated, and other tracts of land that appeared to have been scorched by fire.

"The birds and bees are in trouble. We have seen the changes. Forests have been cleared and no longer provide habitat for the birds. And something is killing the bees. They are not returning to their hives. The younger brother clears out the trees to make room for plants, not to feed his family but to turn the plants into money. He robs the Mountain of its home for the birds, its home for the animals. He sprays his poisons into the air to kill the insects, the very insects that maintain the life of the forest. And he kills the birds. We have seen all this."

He led us back down the path, past the bananas and the fruit trees and nut trees, past the neat gardens of beans and squash and corn. To the left and the right of the path there were masses of colorful flowers. And butterflies.

The Elder plucked a large yellow flower from the ground and held it aloft. I was not at all surprised to see an Owl Butterfly circle overhead and come to rest on the Elder's finger.

"Nothing lives by itself. Nothing lives alone. We are all connected, all interwoven. Without the butterflies, without the birds and the bees, without the flowers, without everything doing its job, everything would die. The birds care for the trees, the trees care for the birds. The birds are the trees and the trees are the birds. The butterfly is the flower, and the flower is you and me. There is no place where one ends and the other begins. We are all connected, we are all one."

The Elder held out the butterfly and set it on my finger.

"You listened to the butterfly and you followed. The butterfly has led you to the Mountain. One butterfly, one bird, one bee - one solitary special wasp - can make all the difference. The loss of one tree can cause the loss of one bird. The loss of one bird can cause the loss of another tree. But one bird, one bee, one butterfly can also make all the difference.

"Just as the nutmeg depends on a single Bird of Paradise to ensure the rhythm of its life, there are birds and plants and animals depending on you and on me. You are the heart of the world. We all are. We have the future of the garden in our hands.

"Everything grows here, but not without the help of others. Nothing survives on its own. And we have arrived at a point in time where the garden will no longer thrive without your help.

"Keep listening. Keep listening to the rhythm of the Mountain. Listen to the water, to the birds, to the wind and the butterflies. Keep turning over the leaves and find all that is hidden among them, waiting for you to discover. Listen to your Earth Mother as she cries out. And listen to your heart. Listen to the Mountain that is calling you to become the heart of the world."

Chapter 11

Magic Mushrooms

The Elders kept walking, kept teaching, kept pointing things out to me so they would not go un-noticed. We followed the path through the jungle until it came to an abrupt end at the edge of a rocky ridge. The Elders wasted no time sliding down the rock ledge to the continuation of the path below. They looked like children on a playground slide, waving their hands as they slid down the grey granite.

I, however, was not so sure about this idea; but if they could do it I could do it. So down I went. The fall felt much longer to me than it had seemed when the Elders were doing it. And with the dense canopy of the jungle blocking the sun it almost felt like I was falling down a hole, not merely sliding down a rock. And I kept falling and falling and falling, or so it seemed.

I bumped my head against the rock wall a couple of times, but for the most part landed safely on my butt. I stood up, shook myself off, and turned to follow the Elders. They were nowhere to be seen.

I started down the path, intending to follow after the others, but was soon distracted by another realization that everything had changed. I had landed on my bottom in a much different jungle than the one I had left on top. There were many more plants and trees, all much more colorful than before, with huge red and yellow and pink and purple flowers, and lots of very big birds and bees and butterflies. Unusually large fruits hung from the trees. There were different mushrooms, too - clusters of big red and yellow and blue and green and purple mushrooms, even polka-dot mushrooms!

I started off, seeking after the Elders. The path was full of twists and turns. As I rounded a corner, I spotted a large twisted tree with a sign hung upon it, a sign just like the one that hung on my farm in the Catskills:

"Fruits and vegetables. Herbs and Spices. Seeds and Plants"

As I walked the garden path, the many fruits and vegetables seemed to also have signs on them - signs that said, "Eat me."

I supposed I ought to eat something or other; but the great question was, what? I looked all round at the flowers and the trees and the plants and the fruits, but I did not see anything that looked like the right thing to eat under the circumstances. There was a large mushroom, a very large mushroom, growing nearby, about the same height as myself; and when I had looked under it, and on both sides of it, and behind it, it occurred to me that I might as well look and see what was on the top of it.

I stretched myself up on tiptoes, and peeped over the edge of the mushroom, and my eyes immediately met those of a large green Caterpillar, that was sitting on the top with its arms folded, quietly smoking a long pipe, and taking not the smallest notice of me or of anything else.

The Caterpillar and I looked at each other for some time in silence. At last the Caterpillar took the pipe out of its mouth, and addressed me in a languid, sleepy voice.

"Who are you?" said the Caterpillar.

Good question, I thought. I replied, not the least bit surprised that I was having a conversation with a Caterpillar, "I hardly know, sir, just at present - at least I know who I was when I got up this morning, and who I was when I first arrived on the Mountain, but I think I must have been changed several times since then."

"What do you mean by that?" said the Caterpillar sternly. "Explain yourself!"

"I can't explain myself, I'm afraid, sir," said I, "because I'm no longer myself, you see."

"I don't see," said the Caterpillar.

"I'm afraid I can't put it more clearly," I replied very politely, "for I can't understand it myself to begin with; and being in so many places and learning so much and experiencing so many things in such a short period of time is very confusing."

"It isn't," said the Caterpillar.

"Well, perhaps you haven't found it so yet," said I, "but when you have to turn into a cocoon - you will someday, you know - and then after that into a butterfly, maybe a big Owl Butterfly, I should think you'll feel a little confused, won't you?"

"Not a bit," said the Caterpillar.

For some minutes it puffed away without speaking, the sweet-smelling smoke from the pipe encircling us both in a cloud. At last the Caterpillar unfolded its arms, took the pipe out of its mouth again, and said, "So you think you're changed, do you?"

"I believe I am, sir," said I.

226

The Caterpillar yawned once or twice, and shook itself all over. Then it got down off the mushroom, and crawled away in the grass, merely remarking as it went, "One side will give you knowledge. The other side will give you wisdom. Eat from both sides."

"One side of what? The other side of what? Eat from what?" I thought to myself.

"Of the mushroom, silly," said the Caterpillar, just as if I had asked it aloud; and in another moment it was out of sight.

I remained looking thoughtfully at the mushroom for a time, trying to make out which were the two sides of it; and as it was perfectly round, I found this a very difficult question. However, at last I stretched my arms round it as far as they would go, and broke off a bit of the edge with each hand.

"And now which is which?" I said to myself, and nibbled a little of the right-hand bit to try the effect. Nothing. So I set to work at once to eat some of the other bit, when all of a sudden a White Rabbit with pink eyes ran close by. I didn't find that so remarkable, nor did I find it at all remarkable when the White Rabbit called out, "Follow me."

I popped the last bit of mushroom into my mouth and continued forth, following the White Rabbit down the path. Still the Elders were nowhere to be seen.

To the left and to the right of the path were more of the most unusual plants, brightly colored and with flowers that looked to me very much like faces. And the colors seemed to be changing, one minute a flower was red, the next minute blue. And my head was feeling a bit light. Maybe it was from bumping it on the way down, maybe it was the mushroom. Whatever, the plants and trees and birds began to appear like a kaleidoscope of changing colors dancing before my eyes.

The White Rabbit was still hopping along before me, and I swear in the distance, well ahead of us on the path, I saw the Owl Butterfly and the Guacamaya. But still the Elders were nowhere to be seen.

The colors of the flowers grew ever more intense, as did the sounds of the jungle. I could hear water somewhere, tumbling down the mountain stream with a continuous rhythm that began to sound like music. And birds. Their colors were also becoming more vivid, and they, too, were singing. Then the flowers began to sing. And the butterflies. And the trees. It was a chorus, and soon a symphony. The whole jungle was singing, even dancing, all around me.

This can't be real. Surely it's just my imagination, I said out loud to myself.

"Imagination is the only weapon in the war against reality."

What was that? I heard a voice but I saw no one.

"Who are you?" I called out to no one in particular.

"Who are YOU?" came a reply from what appeared to be a cat - a cat sitting on a branch of a tree! It was a striped cat, red like a fox, with black stripes around its body and a long tail. Maybe it was a lemur or some other jungle animal like that, but it looked like a cat.

"Who in the world am I? Ah, that's the great puzzle," I replied. "Everyone is wondering who I am. I'm wondering too."

228

"Well, then…it seems you have come to the right place."

"Really? And where is that? Where am I exactly?"

"Why, Wonderland, of course."

Oh my God! Curiouser and curiouser. It must have been that mushroom.

"Wonderland is where everyone comes when they start asking the questions."

"The questions? What questions?"

"Why, the only questions that matter, of course."

The Striped Cat, or what I thought was a cat, was now hanging upside down, suspended from the branch by his long tail. He looked like a monkey now, as he continued:

"Who are you and where are you going? Why are you here? How do you get to there? Where are you supposed to be and what are you supposed to be doing? What is real and what is illusion? What is right and what is wrong? What is your job? Those are pretty much the only questions that matter, right?"

"Yes, I suppose they are," I replied, while still thinking it over.

The Striped Cat or monkey or whatever did a flip on its tail and went from upside down to right side up, and now sat upon the branch, looking very much like one of the howler monkeys I had seen on the mountain.

"If you would seek the answers to the questions that matter you must watch the water, watch the birds, watch the sky, you must listen to the plants and the animals. They are speaking

229

to you, singing to you now - you should never let them go unnoticed. You should dance, you should fly, you should sing. Find your own voice and add it to the chorus, share the cries of your Mother. Always become curiouser and curiouser, take risks, experience adventures. With every new adventure you should grow in knowledge and wisdom - the two are not the same, you know - and never stop asking the questions that matter. If you never stop seeking, your path will lead to where you're supposed to be, to who you're supposed to be - the Heart of the World."

With all of that my head was becoming dizzier and dizzier, the words of the Striped Cat or the monkey or whatever echoing in my ears, the rhythms of the plants and animals beating louder. All the plants and animals and birds were dancing and singing it seemed. And they were repeating the same questions: Who are you? Where are you going? How are you going to get there? What is real, what is illusion?"

"How do I discover who I am? How do I learn where it is I'm supposed to be going and what it is I'm supposed to be doing? How do I know what's real and what's a dream?" I asked.

"The reality is that everything is a dream."

Thanks Striped Cat or mister monkey or whoever you are, but that doesn't really help, I thought to myself.

"Then who am I?" I asked again.

"You are the sum of all your adventures, of all you've ever been in the past and all you've ever dreamed in the future, you are all you would remember."

"But who am I really? I am who I remember myself to be, for sure. But I'm also the illusion, the person I think I am. Am I the person others think I am? I'm not so sure I'm the messenger the Elders think I am, for example. And I know I'm not yet the person I'm supposed to be. Who am I and how do I become the real me I'm supposed to be?"

"Be what you would seem to be. Or if you'd like it put more simply, never imagine yourself not to be otherwise than what it might appear to others that what you were or might have been was not otherwise than what you had been or would have appeared to them to be otherwise. It's common sense."

"Well, I never heard it before, but it sounds more like un-common nonsense to me."

"You really are a bit of a simpleton, aren't you?"

Perhaps he was right. 'Be what you would seem to be,' he seemed to be saying.

"What do I seem to be to you?" I asked.

"What it is that you seem to be to me or others is far less important than what you appear to be to yourself, though it is very worthwhile to strive to be what you wish to be thought to be. But we can ask the others if you like. Sometimes what we think we seem to be is an illusion - very often, in fact. It can be a gift to see ourselves as others see us. Usually when you want to know something, it's best to ask. Why not ask the others?"

Before I could ask anyone anything, the flowers spoke aloud: "You are a flower! You are beautiful and you are growing." Then the birds: "You are a bird - you can fly!" And the trees: "You are one of us! You are alive and you're reaching for the sun." A red snake and a green iguana appeared at my feet: "You are a serpent and a dragon - you are the earth and the wind and the fire and the water." The fruits of the plants and trees were singing now: "You are us, and we are you. You are what you sow and what you tend."

My head was spinning and the entire jungle was singing and dancing. Birds and bees, butterflies and bats were circling above and around me, nudging me forward as squirrels and skunks, monkeys and marmosets, porcupines, possums and armadillos, otters and raccoons, then deer and fox and leopards, even a bear - all danced around me. I was engulfed, one with the crowd of animals and plants, one with of all of nature.

All of nature then took me in her arms and carried me on her shoulders to the waters of the river. I was floating as in a dream, floating on the water under another breathtaking waterfall.

I was a part of the water, a part of the jungle, a part of the nature - I was in it, I was surrounded by it, it was cascading all over me. My body was immersed in the river, my toes were dug into the squishy sand, and the sun and the water were raining down upon me. I wasn't just immersed in nature, I was nature. I had melted into her and she into me.

The rhythms, the music, the singing and the dancing grew more and more intense. The colors - the greens, the yellows, the reds, the oranges and blues, the birds, the plants, the flowers, the trees, the animals - virtually exploded in front of my eyes and in my head.

As I sat under the cascade, one with the water, one with the jungle, a most beautiful Dragonfly circled then came to rest hovering in front of my nose.

"Who are you?" she asked. She gave me no time to answer. "You are the water, you are the birds, you are the sky. You are the flowers and the plants and trees, you are the butterflies and the bees, you are the ants and the fireflies, you are the monkeys, the mangoes and the mushrooms."

I felt that. In this moment I really felt that. It was one thing to have the Elders teaching me that I am nature and nature is me. It's another thing altogether to experience it, to feel it with every bone in your body, to feel it in your heart. My mind, my heart, my body, even my soul, if you will, were one with all of the jungle, with all of the world, with all of the universe. It was a dream, but it was no illusion. It was reality.

The Owl Butterfly appeared before me. "Follow me," she cried again as together she and the Dragonfly led me from the waterfall to the shore. We were joined by Guacamaya and the Striped Cat. They led me up from the river's edge and back to the path.

"Where are we going'" I asked no one in particular.

The Striped Cat answered: "Where do you want to go?"

"Well, I don't really know," said I.

"Then it doesn't really matter where we're going, does it?"

I had forgotten. This was Wonderland.

"We're going to the dark side of the Mountain." said the Striped Cat. "We're going to Uglification."

"I never heard of 'Uglification,'" I ventured to say. "What is it?"

233

The Striped Cat lifted up both its paws in surprise. "What! Never heard of Uglifying!" he exclaimed. "You know what to beautify is, I suppose?" "Yes," said I doubtfully, "it means…to…make…anything…well, prettier." "Well, then," the Striped Cat went on, "if you don't know what to Uglify is, you ARE a simpleton." The Stripped Cat did not seem to have very much patience with me.

We rounded a curve in the path and up a bit of a rise. From there we could see forever. In the distance I could see the black smoke of a fire on one of the hillsides. I felt a burning sensation in my side. On another hilltop a fierce yellow bulldozer was crawling along the ground. It seemed to have a face on its front. It crawled straight into the mountain ahead of it, cutting into the rock with its heavy blade. I felt a sharp pain in my other side. Not far from where we were standing, men with big axes and loud chainsaws were attacking the trunk of a majestic fig tree that was towering above the forest floor. One of them swung his axe into her side and shouted what sounded like, "Off with her head!" and the mighty tree groaned aloud as she collapsed and fell to the ground. My stomach turned.

"This is Uglification," the Striped Cat said, declaring the obvious.

"I don't like this," said a voice out of nowhere. It was Mary! I swear it was Mary! I have no idea where she came from or how she got there, but there she was, standing right beside me.

"I don't like this. I don't like Uglification."

"Mary!" I called out. "How did you get here?"

"I came with you, Adam. I've always been with you. I am you and you are me, remember? And it doesn't matter how we got here, what matters is what we do now."

Yep, that was Mary.

"We need to stop this Uglification. You and me. Together."

The Owl Butterfly was above us now. "Follow me."

Mary took my hand as the Owl Butterfly circled above and led us down the path.

"This is the path that has led us to where we are now," said the Owl Butterfly, circling above the path we had been walking. "There is another path, one that leads away from Uglification. It's a path to your future."

"Then let's take that one," said Mary.

"Not so fast," said the Owl Butterfly. "There are many paths that will get you from here to the future. The secret is in choosing the correct one. If you would avoid Uglification, you must choose the path wisely."

The Owl Butterfly continued to lead us down the path 'til we came to a clearing where our path and several others converged.

"How do we choose the right path?"

"It seems to me that you would do well to listen to the water, listen to the birds, watch the sky. Listen to the plants and the trees and the animals. Listen to your Mother. They have brought you this far. They will help you discover who you are and where you are going."

"Adam, you only need to trust yourself, trust your heart." I don't have to tell you that was Mary speaking.

The wise Owl Butterfly was speaking to both of us now:

"Once you choose, you have to walk the path together. No one walks the path alone. "

Mary squeezed my hand and held me close.

"You will need to lead the others. It's not enough to leave Uglification on your own; you will need to take the others with you. You will need to speak of what your Mother has taught you. You must share the path with the others and lead the way."

I looked into Mary's eyes and she into mine. I continued to have my doubts that I was the one to share the message, to lead the others. It was clear that Mary had no such doubts. Perhaps for me the answer to the question, "Who are you?" could best be found in her clear eyes.

"OK, Mary - let's choose our path."

The path that led us here was behind us and the others lay before us, one to the left, one to the right, and still others in the middle. The first was easy to dismiss. Paths, it seems, have signs attached. If you read the signs, you can usually figure out which paths to avoid. The path on the right had a sign that said, 'Poison.' I had learned as a child if you drink from a bottle marked 'poison,' it is almost certain to disagree with you, sooner or later. The same is true with paths, I believe.

Other paths were not so clearly marked, but still bore obvious signs that they were surely not the way to go. Some led only to darkness, others to light.

"I think it's this one, or that one." Mary, in her infinite wisdom, had narrowed the choice to two, and I agreed. Both paths were beautiful, with plants and trees and birds and cuddly animals to the left and right. A bright golden glow illuminated the horizon at the end of each path. There were rainbows bridging the horizon at the end of each of the two paths. And birds flying over the rainbows. It was the waters, the birds, the sky all speaking to me again. But their message was confusing: two promising paths, two auspicious rainbows.

"I think the trick is to discern what's beyond the rainbows, Adam."

"You think so, Mary?" I said through my smile.

With that the golden glow above the path on the right began to clear. It seemed the earth was turning and the end of the path was coming into view. It was like the sunrise. First what seemed to be the spires of what looked like a fairy-tale castle, then more clearly the tops of shiny glass and steel buildings. As cities go, it looked like one of the most magnificent ever. As the earth continued its turn, the gleam of the city grew in the sun, then erupted in a bright reflection from the ground. The city was floating on a mirror of water! The city was in the water! As the world turned the bright glow faded. The rainbow disappeared. In its place a lone blackbird appeared.

The speck of the blackbird got larger as it flew in our direction. Larger and larger. It wasn't a blackbird at all, but a condor I think - maybe the one from my trip around the world. It seemed to be clutching something in its hooked beak. El Cóndor drew closer and circled us, dropping what turned out to be a parchment paper that floated gently to Mary's hand. She read aloud:

> *The sea was wet as wet could be,*
> *The sands were dry as dry.*
> *You could not see a cloud, because*
> *No cloud was in the sky:*
> *No birds were flying overhead*
> *-- There were no birds to fly.*

As Mary read the words, a great commotion arose from the other path, the one to the left. The river was rushing loudly. Clouds of noisy birds were circling the trees; plants and flowers were singing and dancing. There was music in the air, music in the sky. In the distance, on the bright golden horizon, I could make out the silhouette of woman. She seemed to be coming toward us very rapidly, not walking but gliding above the path. She was dressed all in white, the golden glow on the horizon seeming to follow her as she came closer.

"Adam Joseph Rivera."

It was a familiar voice.

"Follow me."

It was my mother! She was radiant. Like an angel.

"It's my mother!"

I grabbed Mary's hand and we raced down the path toward her. But she turned and began gliding silently back toward the horizon, leading us along the path - the path she had chosen for us.

We ran as fast as we could, but she glided further and further ahead of us. As we ran, my golden figurine was bouncing wildly about my neck. I stumbled and fell to the ground. The golden figurine came to rest on the path in front of my face. "It has always helped me find my way," I heard my mother say. I peered into the mist on the horizon, looking for her. She was nowhere to be seen.

"This is the path we were meant to follow," I said to Mary.

The White Rabbit bounced onto the path as the Owl Butterfly circled overhead.

"Follow me," they said.

And so we did.

Chapter 12

Building Bridges

I was awakened by the woman who had awakened me each day, the Elder, delivering my morning bowl of coffee.

"You slept well?" she asked.

"What a curious adventure I had," said I. She smiled.

"You are walking a path, young Adam. The path is not always easy, not always straight, not always clear. At times the path can appear to come to an end. There are obstacles in our way. Sometimes we need to cross over. Sometimes we need a bridge to make the crossing. Today the Elders have work for you to do. You're going to learn about building bridges and mending bridges. And you're going to learn by doing. They're waiting for us."

I emerged from my hut to see the Elders walking my way in the pre-dawn darkness, the moonlight dimly illuminating the curious procession. The work day begins early in the valley where the sun is born, and it was time to go. The Elders were walking briskly, as they always did, and without slowing for a moment they motioned for me to join the procession.

The Elders were marching with a clear sense of direction and purpose. No one said anything. After some time of me trying to keep up, my curiosity got the better of me and I broke the silence.

"Where are we going?"

"We're going from here...to there."

He gave no indication at all of where 'there' might be.

"This is the path."

It sounded like a confirmation of the choice of paths I had made in my dream.

"But the path alone will not get us from here to there."

It sounded like the lesson had begun. It almost sounded like I was back in Wonderland.

"We will need to cross many bridges."

And indeed we did. We came to the first even as he spoke. It was a simple bridge, spanning a narrow stream, made with wooden planks tied together with vines, the spaces between planks filled with mud and stone. It appeared to be very old, and grass and moss and other plants were growing as though the bridge was just a continuation of the path on the ground.

"No one walks the path alone."

This was becoming something of a refrain.

"The bridge was formed by others' hands. Those hands are carrying you to the other side."

It was a very quaint bridge, a picture-postcard kind of country bridge, but I probably would not have thought twice about crossing it had the Elder not shared his brief teaching. The bridge was the hands of another, probably many others, carrying me across the stream. I'm afraid that simple fact would otherwise have gone un-noticed.

The path took several turns then seemed to end as a rock wall, a fence constructed of large stones, crossed in front of us. It was time for another bridge of sorts, this one not spanning water but helping us to cross the wall, to get over the fence. It was more like a ladder, an A-frame ladder, with wooden steps going up one side of the wall, then down the other. We crossed over. There were goats and sheep and a few cows on the other side. The rock fence was keeping them in. The ladder bridge was our gate, our way over or through the wall. Another bridge. Another hand helping us up and over.

The path led us up and over hills and through little valleys as well. We arrived at the edge of a steep drop, a chasm cut by the rushing waters of the narrow river below. Once again our way forward would have been blocked had it not been for a bridge. We crossed the gap on a wobbly suspension bridge, this one made of long vines, with bamboo tubes all tied together, one after the other, forming the walk under our feet. I confess, the crossing was a bit frightening, what with every step by the Elders and me causing the bridge to bob up and down and sway to and fro, all the while the waters rushing far beneath us. But it was clearly a very strong bridge, one that had been there for a very long time and carried many others before me. We arrived safely on the other side.

"The bridge is alive," the Elder said as he pointed to the thick tree that was supporting the thick vines of the span. "The trees that support the bridge are alive. The vines are alive. The bridge grows stronger every day."

We kept walking. We were higher up the hills now. The air had changed, become cooler and crisper. This was the high village, where the Elders had fled to escape the Conquistadores.

The path had become steeper, the river gorges deeper. Where the river narrowed, we crossed another bridge. It was another suspension bridge, but firmer and more secure than the other one. The support branches or trees were very big around, and the vines of the bridge very thick and woven together very tightly. The floor of the bridge was heavy planks, not bamboo. We crossed over the rushing waters below.

"The bridge can carry us across. It can bring people together. It can also keep people apart. When the younger brother came and attacked us with his guns and his dogs, we fled to the high mountain. Our ancestors built bridges to cross the rivers, to carry them to the highest hills of the Mountain. When all were safely on the other side, they burned the bridges. Without the bridges no one could cross over. The younger brother did not know how to build bridges."

The Elders explained that this was a 'new' bridge, built after the Conquistadores gave up and stopped following. This new bridge was probably only a hundred years old or so! No matter its exact age, no one who first helped build it was alive today. Ancient hands had once again carried us across.

"Our ancestors built the bridge, but it is we who must care for it. It is a living bridge. All the bridges are living bridges. All are doing their jobs, connecting people, carrying the people to the other side. But the bridge needs help, it needs tending. Vines need to be tied, others need to be replaced. Wood dies and needs to be replaced. Grass needs to be pulled, the supports need to be strengthened, straightened. That is our job. The bridge does its job, we do ours. Caring for the land means caring for the bridges we have created. We all work to ensure that the bridges that connect us remain strong."

A group of women and children were tending to the bridge, mending it, when we arrived on the far side. A large mochilla was filled with vines and they were being cut into short lengths and used to tie the vines of the bridge more securely into place. The thick gnarled vines of the bridge were clearly alive, and their rapid growth was sometimes a bit haphazard, vines growing in whatever direction they chose. The children took great delight in tying them back into their proper place.

"It's your turn," the Elder directed. "Hundred-year-old hands have carried you across the bridge, now your hands will be joined with theirs. Whenever we receive something, even if it's a simple helping hand across the water, we must always give something back."

He reached into the mochilla and dug out some pieces of green and brown vine. He picked out the good ones and handed them to me. The children, with their big brown eyes, were giggling now. I think they already knew that this younger brother did not know much about mending bridges. I started to tie what I thought was an errant piece of living vine with one of the shorter pieces. The children giggled and shook their heads. I had it wrong, and the children happily showed me the right way to do it. I had the twist of the knot all wrong. I tied several more vines into place - the right way. How many hands, I thought, have helped build and tend this simple bridge over the years? How many hands were silently carrying folk across to the other side ever day? And now my hands had joined theirs.

We returned to the path and continued our brisk march from here to there.

"Now you are going to help us build a bridge."

Am I? A minute ago I couldn't even tie a knot correctly!

We followed the path down a hill and as we came around a turn I saw many young men gathered at the edge of another ford in the river. There were several thick vines already strung across the river, and a group of boys was pulling another up the hill. The vine was secured to a tree on the far side. It had been tossed across the river, and now the boys on this side were pulling it out of the water, pulling it taught. The Elder motioned for me to join them.

Once again my participation was greeted with giggles. Hand over hand I helped the boys pull the heavy thick vine out of the water and up the side of the hill. Soon it was hung from side to side, sagging deeply in the middle but spanning the two sides of the river nonetheless.

Bunkey was there, not surprisingly acting as something of a foreman of this bridge-building project. He directed us to pull the vine tighter as he wrapped the end several times around a support tree and secured it with a big knot.

There were now four thick vines stretched across the river, two were higher, two were lower. The lower ones already had pieces of bamboo tied between them, spaced a foot or more apart, making it look more like a ladder than a bridge.

The Elder called out some directions after satisfying himself the vine was secure, and Bunkey and a few other boys scrambled onto the bridge, balancing their feet on the bamboo and holding the two upper vines with their hands for support. They looked like trapeze artists, carefully but without fear making their way forward as the make-shift span swung left and right. They were loving it. Me? I was holding my breath! One slip or a break in a vine, and those kids would fall to the river.

"It's your turn."

The Elder had to be kidding!

"Not far. Just take a step or two. It's a test. Show the others you trust them, trust their new bridge." He wasn't kidding.

I watched the boys for a minute or two. The vines held. The boys made their way from bamboo to bamboo. None of them fell to his death. OK, I'd try it. But only a step or two.

I approached the bridge. Actually, it was a hardly a bridge yet - just four strings of vine stretched across the river. I planted my hands firmly on the end of the two vines above, and stood tentatively before the two vines below. The view of the water below was chilling. "Don't look down," I think Bunkey said. My knees must have been shaking, and I know my heart was racing. The boys? They were giggling, of course, the ones before me on the vines, the ones on the bank behind me.

There was no value in waiting. I put my first foot forward, onto the round piece of bamboo. That was OK. Then the other foot. Whoa! This thing was not at all solid. I was swinging on a vine. I flinched noticeably as I felt the vines move under my feet. It really was like straddling a tightrope. I held firmly to the two vines in my hands and gathered my balance. It was a good foot-and-a-half to the next piece of bamboo, with nothing but sky in between. The bamboo was round, and it was slippery. I held my breath and lifted my foot, and balancing on the other foot, put one in front of the other, onto the next piece of bamboo. OK, I was walking on the bridge. Sort of. I took another step, and then another, each time very carefully advancing myself by slowly,

246

carefully placing one foot in front of the other, all the while balancing on little tubes of bamboo a hundred feet above the river. The boys' giggles had turned to cheers. I was doing it!

But I was already ready to turn around and come back. The bridge had run out of bamboo steps. There were only vines going forward. I took a moment to take in the view, and catch my breath. I looked up and down the length of the river, across the length of the vines that were now supporting me. I was flying again, this time supported by the hands that were building the bridge. It was breathtaking, in more ways than one. It was also frightening. This was not one of my dreams. One slip this time and I would fall to my death.

I have no idea how I managed to turn myself around on those slippery bamboo slats, but I did, and I gingerly made my way back, one slow and careful step at a time, back to solid ground. Bunkey and the boys and the Elders cheered wildly. Inside, I was patting myself on the back a little, too. Yes, it had been a test. And I had passed.

"Did I go far enough?" I asked, knowing I had only taken a few baby steps and there were no more bamboo steps anyway.

"You have gone far." said the Elder. "You let go of where you were, and you took a big step forward. You may have been uncertain, but in the end you trusted yourself, you trusted the others. You have made a crossing. You are in a new place."

It's true. I was beginning to trust myself more. I was in a different place, and I was no longer the person I was only a brief time ago.

"What happens now?" I asked. "The bridge isn't finished yet."

"The bridge is not complete. It cannot yet carry people across. It will take a lot of time, a lot of work before the bridge is strong enough to carry people from one side to the other, to connect people. Today the people are divided, some on this side, others on that side. One day it will carry many people from here to there. Many people will have added their little part. The bridge will then be able to do its job.

"Building bridges requires a lot of work. Building bridges takes a lot of time. It will involve the participation of people on both sides. The bridge will connect the people over there with the people over here. The act of building the bridge will help do the same."

We walked to where we could watch the building of the new bridge, the hanging vines more accurately. Already boys were busy down by the river, laying what I figured would be another vine, to be pulled taught across the river to strengthen and support the others. Boys and girls were tying small vines into place at the near end of the bridge. And the really brave ones had walked well out onto the span - which was really not much more than a swing at this point - and were tying more bamboo tubes into place underfoot. The bridge was taking shape.

"The bridge will never be finished. It is a living bridge. The cut vines and the bamboo pieces that shape the bridge now will support the living vines and branches and trees that will be added over time. As more time passes the vines will grow and the bridge will become stronger. It will need constant care, will always need tending. With everyone caring for it, the bridge will grow, become stronger, and last forever."

The Elder motioned for me to return to my job, to re-join the work party. It was like playing tug-of-war on the playground as I helped the boys lift and pull another new vine up the river bank and draw it tight across the gap. These vines are thick and heavy!

Then I returned to tying new vines in place along the side of the new bridge. I think this time I finally got the knots right.

After a little more bridge-building, the Elders again motioned for me to follow and we all made our way to a little slope were we could sit and watch the others. I was struck by the fact that the children were happily working alongside the grown-ups, not playing but having a wonderful time working, working to build the new bridge.

The Elder took a handful of coca leaves out of his mochilla and offered some to me. I offered some in return. He put them in his cheek and continued working his gourd, dipping the stick in his mouth and writing his thoughts on the edge. It seemed to center his concentration as he spoke:

"You don't have the gourd, but you can chew the coca. It will renew your energy after your hard work."

He smiled. Obviously my work had not been all that vigorous.

"I didn't do all that much," I protested. "I only did a little"

"You have done more than you know, Adam."

He didn't usually call me by name. I sensed he wanted to talk seriously.

"You did only a little, it's true. But that's all any of us can do - a little."

He continued to work his gourd, collecting his thoughts and recording them.

"And you did more than you thought you could do, no? You took some risks."

That was certainly true. There was no way I thought I would ever climb out on a vine suspended a hundred feet above a raging river!

"You took a big step forward today. You crossed a bridge of your own making. The living bridge is not complete, you have not yet crossed to the other side, but you have made a crossing of your own nonetheless. And you have used the bridge to take you to a place you've never been before."

I looked back at the bridge, the bridge of vines that was still taking shape. Yes, I had stepped off the ledge and onto that scary bridge and discovered I could do it. In spite of my fears, in spite of the danger, in spite of being unsure of myself, I stepped out on that little path of bamboo hanging precariously in the air, and I helped build a bridge.

"We have called you here, here to the Mountain, to help us build a bridge. We are the heart of the world. We care for our Earth Mother. That is our job. We have never forgotten our job. We have never stopped caring for our Mother."

I wasn't sure where he was going with this.

"But it is no longer enough. We have seen the changes. We have shown you what is happening. The Mountain is suffering, our Mother is in pain. She is gravely ill and may die. We are caring for her as best we can, but it is no longer enough. We need to reach out to the younger brother. But the younger brother's heart and mind are not in the right place. They are over there and we are over here. There is a very wide gap between us. We need to bridge that gap. We need you to help us build a bridge, a bridge to help the younger brother cross over to a new and better place."

Now I understood where he was going. Back to the beginning, back to what he first said when I first arrived on the mountain. I was to be a messenger. I was to help build a bridge.

"The younger brother can build many things. He builds great cities of brick and steel and glass. He builds cars and trucks of metal. He powers his cities and cars and trucks by burning the energy of the Mountain. And he, too, builds bridges - bridges of iron and steel. But they are not living bridges. They are dead bridges. Bridges are supposed to bring people together, bridges are supposed to connect people. The younger brother's bridges may take people across a river in their cars, but they only serve to keep the people disconnected. Bridges of steel will never get the younger brother to where he needs to be."

I thought for a moment of all the bridges in New York. Beautiful bridges. Bridges of iron, brick, metal and steel. I had crossed many of them, crossed them many a time. I had taken them for granted, they had gone largely un-noticed. And it's true. None had ever taken me as far as that little vine bridge had taken me today.

"We have seen the cities of the younger brother. We have seen them in the water, in the bubbles. We have seen what the younger brother has done to the land with his vast cities. We have seen what he has done to the Mountain by taking away the energy and burning it in his cities. We have seen his burning turn the sky black. We have watched as the younger brother has heated his cities and warmed the air and warmed the waters. We have watched as the snows have melted and the ice has disappeared. We have watched as the lakes and rivers and streams have dried up and the seas have risen. Soon the younger brother will need his bridges of steel to carry him over waters where there used to be land."

It was a bleak picture the Elder was painting as he continued to work his gourd.

"The younger brother is killing the planet. He is killing his Earth Mother. There is no other way to say it. The younger brother has lost his way. He no longer knows where he is or where he is going. He needs to find a new path. He needs a living bridge, one that can carry him away from the path he is on now, the path that is leading only to darkness, and toward a new path. If the younger brother does not cross over he will drown in his own destruction."

I looked back at the vine bridge again. The boys were happily adding new vines and new bamboo. They were not the least bit afraid as they scampered along the swinging vines, as they added a little more vine here and a little more bamboo there. I couldn't help wondering what their future might hold.

"We need your help building that bridge, Adam."

There was no more asking 'Why me?' this time. The Elders' teaching had changed direction. What had been eye-opening lessons about nature and about every plant and animal having a job to do - those lessons were over. Now it was about me. Now it was about MY job.

"You are the one. We called you to the Mountain because we knew you were the one who could help us build a bridge."

I had changed. I was a different person than the one who had arrived on the Mountain only a few days before. But I was still uncertain. Yes, I had trusted myself to step out on a scary bridge, but was I really the one who could build the bridge the Elders were speaking of? I had swung from a vine, but did that mean I could save the world?

"You have doubted yourself. Many times you have asked yourself who you were and where you were going, who you were supposed to be and where you were supposed to be going. You asked others, you asked yourself. Don't let the noise of others drown out your own inner voice. You are who you say you are, you are who you wish to become. You had the courage to step out onto that bridge today. You need only to summon that courage to follow your heart. Your heart already knows who you are and who it is you are supposed to become, where you are, where you are going, and what you are supposed to be doing. It is your calling to become the heart of the world. Your heart already knows that."

The Elder was making his case, but I was still uncertain.

"A plant that does not live according to its nature will die. And so it is with people. If you are to live, to truly live, you will become the heart of the world and you will build bridges so others may follow. That is your nature, that is your calling."

The Elder stood up and dusted himself off.

"Watch the water. Think about the bridges."

Chapter 13

The Big Apple

I sat on the grass for some time, watching the bridge-builders, listening to the water as it rushed beneath them, and I watched the birds. The birds didn't need bridges to cross the river.

It was beautiful here on the mountain. I had come to love being so totally one with nature. But I sensed my time here was coming to an end. The Elders had called me to the Mountain because they wanted me to be a messenger. They had introduced me to my Earth Mother in a way I had never known her before. And now they were preparing me to do my job - to be the messenger, to build bridges. Soon they would be sending me down the mountain; soon I would be surrounded by the bridges of New York once again.

New York. It had only been days, but it seemed like years, and it felt as though the city was light-years away. I tried to recall some of my favorite places in the city, even some of the bridges, but it now seemed so strange. The city felt out of place. And for the first time I realized that the city was actually the country, it was actually what I had always thought of as 'nature,' something apart from the city, something over there. I had always loved nature, of course, always loved the country. But I had thought of them as being separate. The city was here, nature was there. But that's not the case, obviously. Everything is on the same little round ball of dirt the Elders call *la madre tierra*, the Mother Earth. It's all dirt, all fertile soil. Everything lives on it, everything grows on it. I'm sitting on it now, I thought. New York City is sitting on it now. The Mountain is rising up from it now. City, country, you and me, we're all on the same dirt. We're all connected, all sharing the same planet.

My daydreaming returned me to my flight around the world. It was probably my little walk above the water on the new bridges that made me think again of flying. I remembered flying over New York and seeing all the bridges. There were bridges all over the world as well. And most were spanning water, connecting two pieces of land that were separated by water. When you fly high above the earth you notice that the whole planet is nothing but land and water. There is nothing else.

Most of us go through the day without ever thinking about that. And how often do we use bridges without even thinking of it? We drive on bridges, we walk across bridges, our trains run on bridges, our groceries are brought to the supermarket in trucks that drive over bridges. The oil that powers it all travels over miles of bridges. Every one, every thing, is going from here to there on bridges. But still we are disconnected. We continue to believe that we are here and everyone else is there, that over there is the city and over here is the nature.

'How can I build a better bridge?' I was asking myself. How can I help people move from there to here? How can I help bridge the gaps, restore connections? And mostly I was thinking again, 'Why me?'

I started picturing bridges in my head. So many bridges I have seen. The Brooklyn Bridge and the George Washington Bridge and so many more in the City, rustic wooden covered bridges in the Catskills. Even right here on the Mountain I had seen so many different bridges. I think I fell asleep counting bridges.

In my daydreaming I imagined myself standing on a bridge in the city, looking out across the tip of lower Manhattan and beyond the water to the Statue of Liberty and the Narrows Bridge over the entrance to the bay. It was the quintessential postcard picture of New York - and its bridges.

"Beautiful view, isn't it?"

I was startled to see another gentleman on the bridge, leaning against the rail, also enjoying the view.

"Beautiful, even with all the water."

I wasn't sure if he was talking to me, or someone else, or no one in particular.

"Yes, it is beautiful," I replied, just in case he was speaking to me. But what did he mean by 'all the water?'

I looked back at the view, at Battery Park. Oh my God! It was under water. The Statue of Liberty was up to her toes in water. Battery Park was underwater, with only treetops and water where the park used to be, where I had walked so many times before. And there was no traffic. There was no street! It was underwater.

"What's going on? Why all the water?" I asked. And as I spoke I noticed there was traffic on the bridge where we were standing, but the cars were all new to me. They were all what I could only describe as futuristic. I didn't recognize a single one.

"You're not from around here, are you?" was his reply.

"Yes, sir, I am from around here. I am from this place, but I don't think I'm from this time."

The gentleman did not seem at all surprised at my answer. He looked at me as though he understood.

"And what time might you be from, young man?"

"From the past, sir."

"From the past? In that case, welcome to your future," he said rather matter-of-factly.

"The water is here all the time," he continued. "This is the new New York. Been this way for some years now."

I recognized him as he spoke. He was thin, with short hair, wearing a black turtle-neck and jeans.

"You're Steve Jobs, aren't you? The Apple computer guy?"

"I was, in the past. I'm different now. I suspect you're different now, different from who you were in the past."

Hmmm. True that.

"Tell me about the water," I persisted, no longer at all surprised at who I might be talking with and when.

"It's been rising for years. Silly people keep building walls, trying to hold it back, but it just keeps rising. And they build bridges. But the bridges don't take them anywhere new, they just lift them above the water. They continue to whiz along in their cars pretending the water below them isn't really there."

"Where's all the water coming from?"

He didn't answer me. Instead he took something he had been holding in his hand and he pointed it toward me. A picture appeared, a picture floating in the space between us. Right before me was an image of arctic ice and polar bears. I could see the picture perfectly, but I could also see right through it. I was looking at polar bears and I was looking at Steve Jobs.

"What's that? How did you do that?" I asked in disbelief.

"It's my Communicator."

He held it up for me to see. It was a smooth oval object, sort of the shape of a bar of soap, and it rested in the palm of his hand. It was polished silver, with no buttons, no lights, no screen - nothing but a smooth oval, like a polished stone.

The pictures floating in front of my eyes were changing now: the polar bears were in one image, but there were new images popping up - pictures of icebergs breaking apart and massive chunks of ice falling into the ocean. There were new images, pictures of hurricanes with waves beating against the shore, and flooded streets. And there were pictures of the Statue of Liberty, many pictures all floating in the air in front of me, and in each new picture Liberty was deeper and deeper in water.

"Wow!"

I didn't know which was the bigger 'Wow' - the images of the rising waters or the magical way they'd appeared in front of me.

"You do that with your Communicator?"

"Yes. I can communicate with anyone anywhere in the world. And I can access pretty much every bit of information that's ever existed. In my mind and with the touch of my hand I ask for the information, for the images, and the Communicator displays them for me to see - and for you to see. They're not really in the air; they're images in your mind that you open with your eyes."

"So they're like windows."

"No, son, it's NOT like Windows," he said sternly.

With his mind or with his touch he kept changing the images.

"You asked where all the water was coming from. Here's where."

There were more pictures of what I guessed was the North Pole - moving images that appeared to be live. I guess his Communicator could do that.

"The water is coming from here," he said, "but it's also coming from here."

Now I was looking at images of parched dry land, maybe Africa. And then more pictures of huge storms, satellite images of monster storms, then pictures of rain and wind and waves, boats washing ashore, flooded streets.

"The planet has been getting warmer and warmer, for years. There has always been the same amount of water on the planet, never more, never less. But now that water is moving to new places. The water of the Arctic ice has melted into the sea. The lakes have dried up and their waters carried to the oceans by the rains. The ocean waters get warmer and warmer, spawning stronger storms, more frequent storms, more rain. It's a cycle, the cycle of nature, repeating over and over again. But now it's out of balance. Everything is more extreme. The dry land becomes drier and drier, and the cities by the sea are flooded."

The images were horrifying. And they seemed to be live, like I was watching the television news floating in front of my eyes.

"Look at your city. Look at your future."

I don't know if it was the Communicator transporting us or what, but soon we were taking a walking tour of New York - the New York of the future. We crossed a lot of bridges.

From our bridge above Battery Park we crossed over to another bridge, and then another. The old streets of New York were wet or under water. The traffic was all on the bridges and new roadways suspended above the ground. And the sleek futuristic cars were silent, electric I assumed. There were trains on the bridges, too, also whisking rapidly by, also almost silent. The City was much quieter than I remembered it.

"You haven't seen this before, right?" he asked.

"No sir. It used to be my City. It's all new now."

"There are no subways. They were flooded out a long time ago. Those trains replaced them. The trains and the cars are all electric, some of them solar, some of them hydrogen-powered. Some are even powered by water. But it's all too late."

We were walking on a bridge that I think was over the old Broadway, heading toward Times Square. Steve Jobs waved his hand - and his Communicator, I guess - and the images on the neon signs of Times Square became the images of the new New York. They were reflected in the knee-deep water.

Then Steve Jobs' image was projected on the signs, and so was mine. I was watching the two of us speaking to each other. We had become Times Square and Times Square had become us, I guess you might say. Weird.

Below the signs and images was the new Times Square. Where there had been cars and pedestrians before was now a suspended plaza, with tables and chairs and people looking down at the water. It was a sidewalk café, with food vendors and street performers and lots of people, seemingly quite content to be suspended above the water. And there were boats - little boats in the water, almost like Venice. The buildings I remembered were still there, but their entrances were now on the second floor, people coming and going on elevated sidewalks - and bridges.

From Times Square we were somehow magically transported to Central Park. That happens in day-dreams, especially when you hold a Communicator in your hand.

Central Park was now more like the Everglades. Plants and trees were now all water plants. The quaint masonry bridges that used to cross over paths below now barely poked themselves above the water. There were raised walkways around the edges of what had become one big lake, and families and couples were happily enjoying their stroll around the park. And there were bridges. There were suspension bridges, swinging bridges of heavy wire cable that were not so unlike the bridge I had just been building. Children were enjoying bouncing and swinging suspended above the water. There were wooden bridges, too, not 'living bridges,' but somewhat natural nonetheless. They were more like paths than bridges, meandering just above the water, so people could walk where there used to be dirt paths.

"Talk to me," I said to Steve Jobs somewhat presumptuously. "Tell me how this all happened. Tell me what went wrong. And tell me about that Communicator."

He walked with me to a little café at the edge of the lake and bought us coffee. We sat at a table with a view. Once again I was watching the water, looking at the bridges. There were no birds, though. Almost no birds.

"All right, first about the Communicator. It responds to your thoughts. Your thoughts are not your thoughts, you know. Your thoughts were in the water before they were in you. And the Communicator can read your thoughts as it rests in the palm of your hand. It reads them from the water in the palm of your hand, from the water in your skin. You hold the whole world in the palm of your hand, and the whole world responds to your every thought."

This Communicator sounded an awful lot like the Elders.

"It's like what the original peoples of the Earth did. They didn't talk to each other, they communicated. For some it was more like mental telepathy. That's what the Communicator enables."

I understood the mental telepathy thing. So did the Elders.

"It's not for talking to one another. God knows there's enough talking in the world already. It's for communicating."

"And the Communicator is almost all natural. We were using tons of fossil fuel energy to make computers and iPhones, and they were becoming tons of waste. They weren't really recyclable. The Communicator is made almost entirely of sand and water - silicone. They're manufactured with solar energy. The

262

water is the source of the thought processes and they are carried on the sands. And over time the Communicator becomes one with the user. After a while he can communicate, display his thoughts without even having the Communicator in his hand. Nothing to throw away, nothing to recycle."

I think he was saying, in so many words, that the Communicator was 'organic.' That was promising.

"As for how all this happened, it's hard to know when it started," he began. He played with the Communicator in his hand and again images appeared before me, images of smokestacks and piles of black coal and crowded super highways, and cities with skies as black as night.

"Maybe with the light bulb, maybe with the automobile, with the invention of factories and machines. I don't know. But somewhere around a hundred years ago we put a price on destroying the planet, and we made a choice - we made the choice to pay that price. It was a tipping point."

I thought of my conversation, if I could call it that, with Henry Ford and Thomas Edison. They understood the tipping point. But they also made the same choice. They understood the promise of the sun, it's true, but perhaps they did not do all they could realize that promise. Maybe they could have made a bigger difference, a different difference.

"A computer operates with only two numbers, zero and one, nothing and something. It can only make one kind of decision: is this number bigger than, equal to, or larger than another number? If the answer is bigger than, the computer responds one way, if the answer is equal to, it responds in another way, and if the answer is it's smaller than the other number it takes the third path. A hundred years ago people looked at cars and electricity and decided they would make the future better than - better than it was, better than it would be without. They were wrong. So now we have arrived at a future that is less than, less than it could have been, less than it should have been, less than it was meant to be. People have been taking the energy from the ground, from the mountains, subtracting from the earth for a hundred years now. They thought the effect would be zero. It's not. The effect has been much more than zero, it's left us with a planet that's less than."

I was never very good at math, but it sounded like he was saying that subtraction and subtraction and subtraction equals Uglification.

"Some people took notice. Somewhere around the nineteen-seventies a few people saw that we were killing the birds and polluting the air and water. For most people, though, it went un-noticed."

For the Elders it hadn't gone un-noticed. I suspect it was about that time that the Elders had begun to see the changes.

"Soon more and more people began to realize that we were on a path to our own destruction. Scientists told us that we were destroying the protective ozone layer, adding dangerous amounts of carbon-dioxide to the air. That was boring, or beyond the comprehension level of many. The warnings went un-noticed. Weather patterns were changing. Plants and animals were dying. Drought in some places, flooding in others were becoming more frequent and more extreme. Still people continued on the same path."

It was the Elders' teachings all over again. Paths and bridges and choices - they make all the difference.

"Somewhere around the turn of the century the changes became too obvious to ignore. Storms were flooding the coastal cities already. New York experienced record storms and flooding several times. Still people ignored what was happening, or more correctly, they chose to ignore, because they had already made the choice that they needed all their things, needed more and better things. They were not about to give up their lifestyle of comfort and consumption, not even to save the planet, not even for their children's sake. In so many words they made the choice to not care about the future, and certainly not to care about the Earth."

"And what about you?" I asked, being once again most presumptuous. "You were rich and famous by then, no? What did you do?"

"That's one of the real paradoxes of my life. I was no different. At Apple we had coined the advertising phrase, "Think Different." But I wasn't different. I wasn't thinking any differently from anyone else. Sure I made different computers, but was I approaching the world any different to anyone else? No. I was all about making better computers, helping people communicate faster with one another. But it was all about profit. I wanted to make and sell bigger and better Apples; I didn't care about their effect on the planet. I wasn't trying to save the world."

That was quite a confession. And what about me? Was I going to try to save the world?

"And what about you, young man? Are you going to try to save the world?"

Everyone always knows the questions I'm asking. Now if only they had the answers for me.

"You say you're from the past. I guess we all are in a way. But it seems you've just arrived from the past. It's like you're a visitor. Why are you here?"

That was another question I was asking. Why was I here? Why was I in the New York of the future talking to a future Steve Jobs?

"I'm not exactly sure. But I do think I'm here for a reason. I think I'm here to learn, to learn from the future. And yes, there are some people who think I'm the one who's supposed to save the world."

"They're right, you know. You are the one who's supposed to help save the world. You're the only one who can."

"Everyone keeps telling me that. I'm not so sure. I'm supposed to be a messenger, but I don't know that people will listen to me. I'm supposed to show others the way. But I don't know that anyone will follow. I'm just a kid from the Catskills."

"Alright, Kid-from-the-Catskills, let me tell you a thing or two. You say you're here to learn from the future. Let me teach you some things I've learned from my future, and from my past:

"I dropped out of college when I was about your age. It felt like a waste of time at the time. I learned what I needed to learn in different places, in different ways. Maybe like you're doing now. I learned the important things, the things that really mattered, the things that could help me make a difference in the world. I learned what I needed to learn, I even learned what I was

266

supposed to do with my life, but I didn't know it at the time. I didn't connect the dots.

"Of course it was impossible to connect the dots looking forward when I was only eighteen. But it was very, very clear looking backwards ten years later. It's even clearer looking backwards now, from my future life.

"You can't connect the dots looking forward; you can only connect them looking backwards. You have to trust that the dots will somehow connect in your future. You have to trust in something - your gut, destiny, life, karma, whatever. This approach has never let me down, and it has made all the difference in my life."

I was learning to do that. The Elders have trusted me all along. Me? It's taken me a little longer, but it seemed I was getting there. I think that's exactly why I was here in my future. So I could look back. So I could start connecting the dots. Maybe it's another way of building bridges.

"You asked me what happened, what went wrong? How is it that we kept destroying the world when we already knew we should be saving it? I'll tell you how. Because you weren't there, that's how."

No, no, no - it's not my fault, I silently protested.

"Everyone was saying it's not my fault, everyone was saying it's not my problem. And worse than that, they were ignoring it. They were ignoring what was happening all around them, they were ignoring everyone who was telling them what was happening. They let it all go un-noticed. And that wasn't easy. They had to make an effort not to notice. They had to look the other way, they had to drown out the messengers. Far too many people thought they could simply ignore what they were doing to the planet, and everything would be alright. They didn't connect the dots. They couldn't connect the dots. In truth, most of them simply didn't want to connect the dots."

"You know what I think the biggest problem was? The real reason we're here, drowning in our future? It's because we didn't have you. The world of my past life, the world that would give birth to my future lives, was a world without leaders, without prophetic messengers, people with a voice who would speak out, who would call others to follow. Oh sure, we had leaders - politicians and others who were called leaders - but no one was leading. No one could see beyond their short-term self-interest, beyond the next election, beyond the next fiscal year. There was a complete vacuum of leadership. The world needed you."

Shit. Everyone thinks it's me. Everyone thinks it's me who's supposed to save the world.

"The world needed me, too. I could have been one of those voices speaking out; I could have been showing people what was happening, what changes needed to be made. But I was kinda shy in those days. I didn't speak out much. And I didn't think it was my job. I thought my job was to make and sell new and better Apples. I thought that was going to change the world. And it did, sort of. But not in the way the world really needed changing. I don't think I ever taught anyone it was their job to care for the planet. I never said it with my words; I never set the example with my actions."

In so many words, it was Steve Jobs' confession, but more

importantly it was his challenge to me.

"You know, we can change our future. We are the ones who create it. The future was first imagined in the past. You can see your future in the water, in all this water that's all around us. You have seen the future in the water. Now you can return to the past and reimagine it. The way to change the world is to change the story. What you see here is not cast in stone, it's fluid. It's water. You can imagine it differently. As I said, you can think different. You can imagine a different future. And it can be."

He hadn't said anything I hadn't already been told. I only needed to connect the dots.

"But I'm only one person," I continued to argue. "I'm nobody famous, nobody important. Why would my vision for the future matter to anyone? You said nobody listened. Why would they listen to me?"

"Maybe they won't. History teaches us that many will not. But they certainly won't listen if you don't speak out. And there are others who will want to silence you, powerful people who would gladly kill you to make sure they could go on killing the planet. You say you're a messenger. I say you need to be a messenger from the heart. You need to speak to those who won't listen and overcome those who would silence you. The world may well die if you don't. The planet may die if people don't hear your message. You need to speak from your heart, you need to speak from the heart of the world. If you speak from the heart, people will listen. History teaches us that, too. "

"Let me share with you some other things I've learned, learned from several lives I can remember, and many more I cannot.

269

"When I was about your age, I was also wondering what I was supposed to do with my life. I read a quote that went something like: 'If you live each day as if it was your last, someday you'll most certainly be right.' It made an impression on me, and since then, for several lifetimes now, I've looked in the mirror every morning and asked myself: "If today were the last day of my life, would I want to do what I am about to do today?" And whenever the answer was 'No' for too many days in a row, I knew I needed to change something.

"It's about choices. Remembering that I'll be dead soon is the most important tool I've ever encountered to help me make the big choices in life. Because almost everything - all external expectations, all pride, all fear of embarrassment or failure - these things just fall away in the face of death, leaving only what is truly important. Remembering that you are going to die is the best way I know to avoid the trap of thinking you have something to lose. You're already naked. There is no reason not to follow your heart."

I was getting another important lesson in living, this time from someone who had already died.

"And you, son, you know things I never knew. You've seen the future. You have seen it in all of this water. And you know that we are killing the planet. You know that our Earth Mother may die at any day. You have a much more powerful understanding empowering your message than I ever had."

It's true. I had been to the Mountain, I had seen the past, I had circled the globe, I had seen the earth in all its beauty. It's true. I had the potential to become a powerful messenger, to help people connect the dots, to fall in love with their Earth Mother all over again.

"People don't want to hear about the ozone layer and greenhouse gasses, they don't want to hear about driving smaller cars or reducing their carbon footprint. They want to hear about hope. They want to hear about love. They want to stop destroying and start healing, they really do. They want to know how they can care for their Earth Mother so their children can have a life, can have a future. They're already looking in the mirror and saying, 'If today were the last day of my life, the last day of my Mother's life, would I want to do what I am about to do today?'"

In so many words that was really my question, wasn't it? And here was one single person, a shy college drop-out at that, helping me figure it out.

"When you return to the past you've come from, back to what you think is your present life, look around you. You will find no leaders. Not a single one. Saving the planet from destruction is a global problem. Sure, lots of little people all around the world have to be making the right choices in everything they do every day - that's important - but the world also needs leadership, global leadership. Look around you. There is no one willing to take the risk. The world needs people speaking out, telling them how to change their ways, how to think different if there is to be a future. But no one is willing to take any risk.

"You are the one. You are the one who has to take the risk. You are the voice they need to hear. You are the messenger. There are no others. All you need to do is step up and fill the vacuum. The world you live in is at a crossroad. You need to lead them across the bridge, show them the better path.

"No one wants to die. Even people who want to go to heaven don't want to die to get there. And yet death is the

271

destination we all share. No one has ever escaped it. And that is as it should be, because Death is very likely the single best invention of Life. It is Life's change agent. It clears out the old to make way for the new. Right now the new is you, but someday not too long from now, you will gradually become the old and be cleared away. Some way, somehow you'll move on to your future lives, whatever they may be. Sorry to be so dramatic, but it is quite true.

"Your time is limited, so don't waste it living someone else's life. You have been chosen - chosen to be you, to be who you have been called to be. Don't be trapped by living with the results of other people's thinking. Think different. Don't let the noise of others' opinions drown out your own inner voice. And most important, have the courage to follow your heart and intuition. They somehow already know what you truly want to become. Everything else is secondary."

"I'm starting to understand that, Mister Jobs."

"Steve. It's just Steve."

"OK, Steve. I'm starting to understand that my heart already knows who I am and where I'm going and how I'm going to get there. And maybe you've helped. You said you didn't make a real difference in the past. Maybe you have, maybe you just did. Maybe one day we will both remember that you made a difference in one person's life, and that he went on to make a difference in another person's life, and another and another. Perhaps that's what we both will remember."

"You're going to do fine, kid. You're going to be the messenger your heart is calling you to become."

Then he reached out and placed his Communicator in the

palm of my hand. "Take this, kid. You're going to need it."

As I cradled it in my hand, images began to appear in the air again. There was Steve Jobs repeating to me, "You're going to do fine, kid." Then an image of Mary. She said sort of the same thing, but in her own inimitable way: "You can do it, Adam. I know you can." Then my mother: "The Earth is calling you. Watch the water, watch the birds, watch the sky." Then an image of the Elders, standing in front of the bridge I had just been helping to build: "If not you, who?"

The image of the vine bridge and the hillside above it grew larger and then faded into reality. I was no longer in New York. I was once again sitting on the Mountain, gazing at the bridge of vines, watching the water, watching the birds, watching the sky.

Chapter 14

Choosing the Future

"Choices. It's all about the choices we make."

Another sunrise, another lesson.

"You will be leaving soon, going back down the Mountain."

I had sensed this was coming.

"You will carry the message to the Younger Brother. You will tell them that our Earth Mother is in danger. You will tell the Younger Brother he must change his ways if our Earth Mother is to survive. And the Younger Brother will ask you, 'How can we save the planet?' The answer is very simple. Choices. It's all about the choices we make. If you would save the planet, first you must pay attention to the choices you make. Pay attention to every choice you make. And start making better choices."

The Elders had a way of making the difficult and complicated sound so simple and easy. Of course people are going to ask how they can save the planet. That's the question I was asking, too. It sounds like a daunting task, overwhelming. The Elders had made it sound so simple. Make better choices.

"We all make thousands of choices every day. Most are so automatic we don't even realize we are making a choice. We choose to breath. We choose to breathe in, we choose to breathe out. We never think about it, but it's a choice. If you don't think

274

so, try holding your breath. You've just made the choice not to breathe. Now stop holding your breath. You've just made the choice to breathe in again. The simple act of paying attention to your breath can help you begin to observe all the other choices you make. Nothing should go un-noticed, certainly not the choices we make."

So simple. If we didn't choose to mess up the planet, we wouldn't mess up the planet. If we didn't choose Uglification over beautification, we wouldn't have Uglification.

"Let's go for a last walk around the Mountain."

I didn't like the sound of that. I had come to love the Mountain. I didn't really want to leave. I didn't want to take a last walk.

"Let's look at your Earth Mother again, and this time let's think about choices."

So we walked. I realized that even our walking was a choice. The Elders' lessons were once again taking hold.

"You're not wearing sandals," the Elder pointed out. "Why?"

"I like feeling the earth under my feet. I've learned that from you."

"So it was a choice? You thought about it, and then you made the choice to walk barefoot on the earth today, no?"

"Yes, it was my choice."

"And it was a new choice for you, no? You used to put your sandals on every morning, put your shoes on, without even thinking about it. It was automatic. But now you've changed. You thought about your choice, and you chose to make a new one."

He hit the nail on the head. That's exactly what I had done.

The first stop on our walk was water, not surprisingly. It always starts with the water. We stopped at a little stream, and the Elder bent down and lifted a small smooth pebble from the water.

"We choose to care for the earth. We choose to care for the water. Here we have planted the seeds for a new river. We plant sacred stones in the ground to encourage the waters to flow toward the trees on this side of the forest. We choose to care for the earth. We choose to care for the water. We help restore the balance. And because of what we choose to do the plants and the trees will grow and thrive. And when the trees and the plants are healthy the animals and the birds are healthy, the Earth is healthy. All because we choose to care for the planet."

Everything is connected. Everything is interwoven. I think that was my first lesson on the Mountain. But I had not heard of planting a river before. What a great choice. Plant a river instead of destroying one.

"In the beginning, everything was water," he reminded me. "It's still all about the water. If you would care for the Earth, if you would choose to care for the Earth, first you must choose to care for the water."

I thought for a moment of a New York City under water. How many millions of choices had resulted in the waters warming and the City flooding? How might the future be different if only people made better choices?

Not surprisingly, I think the Elder heard my silent question. He led us not to a city underwater, but to a lake that was no more.

"This used to be a blue lagoon. That's what our people called it - Blue Lagoon. Now it's mostly dry earth. Far from this place, way beyond the Mountain, the younger brother has been making choices without paying any attention to his choices, and this is the result. We choose to care for the earth, but our choices are not enough. When people around the world are making bad choices the Mountain suffers. The Mountain is the heart of the world. When the Mountain suffers everyone suffers. The people making bad choices are making bad choices about their own world, their own little environment, their own life, their children's future."

From the dry lagoon we walked up and over a hill and down to the gardens in the valley. The corn and the other plants again looked very healthy.

"The garden thrives because we care for it. It has water because we have seeded new rivers, new streams of water that feed the plants. It is not an accident that the garden grows. It is our choice.

"You see the bees on the flowers? The bees cannot make choices as we can. They just do their job. We need to be doing our job, too, but for us it is a choice. We can choose to do our job, we can choose to care for the earth, or not. We can choose to care for the bees, for instance, or we can make choices that cause the bees to disappear, to no longer do their job. Bad choices, no bees. No bees, no flowers. No flowers, no fruits and vegetables."

I knew we were harming the bees and the birds. My mother talked about that all the time back on the farm. I had never thought of it as a simple matter of choices.

From the garden we walked back into the jungle, the forest. I had come to love the jungle. It was so alive, so green, so different from the pine forests of the Catskills. It was teeming with life. With my newly-discovered sense of one-ness with all of nature, the life of the jungle made me feel alive.

"Look at the life. Look all around you and you see everything is alive."

It was so true. Standing quietly for only a few moments in the jungle I could see birds of every color, iguanas climbing the trees, monkeys swinging from the branches, butterflies on the flowers, insects everywhere, everywhere life.

"This is the Heart of the World. And it is home for the birds and animals and plants and trees of the world. If the jungle is not healthy, the world is not healthy. The monkeys don't make bad choices. The birds don't make bad choices. They just do their jobs. But people are making bad choices every day, choices that are destroying the balance, that are destroying the homes of the plants and birds and animals. People are choosing to cut and burn the trees to make room to grow new plants, plants that will make them money, not plants and trees that feed and shelter the animals. Some of the birds and animals are disappearing, dying, because the trees they once lived in, the plants and trees that nourished and protected them are no more. The monkeys did not make bad choices. The monkeys did not choose to burn the trees and replace them with rows and rows of palm trees. The younger brother chose to cook with palm oil. He chose to destroy the forests to plant more palm trees. He chose to destroy the forests that are home to the monkeys, the same forests that sustain all life on the planet. The younger brother made the choices that are destroying his own home as well."

The path through the jungle led us higher up the mountain. Soon we were again on a ridge, once again looking out over the hills toward the highest peaks of the Mountain, toward the snows.

"The younger brother burns the oil, burns the coal. He chooses to burn the energy of the Mountain to power his things, more and more things. Whenever he burns the coal or the oil he is making a choice. He is making the choice to use more and more energy, and making the choice to take it from the earth. He is making the choice to poison the water, poison the birds, poison the air.

"The rains are not coming like they used to. The snows are melting. That's OK. They are supposed to melt. They are supposed to become the lakes and the streams and the rivers. They are supposed to be the waters of life on the Mountain. But the melting snows are not being replaced. There is supposed to be new snow every year, new rains bringing new snows. There is little rain now. The snows are disappearing. We see the changes. We see the changes beyond the Mountain. We see the changes beyond today. We see cities underwater and mountains with no water at all. We see the choices the younger brother is making. We see the results of those choices."

I had seen them, too. I wondered if the Elders knew how bad the future really looked.

"That's the reason the waters will eventually swallow up the cities. It is part of healing, part of killing the disease. Part of nature restoring the balance."

He made it sound so logical, so obvious. The Earth is a living being. If it is injured, it will heal itself. Even if that means swallowing up the cities.

"Tomorrow you will go back down the mountain."

Tomorrow? I didn't want to leave.

"Soon your time on the Mountain will be remembered as only a dream, it will fade from your memory. That's natural. What matters in life is not what actually happens to you but what you recall and how you draw upon it. You will go down the mountain to the lands of the younger brother. You will be the messenger."

I didn't want to leave, and I didn't think I was ready to leave. I still didn't think I was ready to be the messenger.

"You are ready."

He was doing it again! Reading my mind. He was using his ancient communicator.

"We have done our job. We have placed the message in your hands. It is a simple message: Our Earth Mother is gravely ill and she will certainly die if the Younger Brother does not change his ways."

It was a simple message. And the Elders had taught it to me backwards and forwards. But I still worried that I could not get the message across, that the people wouldn't listen. And mostly I worried that I didn't have the answers to the questions I

280

knew I was going to be asked: What can we do? How can we make a difference? How can we change the world?

"If we stop destroying the planet, it will start healing. That's the way it works in nature. That's the way it works with you and me. That's the way it works with our Earth Mother."

Simple. The profound truths are so simple.

"It's all about choices. You have the answers. You know how to save the world. You know what to tell the Younger Brother: 'Make the right choices.'"

Ah, so simple. And such a precipitous challenge. Little ol' Adam Rivera from New York, telling the world how to save the planet.

"But that will not be enough. People acting alone, even making the right choices alone, will not be enough. You need to tell them to speak up, to demand that their leaders make the right choices. We have been trying to care for the Mountain ourselves, always trying to make the right choices. But it's no longer enough. And it's no longer enough for the younger brother to be paying attention to his choices, to be making better choices on his own. The Earth is in trouble. It's a global problem. It will take the peoples of the planet coming together to solve them, to make better choices on a global scale. Whole nations will need to examine the choices they have been making for years, and look for better choices. They will need leaders. They will need leaders who have a heart, leaders who understand they are meant to be the heart of the world. You need to call upon all the younger brothers and sisters of the world to speak up, just as you are going to speak up, and to demand leaders who will take the risks that need to be taken. To risk making the better choices."

I could hear Steve Jobs' voice. The Elders, too, were calling on me to lead. But more important they were calling on me to tell everyone to listen, to speak out, to demand leadership with vision, leaders with a heart. Not easy for an eighteen-year-old.

"By ourselves we can do little. Our younger brothers and sisters, by themselves, can do little. But if everyone comes together, if the Younger Brother joins with the Elder Brother, if they listen to their elders and follow the best among them, if they start watching the water, watching the birds, watching the sky and making better choices, together they can save the world, together we can save the world. It's as simple as that."

Simple? Yeah, right.

"Caring for the world requires little more than looking closely at every choice you make in life, great or small, and making a conscious effort to choose wisely. You must make every choice as though the life of your Earth Mother depended upon it, as though your own life depended upon it, as though your children's lives depended upon it. And you must lead, so that others do the same."

OK, it was simple. The message was simple. But getting the message across to the world, getting a person to listen, to start making better choices, that still wasn't going to be so simple.

"You are ready, Adam. We chose you because you were the one. And now you're ready."

"You believe in me more than I believe in myself," said I. "But I trust you. If you believe that I'm the one who can make a difference, then I'm ready to try."

282

He took my arm and we walked down the hill. Suddenly he grabbed by arm very hard and yanked me back, as a snake lunged toward my ankle. It missed me, but only because the Elder pulled me away. He held my arm tightly as the striped snake slithered away through the grass. I recognized it as a coral snake, one of the most venomous snakes in the jungle.

"There will be snakes along the path. And they will attack you. It's their nature. They defend themselves. When it appears you might step on them, they strike. There are people below the Mountain who are like snakes. They, too, will try to strike you down if they think you are going to step on them. There are powerful people who are making lots of money burning up the planet. If you appear to be a threat to them, they will strike back. That's their nature."

I had thought about those snakes. Billionaire oil barons, to start with. How is an eighteen-year-old kid supposed to protect himself from snakes like that? I wondered.

"You have your whole life ahead of you. The teachings don't end when you leave the Mountain. Your Earth Mother will continue to be your best teacher. As you learn, as you grow, you will find your voice. As you lift up your voice it will grow stronger. As you speak out, others will join you. Soon you will no longer be just a person, you will be a people, people speaking out, people changing people. One snake cannot silence a whole people."

I liked his optimism, but there were a whole lot of snakes in the asphalt jungle, and so far there was only one me.

"You will have to take risks. You will have to step off the ledge and onto many living bridges. While you are hanging on the narrow bridge all by yourself, you will have to add your part, make the bridge stronger, until it can carry you and the others safely to the other side."

He wasn't making it sound any easier. I don't think he was trying to make it sound easy.

"There will be weak and narrow bridges. There will be snakes. But the biggest danger will be yourself. The biggest threat will be doubting yourself. The most important choice you will ever make, and it's one you will be asked to make every day, will be choosing to trust yourself."

The Elders believed in me. They thought I could make the right choices. I hoped they were right.

"When you find yourself doubting yourself, and you will, remember that you have been chosen. You have been chosen to be the messenger, called to care for the earth. You have been called to become the heart of the world - the loving, caring compassionate heart of the world."

With that the Owl Butterfly appeared in the sky above our heads. And then the Guacamaya, flying onto my shoulder. Then the cry of an Eagle, and a Condor. And a White Rabbit came bouncing along the path, though he didn't take the time to stop but kept on going.

"Who has called you, Adam? Who has chosen you and called you?" The Elder was asking me directly.

"You have chosen me, I guess. And the Owl Butterfly and the Guacamaya and the Eagle and the Condor, even the White Rabbit, they all called me. That's why I'm here."

"We have not chosen you. The Elders did not choose you. Your Mother has chosen you. We looked into the waters and we listened to our Earth Mother. She chose you. Like you, we are the messengers. Along with the Butterfly and the Guacamaya and all the others birds and animals, even the plants and trees, we have called you. But you were chosen by your Mother."

I heard the Elder, I heard the water, I heard the birds and the animals and the trees. I looked to the sky and I heard my Mother's voice. She was holding out the golden figurine and it was glowing brightly as she spoke:

> *"This is yours.*
> *It has always been yours.*
> *Like you, it was born from the earth,*
> *Then shaped by the original peoples of the land.*
> *It has always helped me find my way.*
> *But it has always been meant for you."*

The golden figurine floated through the air and landed once again around my neck. It had always been around my neck, but now it was glowing brightly.

"She chose you, Adam, because she knew you were the one. And you must succeed. The life of your Mother depends upon it."

Chapter 15

Awakening the Dream

"The time has come."

The sun was rising over the Mountain. It was spectacular - just enough clouds to fill the sky with color. There was a soft haze over the valley, from wood fires, probably making the morning coffee.

The Elders had gathered, more of them than usual. And others were arriving - men and women and children. I could see lines of villagers all dressed in white and parading briskly down the paths across the valley, making their way to our assembly on the hill.

I was going home. And everyone was coming to say good-bye.

I was a jumble of mixed emotions. Sadness. Trepidation. Even fear. But also joy. I had learned so much. I had become one with nature as never before. There was a calming, almost confident sense within me that I was in the right place at the right time and that I was about to embark on another new adventure. I was preparing to do what I was supposed to be doing. I was ready to go down the Mountain.

I still had doubts. I was still asking the questions of why me. I was still wondering if I was up to the task, could I really be the messenger? Would anyone listen to me? Could I really make a difference? But I was also starting to be at peace with the answers. I now understood what the Elder had said on that very first day. Why you? If not you, who?

The crowd of villagers had grown to a multitude. As the Elder rose to speak, it looked like the crowd gathered for the Sermon on the Mount.

As the Elders prepared to speak, I realized I had received many teachings over the past days, but we had never had any real conversations. We didn't need to. I never needed to ask questions. The Elders knew what was on my mind before I asked aloud. And when the Elders spoke, I listened. And so it was this final morning.

"Adam. The time has come. You have been among us, you have shared meals with us, you have made music with us, you have danced with us, you have learned from us. You have watched the waters, watched the birds, watched the sky. You have re-visited your past and you have seen your future. You have had adventures. You are not the person you were when you first arrived on the Mountain."

That was the truth.

"And now it is time for you to go. When we called, you came. When we taught, you listened and learned. When your Earth Mother cried out to you in her pain, you embraced her. You have become one with *la madre tierra*. And now it is time for you to do your job. It is time for you to be the messenger. It is time for you to carry the message from the Heart of the World to a world that is suffering. When our Earth Mother cries out in pain, it is the world that is crying, the whole world that is in pain. Our younger brothers and sisters have for too long believed that the path to happiness was to be found in more and better things. You carry the message that will bring them true happiness, the happiness that comes from doing what we are all called to be doing, the real happiness that comes when we become the heart of the world, when we join with our brothers and sisters and take responsibility for caring for the Earth. That is the true happiness. Balance and harmony. Doing what we have all been called to do."

I was surrounded by children now, smiling wide-eyed children. They had been watching me from behind their mothers for days and now they wanted to get up close to this odd stranger. They wanted to be a part of saying good-bye. And for me they were a poignant reminder of what it was the Elders were charging me to do - to help ensure a healthy world for my future children and my children's children.

"We have shared with you the key to healing your Earth Mother. Saving the world requires little more than looking closely at every choice you make in life, great or small, and making a conscious effort to choose wisely. You must make every choice as though the life of your Mother depended upon it. And you must lead, so that others do the same."

The Elder was repeating himself. This was the one important lesson he wanted me to carry down the mountain. As he said, it was the key. And now it was my job to share it.

"We cannot tell you every choice to make in every situation. And you cannot tell the younger brother. But you can, and you must, awaken everyone to the need to examine every choice and strive to make the choices that can make a difference."

This was becoming the final lesson, a recounting of all the others.

"Our Earth Mother is gravely ill. But she can be healed. If everyone will stop destroying and start healing she will recover."

The Elders were quick to sound the warning, but they were equally quick to lift up hope.

"You are your Mother's hope, Adam. The time has come for you to go down the Mountain, to return to the lands of the Younger Brother, to build bridges and to help people cross over. It's your turn to share all that we have shared with you, all that you have discovered. And you will not be alone. Whenever you need help you need only watch the water, watch the birds and watch the sky. We will be with you. Your Mother will be with you."

I knew that. I felt that. I would never be alone.

"We know you are still not sure you are ready to be the messenger. We know you are still not sure you are the one. We have told you that you will encounter those on the path who will want you to fail. But you have listened to us and listened to your Earth Mother. You are armed with new and ancient wisdom and knowledge. Your Mother does not make wrong choices. She has chosen well. You are the one. We have seen it in the water. You will prevail."

I was still not as certain as my new teachers. But I was accepting my new role. I had come to the Mountain looking for answers to the big questions: Who am I? Where am I going? What am I supposed to be doing with my life? The teachers on the Mountain had given me the answers. My Mother was trying to give me the answers. It seemed it was time for me to start listening, and believing. It was time for me to start down the Mountain.

"Soon it will be time for you to go. But first we want to say good-bye and to confer upon you our blessings and our empowerment."

The Elder lifted a large conch shell from his mochilla. He pressed the shell to his lips, drew a breath, puffed his cheeks and blew out a loud call to the sky. It echoed across the hills, up and down the Mountain. Three times he sounded his trumpet. As he did, the children and then the men and the women assembled all stood up and began chanting. Then, right on cue, the Owl Butterfly appeared in the sky. And Guaca, and the Eagle and the Condor.

The Elder led me to a large stone, a boulder that sat atop the rise. He took me by the hand and directed me to stand upon the rock so all could see. Once again, as they had done when I first arrived on the Mountain, each of the four Elders drew a colored cord out of his or her mochilla. Each took his turn wrapping a cord around my wrist and this time tying it with a colored bead attached. Once the band was secured, the Elder gently held my head and pressed his forehead to mine. It was a powerful blessing.

"Every moment is a sacred ceremony," he intoned. "With these sacred threads we are now bound together. Just as the mother first stuck her spindle in the ground and spun the first thread, may these threads mark the beginning of a new creation."

The people of the Mountain were not given to wild celebration, but the Elders' blessing was understood by all and resulted in a collective cheer of approval.

The two women Elders stepped forward. One took her mochilla from around her neck and together the Elders presented it to me, placing it over my head ceremoniously. I was certain the women had woven this special mochilla themselves and just for me. I had never seen it before. It was more colorful than most, with a striking geometric design.

"You arrived with a mochilla, now you have two. You are a *mochillado,* one who wears the mochilla. A true *mochillado* carries two - one for his possessions, one for his medicine, his coca leaves and food. The design woven into this mochilla represents the water and the birds and the sky. It is meant to help you find your way."

I thanked them both with a big hug, even though the Elders were not so big on public displays of affection. The women had treated me like their grandson during my whole time on the Mountain. This was my good-bye, and my thank you.

The Elder continued the blessing and the charge. He reached out his hand and placed it on my head as if anointing me:

"We are the people of the Mountain. You are the messenger. We have shared with you all that you need to know. Your Earth Mother has chosen you and we have empowered you. Now you must speak to the people of the planet. Help them to hear the cry of their Earth Mother.

"You are the sun and the rain, the water and the plants, the birds and the animals. There is no such thing as 'nature,' apart from you and us. You are nature, we are nature, just as you are us and we are you. We are all connected, we are all one. The future was born in your past, and now it has been shaped by your time on the Mountain. Go forth, Adam Joseph Rivera, imagining a new future and making the choices that will awaken it."

If that was supposed to be an empowerment, it worked. I felt it all through my body. It felt as though all my self-doubt had just fallen off me and I was standing on the Mountain clothed in a new confidence.

The Elder called out loudly to the crowd. A big cheer went up and there were hugs and handshakes for everyone, myself most certainly included. And then the horns and the drums and the flutes. The party had begun.

Food appeared from nowhere once again, great quantities of food. It was still morning, but in this part of the world breakfast, lunch and dinner can often all look the same: a great pot of flavorful soup with everything in it - meat and potatoes, corn and platanos, avocados and yuca - pretty much everything from the garden. And the dancing had begun. Men and women, even the children, swaying to and fro in big circles, holding hands and responding to the gentle rhythm of feather flutes and drums and more.

Again I was invited to join in, to join the drummers. As the music played and I tapped into the rhythm of my heart, I thought of my dad. I had come wanting to learn more about my father, to discover my roots. Instead I had found myself.

It felt not unlike a family celebration at a baptism, and maybe it was. I had been baptized into a new family, and given a job to do. I had been anointed and had received their blessing. Now the community was welcoming me and sending me off at the same time.

The Owl Butterfly and Guacamaya, the Eagle and the Condor, even the Pelican and the White Rabbit were there, too - just to make it official.

The celebration continued for some time, well past noon, but soon it became clear that things were winding down and it would be time for me to go.

The Elders converged and each offered a hug and a pat on the back. And then Bunkey. He came with the mule, just as he had done days ago, not saying a word but indicating it was time to climb aboard and start down the Mountain.

As he helped me up, I swear I heard him say, "Are you ready, Capt'n?" He smiled. I laughed.

Another round of handshakes and we were on our way. "Follow me," said the Owl Butterfly. And so I did. Once again.

We headed down the hill into the valley, Bunkey leading the mule as I rode, with Guaca perched on my shoulder. We crossed over the river on a very sturdy bridge. I looked back. I couldn't help thinking I had truly made a crossing. I was not the same person going down the Mountain as I had been going up.

From the river we climbed the hill on the other side. From the ridge I got my last look at the snowy mountains in the distance. Then it was down the Mountain.

As we rode along, I knew I would never again look at a plant or a flower or a tree in the same way. They all seemed to be talking. And I was listening. They seemed to be saying good-bye. I couldn't help thinking that they were also counting on me. I was on a mission now. I was the messenger. If the little plants and flowers were to survive I had to succeed.

The Owl Butterfly was leading, Bunkey had the mule and me in tow. Guaca had left my shoulder and joined the Owl Butterfly in the air and I thought I saw the Eagle and the Condor high in the sky, way ahead of us. We were again an odd procession. We were all connected, and I understood for the first time that we had all been connected all along. I had traveled the world with them. With their help I had come to view my planetary home in a whole new light. It had all been a dream, I know. But it had also been very real.

I reached into my mochilla to retrieve the golden figurine I had tucked securely away. As my hand fumbled for the figurine it found instead what felt like a smooth stone. It was the Communicator! This didn't make any sense. The Communicator had been a figment of my imagination, something in a dream. But here it was, now resting in the palm of my hand.

Just as Steve Jobs had said, it read my thoughts. Without me doing anything, images began appearing in front of my eyes. They came and went, all sort of passing in review in front of me. There were the Elders, waving good-bye. And the snowy mountains. And the Lost City. Images of the river and the valley, the gardens and the plants and the trees. Images of the birds - lots of birds. Then began a full review of my adventures of the past days. Images from my flight around the world, just as I had seen it - continents to oceans, icebergs in the Arctic to snowy mountains in la Sierra, smokestacks to hay stacks. Then there were the Conquistadores, and Bunkey and Mary - I mean Maria. The images began talking to me, communicating on my Communicator, I guess you'd say. First was Mary. Not Maria this time but really Mary.

"I'm waiting for you, Adam," she said. "You've had such an adventure, and now you have a job to do."

Mary's image faded, replaced by others. There was Henry Ford and Thomas Edison, each one saying in his own words

294

something like, "It's your job now, Adam. Tell them how they must make the choices that will shape their future. If you speak from your heart, they will listen." And then Thomas Edison added, "And tell them about the sun."

"Then there was the White Rabbit, and then the Caterpillar and the Striped Cat. The Caterpillar called out, "Who are you? Who are you now? Where are you going?" Well I was certainly someone different than I had been before. And I didn't know exactly where it was I was going, but I was now certain I was on the right path.

And there was an image of the path, right in front of me, and my radiant Mother in the distance calling me on. "Follow me," she seemed to be saying.

Her image faded and then there were bridges. There I was swinging in the air, suspended over the river. And then the Elder again: "You are the one. We called you to the Mountain because we knew you were the one who could help us build the bridge."

From the vine bridge the images changed to the bridges of New York.

There was Steve Jobs repeating to me, "You're going to do fine, kid. Speak to them from your heart and they will listen."

The images continued changing. Steve Jobs faded and a carousel of images of world leaders began passing in front of me. Some spoke out, some didn't. There were images of President Ronald Reagan and Vice-President George Bush and then the other President Bush. I don't think they said anything. Then Jimmy Carter: "I was just a peanut farmer from Georgia when I was called. You're gonna do fine, kid."

Then Al Gore: "It's an inconvenient truth you carry, kid, but they'll listen if you speak from your heart."

And John Kennedy: "Ask what you can do…"

And then the Dalai Lama, with the snowy peaks of the Himalayas behind him, I think, speaking directly to me:

"Adam, you are a messenger now. We must all be messengers. You and I and our brothers and sisters. As the only beings on the planet who are capable of making choices, we must choose to care for this world. We have recklessly polluted the world with chemicals and waste, selfishly consuming and destroying its natural resources. Humanity must take the initiative to repair and protect the world. The decision to act must come from our hearts. All of us need to develop a genuine sense of universal responsibility, not only toward this beautiful blue planet that is our home, but also toward the innumerable sentient beings with whom we share it. That is the message you must share. And if you speak from your heart, the people will listen."

Now it was me. I was the one in the image before me. I was speaking, and as the image grew it looked like I was speaking to some grand assembly. The audience was dressed all in coat and tie, seated in polished oak chairs, and nodding at each and patting each other on the back as I spoke:

"Caring for the world requires little more than looking closely at every choice you make in life, great or small, and making a conscious effort to choose wisely. You must make every choice as though the life of your Earth Mother depended upon it, as though your own life depended upon it, as though your children's lives depended upon it. And you must lead, so that others do the same."

The images continued to change as I spoke - the Halls of Congress, the Houses of Parliament, the General Assembly of the United Nations. I was speaking as though I had found a new voice:

"Our Earth Mother is gravely ill. The world needs healers. The world needs leaders. Remember that you have been chosen. You have been chosen to be the messengers, called to care for the earth. That is your job. You have been called to become the Heart of the World - the loving, caring compassionate heart of the world - and to lead others to do the same."

There was a buzz of agreement among the black suits and ties as they nodded in agreement.

Bunkey was still leading us down the path. He may or may not have been able to see the images, may or may not have seen me speaking. In any case, he smiled. And the Owl Butterfly and Guacamaya were still ahead of us.

The collage of images in front of me all faded, replaced by a panoramic image of the four Elders, standing on the ridge with the snowy mountains in the distance. I didn't see their lips moving, but I heard their voices in my head:

"You are the sun and the rain, the water and the plants, the birds and the animals. There is no such thing as 'nature,' apart from you and us. You are nature, we are nature, just as you are us and we are you. We are all connected, we are all one. The future was born in your past, and now it has been shaped by your time on the Mountain. Go forth, imagining a new future and making the choices that will awaken it."

Suddenly the mule bolted. There was a snake in the grass on the side of the path. It lunged at the mule's leg. She reared her

297

legs and I was thrown to the ground, my mochilla going one way and me the other.

That's the last I remember of the Mountain.

I must have hit my head because everything appeared to swirl around me, and then all went dark. Either I fell into another dream, or I began to awaken. I'm not sure which.

I was only once again aware of my surroundings when I heard my sister's familiar voice.

"Are you O.K?"

I was a bit startled and disoriented, but as I instantly recognized, I was again laying on the grass in my own back yard.

"Were you sleeping? Sleeping on the grass?" asked Sarah with a puzzled look on her face.

"I guess so. I'm not sure. I guess I was."

As I looked around the familiar grassy field, I quickly became aware of how similar yet clearly different it was to the mountain in my dream. It was the Catskills again, not the lush tropical jungle. Then I caught myself looking around for a butterfly. No butterflies here, not this time anyway.

"Mom seems to have taken a turn for the worse. She wants us to come to the hospital," Sarah said with a concerned sadness in her voice.

Still no butterfly. Something was very strange. And the dream - or whatever it was - continued to seem very real. In fact, it seemed to be continuing, even re-playing itself.

I got up from the grass and dusted myself off and followed my sister back to the house.

I didn't know what to make of it. I knew I had been dreaming, but I also knew it had been real. Now what was happening? Was this a dream or was this reality?

Sarah and I started the drive to the hospital.

Sarah was especially quiet as we drove. Me, I just kept silently re-playing my dream, if that's what it was, of the Mountain. I saw it all. I heard every sound, every word. I knew it had been real.

Sarah was the first to break the silence. "I think Mom wants to tell us she's going to die soon." What was happening? It didn't make any sense.

As we got to the hospital, the sun broke through the dark clouds for the first time. Aunt Susan was already there. "Your mother is gravely ill, kids. She wants to talk with you. I'm afraid we're going to lose her soon."

It was déjà vu all over again.

When we got to her room, she still looked very ill, but she was smiling as we all came into the room and sat down beside her.

"You know the doctors have said I haven't got much longer to live," she said once again. It was like an out-of-body experience. I was listening to my mother but as an observer who knew she had already died.

"Something has changed. The doctors don't know what has made the difference, but something is different. The cancer that was spreading out of control has started to heal."

I didn't know what to think. I was overjoyed, of course, tears welling up in my eyes and starting down my cheek, but I was also totally confused.

"The future has changed. I've been given a second chance," she continued. "There are no guarantees that I will be healed completely, but it looks like I'm going to be around for some time now. There is hope."

Maybe it had all been a dream. I had seen this all before. It had been real, I'm sure of it. But that was somehow in the past. This was a new reality. Something had changed. I no longer knew if I was in the past or the present or the future, but the story had been changed.

The tears were running down my cheeks now. There was hope for my mother. The future had changed.

We were all hugging each other now, and laughing and crying at the same time.

"My biggest fear all along was that I would never see you two grow up to be all I know you are going to be." My mother's voice sounded stronger even though it was trembling with emotion.

"Sarah, we're going to be able to tend the garden together after all. But I know you'll follow your heart wherever it may lead you. The whole world is your garden. Don't ever feel you have to stay on that old farm. You have a bright future ahead of you. You can make of it whatever you wish, whatever you can imagine. No matter what, I know you'll always be tending gardens, caring for the world.

"And Adam. I'm going to be around for a little while longer now, long enough to watch you become the man you were meant to become. The world is calling you, my son. You're destined to see the world as you've never seen it before, to watch the water, to watch the birds, to watch skies the world over, to experience adventures like you've never dreamed. Trust me, these things will come to pass and you will remember. You're going to make a difference, Adam Rivera. You are the sun and the rain. You're going to touch people's hearts. You're going to change the world."

As she spoke, the monitors on the wall began to sound a warning. Nurses filled the room. "Your mother is healing, but she is still gravely ill," one of them said. "She has a long recovery ahead of her. She is still in pain, she is still weak. I'm going to have to ask you all to leave for now. But please come back, after she's rested. She's going to need your care now more than ever."

Mom had closed her eyes. She managed to reach out her hand and take hold of mine before she fell back asleep.

"She's all right," said the nurse, sensing my concern. "But we need to care for her."

We all filed out of the room, and as we did Mary came running up the hall.

"Mary! Mary!"

"I came as quickly as I could. I don't know how, but I heard you calling. Is she OK?"

"She's OK, Mary. She's better than OK. Something has changed. The cancer is healing, not spreading anymore."

"Oh that's wonderful, Adam."

301

I took Mary's arm and led her outside.

"Mary, I am so happy to see you again. I have had such an amazing adventure."

I gave her a big hug and smothered her with a kiss. She looked puzzled, but I continued:

"And I think I know what has changed, how it is that my mother may have started to heal."

We walked out into the hospital's beautiful memorial garden. We found a bench and sat beside the little pool of water. The sun was shining brightly now. The sparkling sunlight dancing on the ripples of the water did not go un-noticed.

"Mary, I've had the most curious adventures. And you were there. It was like my mother predicted, like the Owl Butterfly said."

"What adventures? And where did you get that bag?"

My mochilla! I was wearing my mochilla. The one the Elders had given me. I hadn't been wearing it the hospital room, I don't think. I'm sure I didn't have it before. But I was wearing it now. The one I had hidden the golden figurine in. I reached inside to find the figurine and the Communicator.

"It's gone!"

There was no Communicator. And no golden figurine either.

"It's all so strange, Mary. My mother gave me a golden figurine. But this time she didn't. She spoke the words, 'Watch the water, watch the birds, watch the sky,' but no golden figurine.

Maybe there was never a golden figurine. And there's no Communicator. Maybe there was never a Communicator either. But I do have my mochilla."

"You're not making any sense, Adam. What figurine? What's a communicator? And what about that bag?"

The mochilla! I did have the mochilla. The mochilla the Elders gave me. On the Mountain. I had that. It was real. I held the mochilla in my hands, and as I did I spotted the threads around my wrists. Four green cords, eight actually, four with a bead, and they were real.

"It was real, Mary. It may have been a dream, but it was real."

"I still don't understand, Adam. But I think you're wearing the golden figurine."

I looked. She was right. I know I hadn't been wearing it a moment ago - I'm sure I hadn't - but it was hanging around my neck now, as sure as gold. And it seemed to be glowing.

"I don't understand, either, Mary. There's a lot I don't understand. But I know it's all real."

I didn't know what to think. Maybe it had all been a dream. Or, just as possibly, maybe it had all been real.

"My Mother has a new future, a new chance of surviving. And I know why. It's because there are people on the Mountain who are caring for her."

"OK, Adam - if you say so."

"My mother was right. Just now she held my hand and said I would become the man I was meant to become. She said, 'The world is calling you, my son.' It's true - I have been called. She said I was destined to explore the world, to have incredible adventures. She said I was the one, I was the one who was going to make a difference."

"I have always believed in you, Adam Rivera. I do believe you're going to make a difference," said Mary, sounding so very much like Mary.

"The Elders believe in me too."

"Who are the Elders?"

"Don't worry, I'll tell you later. I'll tell you all about the Mountain and the Elders. I have so much to share with you Mary. I AM going to make a difference, Mary. I am going to help my Mother heal. And you're going to be with me. You were with me on the Mountain, you're going to always be with me and I with you. You and I together, we're going to make a difference."

"I still don't understand. But I trust you."

"Mary, together we're going to change the world, I know we are. We're going to change the world together. We're going to care for the world together, to heal the world together. The Elders taught me, we're the only ones who can."

"That sounds very noble, Adam, and I will be with you, all the way. But why you? Why me? Why us?"

"If not us, who?"

With that the Owl Butterfly reappeared. (You knew it had to end this way, right?) Búho circled above me and then circled above both of us, three times. He came to rest on my finger.

"It's Búho! I told you about the Owl Butterfly, about my dream, remember?"

"Not really. It was your dream, remember? But somehow I know I was a part of it. I know I've always been a part of it."

The Owl Butterfly left my finger and landed gently upon hers. The Búho began to speak, but this time I knew it was the Mountain I was hearing:

"You are the sun and the rain, the water and the plants, the birds and the animals. We are all connected, we all are one."

"Can you hear that, Mary?"

"Yes I can, Adam."

"That's the Mountain. That's our Mother. That's the Elders. They're speaking to me. They're speaking to you."

Images appeared in the air, images of the Mountain, of the Elders, and the voice continued:

"Saving the world requires little more than looking closely at every choice you make in life, great or small, and making a conscious effort to choose wisely."

"Adam, how are you doing that? Where are those images coming from?"

I remembered what Steve Jobs had said, about how it would work without it even being in my hand.

"We're communicating, Mary."

305

Then an image of my Mother, golden and radiant, as the voice continued:

"You must make every choice as though the life of your Mother depended upon it. And you must lead, so that others do the same."

The image of my Mother was joined by an image of my father. I swear it was my father, just as he looked in one of the old photos I had seen of him so many times before.

"Adam, that looks like your father!"

The images all faded and became a CNN news broadcast, the voice became that of a television news anchor:

"In other news, Adam Rivera, the President's Special Advisor on Environmental Affairs, today announced that for the first time in decades the average temperature of the planet has fallen rather than risen."

My father's photo came to life, and there he was - no, there I was - speaking to a crowd of reporters as the broadcast continued...

"The drop has been attributed to the many visionary choices made by leaders of the global community of nations in recent years," Rivera said, adding, *"We may have given the Earth a second chance."*

"Adam, that's you!"

It was. And as I spoke, as my father spoke, as the future me spoke or whatever, all the images blended into one, a giant panorama of the Mountain - the jungle, the valley, the hills, the snowy peaks. And the Mountain spoke...

The future was born in your past, and now it has been shaped by your time on the Mountain. Go forth, imagining a new future and making the choices that can awaken it.

The End. The Beginning.

Acknowledgments

First and foremost I offer thanks and blessings to my many indigenous friends in la Sierra Nevada de Santa Marta in Colombia, for their warm hospitality, the gift of their sacred teachings and their gracious invitation to join them in their villages and homes and to share their spiritual and environmental message with the world.

Particular thanks to the Elders - the Mamos and other Spiritual Leaders - of the Kággaba (Kogui), Ijka (Arhuaco), Arzario (Wiwa) and Kankuamo, including among others Ñankwa Chaparro, Arhuaco Spiritual Authority; Mamo José Gabriel Alimaco, Kogui Spiritual Authority; Mamo Pedro Juan Noevita, Kogui Spiritual Authority; Mamo Julio Pinto, Wiwa Spiritual Authority; Mamo Jazinto Zarabata, Kogui Organizational Leader; Mamo Pedro, Arhuaco Spiritual Authority; Mamo Quintero, Kogui Spiritual Authority; Mamo Benencio, Arhuaco Spiritual Authority.

Additionally, special thanks to "Chiqui" and all the wonderful peoples of the Arhuaco village of Nabusimake, and to my very special Arhuaco family in the village of Gunmaku.

Thank you to the Directors and Staff of Organización Gonawindúa Tayrona and Casa Indigena de Santa Marta for their cooperation and assistance.

Nelson Caraballo, Miguel Echavarria, and Felipe Andres Echavarria who introduced me to Colombia and led me to the Mountain and to the indigenous peoples of la Sierra Nevada, and who assisted with translation as needed.

Thanks to Vladimir Agudelo Montoya, Curator of Butterflies at la Casa de las Mariposas at the Jardín Botánico de Medellín, who graciously invited me into the House of Butterflies after hours to offer me a private education into the world of Colombia's amazing butterflies - including most notably Búho, the infamous talking Owl Butterfly.

The Curators and Staff at the Museo del Oro in Bogotá and in Santa Marta, thank you for welcoming me into your museums and research library so many times.

Posthumous thanks and acknowledgement to several voices from the past whose words and literary style have woven wisdom and much-needed humor into this fantasy adventure: Lewis Carroll, *Alice's Adventures in Wonderland*; Robert Luis Stevenson, *Treasure Island*; Steve Jobs for his *Commencement Speech to the Graduating Class of Stanford University* in 2005; Henry Ford and Thomas Edison as quoted in *Uncommon Friends: Life with Thomas Edison, Henry Ford, Harvey Firestone, Alexis Carrel & Charles Lindbergh*, by James Newton (1987).

A very personal Thank You to the staff and friends of Menla Mountain Retreat Center in the Catskills of New York who hosted the historic gathering of Native American Elders from throughout the Americas that literally gave birth to this book.

And finally to my friends and neighbors in Minca, Colombia, the beautiful eco-village in la Sierra Nevada that has been my home for these past three years, thank you for making me feel at home and for allowing me to experience what it is to truly be one with *la madre tierra*.

- John Lundin

la Sierra Nevada de Santa Marta, Colombia

CPSIA information can be obtained
at www.ICGtesting.com
Printed in the USA
LVOW13s1915010517
532859LV00013B/1017/P

9 781539 514923